BYZANTIUM

ASIA MINOR

TARSUS

ANTIOCH

CYPRUS

TYRE

BOSTRA

CÆSAREA

PELLA

JERUSALEM

GAZA

ARABIA

ALEXANDRIA

RÆTONIUM

WADI NATRON
DESERT

NILE RIVER

RED SEA

AFRICA

NTURY A.D.

ORIGEN

ASWAN

MAP BY LINOS DOUNIAS '77

D0930583

# ORIGEN

Other books by Theodore Vrettos

HAMMER ON THE SEA

A SHADOW OF MAGNITUDE

# ORIGEN

*a historical novel by*

## Theodore Vrettos

CARATZAS BROTHERS, PUBLISHERS
New Rochelle, New York
1978

*First Edition*

CARATZAS BROTHERS, PUBLISHERS
246 Pelham Road, New Rochelle, N.Y. 10805

ISBN 0-89241-079-5
Library of Congress Catalog
Card Number 77-91602

To Lawrence Durrell
and
"the dead horse."

# A Note

I had much help in the research and writing of this novel. I especially want to thank my wife Vas for her invaluable assistance and editorial counsel.

Many libraries came to my aid, particularly Harvard's Widener Library, the Harvard Divinity School Library, the Library of Congress, the Hellenic College Library, and the Peabody Institute Library.

With his keen foresight, my publisher Ari Caratzas has given Origen his long due recognition, and I am very grateful to him.

*Theodore Vrettos*

## Prologue

In the third century A.D., Alexandria still basked in a rich tradition of science and art. As the capital of the Eastern Roman Empire, she possessed unlimited sources of wealth and was the main contact between East and West.

She was far more lively and interesting than imperial Rome. Her great library, college and Museum gave birth to poets, scientists, artisans and craftsmen. Euclid's mathematical school continued to flourish at this time, Alexandrian geographers and astronomers already knew that the earth revolved around the sun and that it was round (the astronomer Eratosthenes even estimated its diameter and was off by only fifty miles), Egyptian cartographers included China on their maps of the world, and Erasistratus the physician discovered a link between nervous illness and sexual problems.

The history of this remarkable city begins with her founder, Alexander the Great, and passes nobly through aeons of time . . . to the Ptolemies, Cleopatra, Berenice, Philo, Plotinus, Porphyry, Hypatia . . . the names are legion.

And finally there is Origen.

# I

The old Arab woman put down her basket of hyacinths and pointed toward the awakening breeze in the eastern harbor. "Riyeh Bahri!" she cried. From the time he was a child Origen remembered her this way, chained to a blot of shade beneath the Gate of the Moon, selling her flowers for two obols, always with that same suffering look in her eyes.

With a surge of anticipation in his heart, he sped down the full length of Canopic Way, through the clouds of hot dust that had gathered over the city. Alexandria was an inferno. For an awesome moment his thoughts converged upon death and he envisioned himself alone in a flaming world, scorched by the holocaust of a thousand suns, wanting to die but unable.

The cool breath of the sea refreshed him when he reached the promontory at the entrance to Alexandria's harbor, a wall of solid granite extending the length of seven stadiums. It stood directly before Pharos Torch and connected the city to the small island. From the deep hold of a sagging barge a weather-beaten old fisherman looked at him and smiled. Three young lads dashed past, arms frolicking, their hearts panting for Pharos Torch. When he was their age he had a great desire to climb Pharos and look down at Alexandria with the eyes of God. He would never forget the day . . . the loud bargaining with one of the donkey-men on the marble steps, the eventual agreement, the endless climb up the hollow smelly ramp, past twisting caravans of laborers carrying heavy bundles of wood that would feed the insatiable flames of the lighthouse. When the donkey reached the Triton columns, he coaxed it into a broad marble terrace where bustling tradesmen converged upon him with pomegranates, lemon juice sweetened with honey, and small morsels of roasted meat on sticks. But he had only enough money to buy the lemon juice. After drinking half the cup he offered the rest to the donkey and then to appease his hunger he attached his thoughts on the Greek inscription high above him:

'*Sostratos of Cnidus, son of Dexiphanes, to the savior gods for sailors.*'

It took him one full hour to reach the top of Pharos. The glare from the immense lamp almost blinded him. Its fierce flames lashed at the howling wind, while ageless Poseidon braced himself on a marble arch, trident in his right hand, his sleepless eyes fixed on all ships at sea. A wide platform, protected by a high wall of granite, circled the base of the lamp. Several visitors had huddled together along one side of the wall, afraid to look down, but he stepped boldly forward and moved to the very edge of the platform. Far below him lay an awesome sight, a microcosm of people, temples, ships, hills and lakes intertwined with the swollen gray veins of the Nile. All of Egypt was kneeling at his feet.

2

Memories tarnished by the rude pull of time.

And now the soft lapping of waves against the Heptastadion beckoned him. He took off his sandals and white robe then plunged into the cool water, swimming tirelessly into the open sea for several hundred yards before turning back. He slipped into his robe then sat on a slab of granite. Toward the eastern harbor, long rows of stone warehouses lay sprawled along the yellow sands. On his right hand, the reefs of Lochias stretched into the Great Sea like fingers of a drowning god. The lemon groves in the royal gardens were already drenching the inner harbor of Antirrhodos with their fragrance. The season of Sefi was upon them.

Fleets of barges and galleys invaded the sea, capping the water with multi-colored sails. Origen was spellbound. Clearly he saw the ships of Caesar and Antony cloaking the waters around the Timonium while cries of battle rose like veils of incense toward the roof of a muted sky. He saw Golden Alexander on this same mole, slicing out the streets of his city with a quick stroke of his finger in the sand—streets wide enough for eight carriages to course unmolested—marble avenues that once beheld the majestic hair of Berenice, the carpricious smile of Cleopatra.

His mind was a hornet's nest. In a few weeks he would complete his course of study at Clement's college, along with his best friend Alexandros. From the time they were young boys they had made a solemn promise to each other to go to Athens and study philosophy at its source. It was this hunger for knowledge that brought him to the Heptastadion every day after classes. Together with his father Leonidas, who was a teacher of rhetoric at the Academy, he discussed poetry, music, art, history, and science. Whatever was Greek he owed to his father. Everything Jewish, to his mother.

A solitary figure was approaching the Heptastadion. If there were ten thousand men in a stadium he would

3

recognize his father immediately: tall angular body, sinewy arms and shoulders, proud stature, confident gait.

"Have you been waiting long?" asked Leonidas, glancing at the sea for a moment. "I could not free myself from those insatiable students."

"What shall we discuss today?" said Origen.

Leonidas spoke to the sea. "What is it about the young? They expect to solve life's problems with questions." He fell into a long silence then snapped, "Today we shall discuss you."

"Me?"

"I must know what you intend to do with your life."

With nervous eyes Origen followed the gilded barge that had just swung around Pharos and was about to enter the harbor. Its bright red sail clashed momentarily with the sun. At the bow stood two men, their harpoons aimed toward the water, while overhead a multitude of gulls circled and shrieked.

"Well?" exclaimed Leonidas.

"You know my feelings about philosophy," said Origen.

"Philosophy does not buy bread!"

Origen studied the sky.

"This is the third century," said Leonidas. "Great opportunities await you. It is insane to bury yourself in dead theories!"

Origen's mind wandered to a sad tale about a Greek fisherman who saw a strange vessel approach his barge one day. As was the custom, the fisherman hailed it with the ancient greeting, *'Where is Alexander the Great?'* The stranger responded with a sardonic laugh, *'He is dead. He has been dead for hundreds of years!'* The words no sooner left his mouth when a sudden storm erupted, his vessel overturned, and he was drowned.

Leonidas raised his voice. "What are you thinking?"

Origen kept his eyes on the red sail.

4

"There are more important things in life," Leonidas fumed, "You will take a wife someday. Where will you live . . . in an earthen vessel like Diogenes?"

Origen's silence inflamed Leonidas. "What do you hope to find in philosophy?"

"I do not know," said Origen.

"But you must be seeking something. What is it?"

"Truth perhaps."

Leonidas ignited. "Truth has already been revealed, once and for all. Every word in Scripture is inspired of God!"

"I too can be inspired."

Origen's body began to tremble. "I cannot sit idly back and expect Isaiah to speak for me, nor Moses or Christ. I am not a cipher!"

Leonidas seized him by the arm. "I will not tolerate your insolence. You must accept what is written and nothing else. Do you hear me? Nothing else!"

From under his robe Leonidas pulled out a scroll. It was yellow with age. Untying it fiercely, he brought it to his eyes and began to read, *"If thy right hand offend thee cut it off. It is better to enter into life maimed than having two hands to go into Hell. And if thine eye offend thee pluck that out also, for it is better to enter into the kingdom of God with one eye than having two eyes and be cast into hell fire. . . . "*

Origen picked up a small stone and hurled it into the sea. It skipped over the surface of the water four times before it sank.

"Not too long ago you begged me to read from blessed Mark!" Leonidas yelled. "You committed his entire gospel to memory when you were only ten. We spent whole nights together, devouring every word, and after falling exhausted on our beds I would crawl near to kiss your breast and thank God for enshrining it with His divine spirit."

Origen threw a second stone into the water. A third.

5

"For this reason have I labored with you, as your mother has labored also, teaching you Hebrew letters so that you might converse with David in his own tongue!"

Origen was unable to restrain himself any longer. "You would glue my heart to a withered sheet of parchment, clamp it forever on a stale blot of ink and say, *Enough. Breathe no more. Here is eternity! Here is peace and fulfillment!*"

Leonidas' face paled. "The Church is not a sheet of withered parchment. She is God's merciful hand on earth."

"God has nothing in common with her!" Origen exploded. "She has desecrated His name and made His temple an abominable market place for money-changers, dispensers of tapers and miraculous oil. Everything He warned against, she does . . . droning out one *Kyrie eleison* after another, worshipping human bones and relics, adorning herself in the purple robes of pride and vanity!"

Leonidas swung away. "I will not listen to this. God has chosen you, prepared you. His finger has been on your head from the day of your birth."

"I refuse to become a priest!"

Angrily Leonidas tied the scroll and shoved it into the sleeve of his robe. "It is getting late," he muttered.

Origen wanted to say something further but Leonidas cut him off. "No son of mine shall be a heretic! For the last time, I demand that you put an end to your profane questions . . . to open your heart and believe."

"In what?"

"God."

Origen fell silent.

"In His Son also," exclaimed Leonidas.

"We are all His sons."

" . . . born of the Virgin Mary, crucified under Pontius Pilate, resurrected in all His glory. . . . "

Origen struggled to fight off the turbulence that was

swirling around in his brain. 'You cannot touch me, nor really see me. My breath is inaudible, even to God!'

Leonidas did not say another word. With long angry strides, he sped down the Heptastadion and turned into the Street of the Soma. Origen tried to keep up with him but finally he realized that it was futile. At the first street inside the Greek Quarter Leonidas disappeared from view, and once again Alexandria smouldered under the cruel blasts of an African wind.

2.

Alexandros came for a visit during the evening meal.
When little John saw him he ran screaming into Alexandros' arms almost knocking him down. Alexandros was
shockingly thin. His innermost thoughts betrayed themselves through his sensitive face, his delicate eyes and lips.
Origen's mother offered him something to eat but Alexandros said he had already eaten.
    "I wish you had a little brother," cried little John.
    "Why?"
    "So I could play huckle-bones with him."
    Alexandros sat down.
    "You only have a mother," whimpered little John,
accepting Alexandros' tender pat on the head. "But I have
a mother and a father, also six brothers . . . Origen,
Photius, Barnabas, Soterius, Stephanus and Philippus!"
    Origen's mother commanded little John to be quiet,

and then against Alexandros' protest, she handed him an orange. "We have not seen you in several days," she said. "How is your mother?"

"In good health, praise God."

Origen cringed everytime Alexandros spoke this way.

"Tell me, what do you plan to do after you leave the college?" aked Leonidas, glancing up from his platter.

Alexandros did not reply.

"Is anything troubling you?" said Origen.

"I thought perhaps you might want to come with me. . . ."

"Where?"

"To Natron," said Alexandros.

Origen laughed. "Natron is a full day's journey from here."

Alexandros put down the orange. "But we may never have another opportunity to see him."

"Who?"

"Holy Abouk."

Origen let out a disgusted sigh and was instantly reprimanded by his father. "Holy Abouk is gifted with prophecy. His visions and miracles of healing are known throughout Egypt."

"Sitting on a pole like a crow hardly makes a man gifted," Origen retorted.

Leonidas stood up. "A little knowledge has made you impudent. Holy Abouk does these things not because he wishes to be a spectacle unto men."

"Why then?"

"To glorify God."

"I want to see Holy Abouk!" wailed little John, leaping up from the table again. "May I come with you, Alexandros? May I?"

His mother retrieved him as Leonidas bowed his head and made the sign of the cross. Turning to Origen, he said, "If you were not so blinded by your audacious spirit you would realize that only a man of deep faith can accomplish such miracles. When Holy Abouk was but a lad of sixteen he spent an entire summer buried up to his neck in sand."

"Why?"

"To show his disdain for physical comfort."

Origen frowned. "Christ ate and drank."

"He also fasted for forty days and nights," exclaimed Leonidas. "He knew that only through complete humiliation of body could His soul be set free."

Alexandros entreated him, "Please say that you will come, Origen."

"It is out of the question. We have the college."

"But the three-day festival of blessed Mark begins tomorrow. Classes have been suspended."

"It will do you no harm to go," said Origen's mother softly.

"If we leave at sunrise we can be at Natron tomorrow evening," Alexandros declared, his hopes rising.

Leonidas washed his hands. "Alexandros, you had better stay the night with us. That way you can have an early start in the morning."

"But I did not say that I was going," Origen objected.

Leonidas paid no attention to him. "I will stop by your house on my way to the agora, Alexandros. Your mother must be told."

Origen's mother became alarmed. "Must you go to the agora tonight?"

"There is no cause for fear."

"But the populace has not taken kindly to the new religion. You cannot stuff it down their throats."

"Our discussions harm no one." said Leonidas firmly.

"Leonidas, I implore you. The streets have ears. Be careful."

"Nonsense," scoffed Leonidas, drying his hands on a towel. Origen trailed him to the door. "I really have no desire to go to Natron, father."

Leonidas opened the door. "Not another word. You

10

are going with Alexandros at daybreak . . . and that is final!"

His mother worked far into the night baking millet cakes for the journey. After breakfast they packed food and water into two goatskins, took a large blanket of sheep's hair and set out toward Rhakotis Hill, moving first along the Street of the Soma until it brought them to the race course. It was not yet daybreak. Along the western horizon Pompey's Pillar was casting its shadow upon the Temple of Serapis. After crossing the canal, they entered the Great Western Cemetery and walked for an hour through ankle-deep sand, until they came in sight of a desolate hut that hugged the side of a hill. Nearby a small herd of camels and dromedaries grazed leisurely on thorns and desert grass.

An old shepherd lived inside the hut. He accepted their first offer without argument then came outside in his bare feet and selected two dromedaries, explaining they were swifter than camels and of better disposition. He volunteered to strap their belongings to the beasts' sides but Origen told him it was not necessary. His name was Loukas.

"Are you Greek?" asked Alexandros.

"Although I speak the Greek tongue, I am Egyptian by birth, and came originally from Paraetonium. In the name of Serapis, you will never encounter a more beautiful place in all the world, white waves dancing in pure sunlight, sand dunes the color of gold, hundreds of galleys riding peacefully upon the clear blue water!"

"Why did you leave there?" asked Alexandros.

"Fate so ordained it, my child."

It was from Parateonium that Golden Alexander set out to find the oracle of Zeus Ammon, traveling twenty days across the desert, and guided throughout by two vigilant crows. As a young boy Origen had often placed himself near his king on this long trek, retracing every

11

step, listening to the commands, watching with boundless joy that first sigh of wonder to escape from Alexander's mouth when he at last came face-to-face with the ram-headed god.

" . . . I tell you, my children, the sea has the appearance of grapes in harvest, and our sponges are not like those undernourished waifs sold on the docks of Alexandria. Indeed they are large enough to contain all the waters of the world!"

Alexandros stepped cautiously toward one of the dromedaries. "Have you adopted the new religion?"

"What religion, my child?"

"That of Christ Jesus."

Loukas peered at the sky which already had begun to brighten. All around the hut lay an enchanting world of sand and flaming red hills. "I am too old for new things, my child . . . too old and too tired."

"Surely you do not cling to Serapis?" exclaimed Alexandros as he guardedly patted the dromedary on the head.

"I cling only to what I can see or touch," scowled Loukas. "There are no chambers in my heart for demons or gods."

Alexandros wanted to converse further but Origen mounted his dromedary and asked Alexandros to do the same. As the beasts straightened up, Loukas said, "You did not tell me where you are bound."

"To Natron," said Origen. He felt as though he were sitting on a sack of rocks. The dromedary was skin and bone.

Loukas snickered. "Ah, I should have known. You are seeking that new God. But you will be disillusioned, my children. He does not howl in the desert like a starved dog."

Alexandros jabbed his heels into the dromedary's side but it refused to move. Loukas came forward and slapped its bony rump. "Go, ill-fated son of the desert. Go with the wind!"

Origen had one last question for Loukas. "Perhaps you know where He might be found?"

"Who, my child?"

"God."

Loukas spat at the sky. "I have twenty-two camels, seven dromedaries, enough food to see me through the day, and that aged hut whose fragile roof still protects me from the desert winds. This is all I know."

Alexandros swerved his dromedary around. "What will you answer when the Bridegroom knocks on the door of your sleep?"

"Who?"

"The Bridegroom!"

"Ah, you mean that new god whom you seek. My child, life is too brief to be dealt with so seriously. I do not mean to be disrespectful but when I was your age I too sought after many things and just when I was certain I had found them behold they disappeared into the air. The quest is futile. Take counsel from this old man. Nothing is eternal but death."

Loukas remained in front of his limping hut and waved to them until the sand finally swallowed him. They traveled some ten miles in silence through flat stretches of endless dunes that rose up from the bowels of the desert. Origen's robe and headdress were saturated with sweat. He was unable to understand how an old man like Loukas could live in such misery after knowing Paraetonium. Nor could he comprehend how a herd of beasts lay content on burning sands, munching on dry thorns, sleeping under the stars, day after day, year unto year.

By mid-morning they were well into the heart of the desert and saw no further sign of life until late afternoon when a handful of sheep tended by a family of impoverished Bedouins drew near them. One of the sheep had strayed from the flock and two small boys with scrawny arms and legs were trying to recapture it. Origen suggested that they rest for a while but Alexandros was anxious to move on.

Another hour passed.

The dromedaries kept ambling along at a steady pace and within another hour they had reached the summit of a high ridge. Below them, stretched out as far as the eye could see, lay the parched valley of Natron.

3.

The hard beds of the waterless lakes were surrounded with tents and people. As the dromedaries eased their way through the encampment Alexandros remarked, "We are walking on the veins of history. These deposits under our feet were used by our ancestors for mummification, and for the manufacture of glass and medicines." He leaped from his dromedary and scooped up a chunk of earth with his fingers. Suddenly he put it into his mouth and began chewing.

"What are you doing?" Origen exclaimed.

"Try some. It is therapeutic."

Origen threw him a wry look. "Are you sure you do not mean thaumaturgic?" He found delight in teasing Alexandros. Alexandros did not mind. He remounted his dromedary and they wound their way through the crowded encampment. The air was heavy with the scent

15

of food. Vendors and tradesmen snaked through the multitude selling their bread, sweets, carved wooden relics and religious medals. Commanding his dromedary to halt and kneel down, Origen slid off and led it by hand. Alexandros did the same.

"It is claimed that this whole area is filled with the Nile waters during the inundation," Origen recalled.

Alexandros' face still sparkled. "I have seen it with my own eyes. I came here with my mother three years ago. The waters form the most beautiful lakes in the world!"

"More beautiful than Mareotis?"

"A thousand times."

"Where do we find Abouk . . . I mean, Holy Abouk?"

Alexandros pointed toward a small valley just beyond the encampment where a great throng was milling around a high platform that was braced together with poles and thick planks of wood. They saw a solitary figure standing on the platform wearing a brown sackcloth, his bearded head arched toward the sky while his arms remained rigidly at his sides, palms extended outward.

"We have arrived just in time," said Alexandros. "Holy Abouk is at his hour of prayer. Soon he will give ear to the needs of the populace and heal them."

Origen gazed at the hundreds of faces before him, men and women pale from sickness and despair, lying prostrate on the scorched earth, their sunken eyes raised toward the platform, uttering faint prayers while their children played in the sand. His heart soured. Only yesterday Egypt danced. She sang and laughed and was not ashamed of life. But now Christ had turned her into a useless old woman reeking with fear and superstition. A strange and unfamiliar land clouded his eyes, forsaken, abandoned, buried up to her neck in sackcloth and ashes. Mummified. . . .

A young pilgrim, agile and wiry, started climbing up

the planks. Slung over his shoulder was a canvas bag filled with bread and fruit. Abouk looked the other way as the throng cheered. When the youth persisted, Abouk stepped forward and in a wild voice ordered him to leave. There were more cheers.

"How does he sustain himself?" asked Origen.

Alexandros had his eyes glued to the platform. "Holy Abouk has been known to go without food and water for a period of thirty days."

"I am hungry," said Origen. He opened one of the bags and drew out the food. An old woman was sitting on the ground behind him and he asked her if there was any water nearby.

"You'll find a small spring behind that slope," she rasped. "The water is very cold."

Origen unstrapped the goatskin from the dromedary's side and went toward the slope. There was a long line of people waiting at the spring. When it came time to fill his goatskin he looked up and saw a young girl carrying a large earthen jug on her shoulder. Her spotless white robe fell in soft folds as she walked toward him. Clumsily he stepped aside and permitted her to fill the jug but when the others saw this they began to grumble. In time he filled the goatskin and ran to catch up with her.

"What is your name?" he stammered.

"Herais."

"Where is your home?"

"Heliopolis."

"You came all this distance?"

"Yes, with my father. He is sick with palsy."

"Do you expect Abouk to heal him?"

"Of course."

"Is your mother here also?"

"She is dead."

"That jug is heavy. Let me carry it."

She was horrified. "No, it is not permitted. In Heliopolis only young maidens go to the spring for water."

Origen laughed.

"Have you come here for healing also?" she asked.

"Do I look ill?" he exclaimed.

She lowered her eyes. "No. You are unusually tall and very strong of body."

As they walked past the platform, Origen looked up. Abouk was still at prayer but the crowd had scattered. Boldly he touched her arm and said, "Where is your father?"

She became uneasy. "In our tent. I must go to him and prepare supper. Holy Abouk will begin with his healings soon."

Origen stood in front of her. "What if . . . he cannot heal your father?"

"He will. We have faith in him!" Defiantly she walked away. Origen waited until she reached her tent then made his way back to Alexandros. Somehow he felt that he had to offer him an explanation. "There was a large multitude at the spring."

Alexandros said nothing.

The millet cakes were dry and tasteless but they each ate half a dozen. Origen drank from the goatskin then led the dromedaries to the spring. No one else was there and the beasts drank at leisure. Returning to Alexandros, he waited until the dromedaries settled down then he picked up a handful of earth and brought it to his nose. It gave off a sharp repugnant odor and he flung it away. He took a few restless paces.

"Where are you going?" Alexandros asked.

"For a walk."

"But we must decide where to sleep tonight."

"Anyplace will do," said Origen. "Perhaps Holy Abouk can make room for us on his platform," he added with a mischievous grin.

Alexandros wore a grave look on his face. "Origen, I saw you talking to that girl. . . . "

"So?"

"Do you intend to go to her now?"

"Alexandros, you are not my keeper."

"Your body is the temple of God, a vessel of holiness and purity."

"You sound like a hermit," snapped Origen. He took several more paces.

"I wish now that we had not come here." said Alexandros. "This place overflows with the daughters of Satan. They are here not to see Holy Abouk or feel his healing hand, but to tempt and ensnare!"

Origen walked away from him. When he came to Herais' tent he softly called out her name but received no reply. He tried once more and was rewarded by the sight of her face. "I came to see your father," he said.

She drew back as he crawled inside. A small man sat propped against two pillows near the center pole of the tent. He looked emaciated. His right arm had no life, one side of his face had fallen, strands of saliva dripped from his mouth.

Origen pulled him up by the arm-pits to a better position as the twisted mouth tried to speak.

"I wish you had not come here," said Herais. She nervously began washing some wooden bowls.

"How did you manage to bring your father to Natron?" asked Origen.

"By mule and cart."

"Tell me, what kind of place is Heliopolis?"

Herais did not look up from her work.

"Is it true that Cleopatra once planted a grove of balsam trees there?" said Origen.

She did not reply.

"The trees came originally from Jericho and were gifts of Antony. It is said that he even brought Jewish gardeners from Palestine to tend them because balsam trees are

19

rare in Egypt." Origen swung around the tent and came by her side. "I have heard many fables about Heliopolis. When the holy family entered Egypt they sought refuge in your city and that same day a strong wind lashed the country, tearing the earth open and causing all the pagan idols to crash from their pedestals."

Her eyes caught fire. "This is not a fable. It truly happened!"

"It is also claimed," Origen went on, "that at harvest time the endless fields of sugar cane surrounding the obelisks send forth a fragrance that reaches to the shores of the Great Sea."

She looked stunned. "How can you know all these things about Heliopolis when you have never been there?"

Origen smiled. "Two of your obelisks now stand in Alexandria. The emperor Augustus ordered them removed from Heliopolis. I walk past them every day. They are high above the Street of the Soma, near the Caesarium. We have an appropriate name for them, *Cleopatra's needles.*"

"You did not tell me your name," she said in a timid voice.

"Origen."

"It is a strange name. What does it mean?"

"Son of Horus."

Her face brightened. "We have a beautiful temple in his honor at Heliopolis. It is located on a high hill overlooking the great obelisks. Horus is my favorite god."

"But you are a Christian."

Herais did not respond to this. She finished with the bowls, dried them, then turned to her father. Origen touched her on the arm. "Why is Horus your favorite god?"

"Because he defeated darkness."

"Are you afraid of darkness?"

She retreated into silence.

20

"Did you know that Horus reclaimed the ancient Egyptians from slavery and taught them how to use their hands in skillful work?" said Origen. "But he did this through the intervention of his father Osiris, who was hated by his brother Set. One day Set invited him to a banquet and then persuaded him to step into a cunningly-devised coffin made exactly to Osiris' measure. . . . "

Herais glanced toward her father.

"As soon as Osiris stepped into the coffin Set slammed shut the lid and cast it into the Nile. Isis heard of this and set out to search for her dead husband's body. After many wanderings, she succeeded in finding it but Set once again seized possession of the corpse and this time cut it into fourteen pieces and scattered them over Egypt. Isis collected them, joined the limbs together with her miraculous hand and brought her husband from the dead. This is why Osiris is honored as god of the nether world."

"What has all this to do with Horus?" she asked.

"When Horus grew up he went forth to avenge his father's death. Soon he conquered his evil uncle and dispossessed him of his kingdom." Suddenly Origen stopped. In a hollow voice, he added, "Christianity has borrowed much from Osiris. He too was resurrected, and the dead of the nether world partake of him in the same manner as Christ is partaken at the Eucharist."

"You speak like a student."

"I am."

"Where do you study?"

"At Clement's college in Alexandria."

"I have an uncle who lives in Alexandria. His name is Nichomachus. He is a wealthy grain merchant."

"I know of him," said Origen.

"It is almost time for the healings," she whispered. "I must arrange to find some bearers."

"Why?"

"My father has to be carried to Holy Abouk."

"I can do it," said Origen.

"He is very heavy."

"Throw a cover over his shoulders. I will carry him."

Herais did as he bade. He picked up the willing body and carried it out of the tent. He looked for Alexandros but could not find him. Several young acolytes dressed in bright yellow robes and carrying lit tapers had formed a small circle beneath the platform and were chanting hymns. An old woman with a sallow face hobbled on a crutch through the multitude and shouted hoarsely, "Holy prophet, have mercy upon me!"

Her threnody touched off a chorus of anguished cries.

"Heal my daughter, Holy Abouk . . . touch the withered arm of my son . . . cast out the devils from my heart, holy prophet!"

The sun sank into the desert. Night fell on Natron. One of the acolytes stepped into a nearby tent and brought out a large pan filled with oil. Someone set a torch to it. Hand lamps were lit. Origen found himself in a sea of drowning faces, each straining with fear and hope. He could not bear it. "This is insane," he said to Herais. "I am taking your father back to the tent."

"But the healings have not begun."

"God cannot manifest Himself in this wild circus!"

She began to tremble. "Did He not feed the five thousand with only a few loaves of bread and two fishes. . . ? "

Origen fought to curb his tongue. *Do not speak to me of two-cheeked Saviors, walkers-upon-the-sea, healers whose own flesh can be punctured by a soldier's lance!*

The woolen cover slid off her father's back and Herais stooped to pick it up. Origen's arms ached. "What do you want me to do with him?" he asked.

"Please put him down . . . here beside me."

Against the shimmering lights, several pilgrims hoisted a young man on their shoulders then handed him

22

the largest lamp. Using the planks as a ladder, he climbed to the platform, placed the lamp at Abouk's feet and quickly scrambled back to the ground. The prophet's thunderous voice tore the night asunder:

"Great is the Lord and highly to be praised. Yea, verily He is great and more lovely in beauty than the sons of men. Great is He who doeth wondrous things. Yea, glorious and marvelous things of which there is no number. Great is He who changeth the times and the seasons . . . who hath put down princes from their thrones and hath exalted those of low degree!"

"I must leave," exclaimed Origen.

Herais clutched his arm. "Please stay. I need you here."

" . . . Be glad, oh thirsty desert. Rejoice and blossom like the lily. Be strong, ye hands that hang down, ye palsied knees. Behold, your God will come and heal you. Yea, He will send His water into the thirsty ground, and hands that before hung down shall become strong, and knees that long ago were diseased shall walk straight!"

Origen moved away. "I must attend to our dromedaries," he said. "Wait here. I shall return in a short while."

She looked crestfallen. He waited until she had settled beside her father and then he edged away. Seeking the loneliest corner of the night, he fled to it, convinced more than ever that his life was drowning in illusions and contradictions.

"Origen. . . . "

"You left your father alone?" he cried.

"I was afraid," murmured Herais.

"But I promised to return quickly."

"You did not go to the dromedaries. . . . "

"Please go back to your father."

Behind them, Abouk kept shattering the night. Loud cheers erupted. Now silence.

"Are you going to the dromedaries soon?" she asked.
"Yes."

Slowly she walked away.

An hour later he returned to the encampment and found only a few stragglers huddled around the platform. Herais and her father were at the same place where he had left them. She was weeping. He hurried toward her but an obese old man in a tattered robe stepped in front of him. "Did you see it, my son?" he shouted. "Did you see the miracle?"

"What miracle?"

"When the oil in the large pan failed, Holy Abouk raised his hands and ordered the acolytes to go to the spring and fill their coffers with water. After they returned, he blessed them and straightaway the water in the coffers was transformed into oil!"

"Nonsense," cried Origen. But the old man was hard of hearing. He lifted his glazed eyes toward the platform and intoned in a heavy voice, "Great is the hand of God. Great is His prophet, Holy Abouk!"

"Were there any healings?" Origen yelled into his ear.

"Of course, my child. A certain woman whose daughter had an unclean spirit besought Holy Abouk to cast it out and he did so. There were many other healings also. A young boy with an impediment in his speech was brought to Holy Abouk. The prophet spoke to the boy's infirmity in the same manner as the Master and immediately the string of the boy's tongue was unloosed. . . . "

Herais was suddenly standing beside them. "He did not heal my father," she sobbed.

The old man did not hear her.

Origen went to Herais' father and picked him up. When he got to the tent he put him down then tucked two pillows under the trembling head. Herais followed him outside. "Will you come again tomorrow and carry my father to Holy Abouk?"

Origen did not answer.

"Perhaps it was my fault that he was not healed."

"Why do you say this?"

"I should not have left him alone. . . . "

Origen touched her on the arm and walked away.

Alexandros was lying on the ground, the sheep's hair cover draped over his body. The dromedaries stirred when they heard him approaching. He sat down beside them and clasped both hands over his knees. Alexandros' voice startled him. "Where have you been?"

"Walking" said Origen.

"If you wish, we can leave tomorrow,"

"Why?"

"I should not have asked you to come. It was wrong."

"Go to sleep, Alexandros. We can discuss this in the morning."

"Holy Abouk performed many miracles tonight."

"I heard," said Origen, smoothing down the sand behind Alexandros. The night had turned very cold. He took the cover and pulled it over his body but he could not close his eyes. Herais' sobbing face tormented him. When he was certain that Alexandros had fallen asleep, he got up and crept quietly around the dromedaries. At the poles he reached for the first plank, jumped, and grabbed hold of it. He worked his way up to the next plank. In the distance a dog howled. Climbing on to the platform, he saw the figure of Abouk silhouetted against the full moon, facing the east in prayer. An offensive odor attacked him as he crawled near the prophet. "I must talk to you," he said.

"Who comes here?" cried the hollow voice.

"I have something to ask you," said Origen.

The prophet did not turn around. "No one is permitted on this platform. Leave!"

"But I have to know. Did you truly transform the water into oil? Were those people healed?"

Abouk kept his head high, threatening the night.

"I must know!" shouted Origen.

"You are the son of Satan," bellowed the prophet. "The spirit of God cannot enter into the house of pride, the house wherein are found worldly pleasures; for as the body grows the soul becomes weak. Yea, it is sufficient to eat only grass, to wear grass, to sleep on grass. I will not allow even the sparrow's twitter to prevent me from that repose of heart which only You can give, oh Lord. No, I will not fall victim to that arch-enemy called sleep!"

Origen crawled over the side and worked his way down the planks as the monotonous voice kept ranting, "Your countenance is known only to those who worship You in unceasing prayer . . . in fasting, purity of soul, self-abnegation, humility. . . . "

When the earth finally accepted Origen's feet he raced to the spring and feverishly washed his hands and face. But he still felt unclean. Hurrying back to Alexandros, he shook him awake. "We are leaving this place at daybreak," he shouted hoarsely. "Do you hear me, Alexandros?"

4.

Alexandros did not attend college when classes resumed several days later. Origen was relieved. His brain still burned from the disgusting events at Natron, and he kept chastising himself for allowing Alexandros to drag him there. But now everything had changed. He was back in Alexandria, listening to Titus Flavius Clement. Lean, white-bearded, inexhaustible. It was Clement who first opened his heart to philosophy by insisting that scientific knowledge was far superior to dogma.

Clement's college was a large two-storied house of granite in the Greek Quarter, adjacent to the Oratory of Blessed Mark. It had a spacious courtyard with flower-beds, fig and palm trees, a fountain, and several busts of Greek philosophers. Classes were conducted in the two large rooms east of the courtyard. The course of study continued for three years and from the first day Origen craved to put his heart on truth, wiggling with impatience whenever Clement tried to tie the anchor of discipline to his quest. 'The sincere philosopher,' Clement warned, 'has two obligations, the study of wisdom and the duty to teach.'

Seldom imposing any demands other than a strict obedience to sincerity, Clement constantly thrust his students against the wall of earnest study and self-examination, encouraging them always to look daringly into their hearts. It was an apprenticeship Origen never shunned but like Odysseus after a long siege of trials he longed for the sight of his own Ithaca.

Throughout most of the morning Clement spoke on martyrdom. "There are far too many ill-advised people in Alexandria who feel they must sacrifice their lives for one cause or another. But only the fool seeks death. The true martyr is that man who comes to the end of his days after courageously exhibiting the perfect works of love."

Clement's words stabbed at Origen's memory because as a young boy he had yearned with all his heart to die a martyr's death and even imagined himself walking proudly down Canopic Way to his martyrdom as thousands cheered.

At the end of the lecture the students gathered around Clement and beleaguered him with questions. Philimon was the first to speak. "Master Clement, I do not agree with your statement that God endowed the Greeks with the gift of philosophy in order to prepare them for the new religion. I say that it is wrong to devour Pagan literature, seeking to discover seeds of truth in it. There can be no truth in heresy."

Clement did not look up from his table. "Who speaks here . . . Philimon or the Carthaginian philosopher Tertullian? At any rate I hasten to answer you. We borrow from philosophy not so much its content as its method. All knowledge proceeds from the Creator. If we accuse philosophy of heresy it must be concluded that God is a heretic, for it is He who first imbued us with the search for wisdom."

Philimon flushed. Because he had always nourished a disdain for physical demeanor he suffered from an excessive amount of flesh. But he was liked by most of the students. Just as another student named Heraclas was about to inject himself into the argument Origen put his hand on Philimon and said, "Come walk with me."

They sauntered around the courtyard, stopping before a marble bust of Plato. "I cannot understand this inordinate affection you have for Tertullian," said Origen.

Philimon's face twitched with resentment. "Tertullian is an acknowledged man of genius. . . . "

"He is also a religious fanatic who closes his mind entirely to all the wonders of the universe, particularly man. He is unjust, cynical, and without mercy and love." Origen wanted to say more but stopped when he saw Clement drawing near.

"What is wrong?" Clement asked.

Philimon struggled with his face, trying to hold back the tears.

"Are you upset?" said Clement in a softer voice.

Philimon could not speak.

"But why?"

"Perhaps because the class laughed at him," said Origen.

Clement shrugged. "The class requires little encouragement for laughter. We must all learn that we cannot approach the flames of wisdom without scalding our fingers." Tenderly he touched Philimon on the head. "Go in peace, my son. In the future, try to speak with your own tongue, not that of others."

Soon after Philimon departed, Clement said to Origen. "It is unbearably hot in this courtyard. Let us move away from here."

The sun was even more relentless when they came into the street. Students scurried to seek refuge within the sprawling shadows of the Museum. Merchants had already closed their shops and gone home. Stopping a moment to wipe the sweat from his face with the back of his hand, Clement remarked, "Alexandros has not been to class for many days. Is anything wrong?"

"I have not seen him since we came back from Natron," said Origen testily.

Clement laughed. "You went to Natron?"

Origen did not find this amusing.

"Perhaps you should go to his house tonight," Clement added. "He may be ill."

"If you say so."

Clement gave him an austere look. "Is something bothering you?"

"In a few weeks I hope to be on my way to Athens. . . ."

"I wish you would remain here."

"What is there for me in Alexandria?"

"This college."

"What do you mean?"

"I want you to assist me next year," said Clement.

"Be a teacher?"

"Yes."

"But I am only seventeen."

"Your age has nothing to do with it."

Origen plunged into deep thought.

"Well?" asked Clement.

"Surely you do not expect an answer this minute?"

"Of course not. Speak first with your father."

"I need not discuss it with him."

Clement hunched his shoulders. "But I must have your decision soon otherwise I shall have to ask someone else."

"Alexandros and I promised each other. We intend to go to Athens as soon as we finish our course of study here."

30

"Athens can wait. Besides, Alexandros will understand."

They walked as far as the Museum then turned back. In the courtyard, Clement's voice softened. "Let me tell you what I have been writing. I call it STROMATEIS. It is a collection of incidents that I have stored up for my old age as a remedy against forgetfulness. As you know, I was priveleged to hear many discourses of blessed and remarkable men but to enumerate them all is impossible. It is sufficient that I mention only that Sicilian bee whom I tracked down while he was concealed in Egypt, gathering honey from the flowers of prophetic meadows. I speak of my esteemed teacher, Pantaenus. It was he who carved into my mind the lasting impression of morality and Greek thought. His gift I have tried to pass on to others, particularly you, my son. Indeed how mighty is philosophy! It makes men out of wild beasts, gives life to the dead, opens the eyes of the blind."

The heat was oppressive. The leaves of the lemon trees in the courtyard looked parched. Not one bird was in sight.

"I hope you find Alexandros in good health," sighed Clement. He lifted his hand in blessing but Origen, anticipating this, turned to wave at a student who was not even looking his way.

## 5.

Alexandros' mother was pleased to see Origen. She invited him into the front room and then put a small platter of figs and dates before him. She was a slight woman whose face always reflected pain. Her husband had died of a plague that had swept through Alexandria during the reign of Commodus. Alexandros was her only child.

"I came to talk with Alexandros," Origen said, pushing aside the platter.

Her eyes clouded.

"He has not been in class for many days. Is he ill?"

She sat down. "I have something to tell you, Origen . . . Alexandros has become a priest."

"What?"

"When he came home that night from Natron he was very pale and unable to sleep. In the early hours of morning I heard him cry out in anguish, 'I hear Thee! I hear

Thee!' It sent terror into my heart and when I rushed to him I found him rolling over the floor in a convulsive fit. I tried to console him and whisper reality back into his ears but he pushed me away. I then ran to bring him some water and as I put the cup to his lips he smashed it against the floor. With loud moans he fell among the broken pieces, wailing and thrashing his body. Not knowing where to turn, I closed my eyes and spoke to God. Soon Alexandros came to himself and I helped him to his bed but he did not remember what had happened. I asked him what he meant when he said 'I hear Thee! I hear Thee!' and he refused to answer. With heavy fear in my heart, I went with him to the house of Bishop Demetrius at day-break. He talked privately with Alexandros while I waited, and when at last they came out of the room I saw an immediate change in my son. His face was serene, his eyes peaceful. 'It is God's voice that Alexandros hears,' the bishop announced to me. 'God leaning over his ear, hounding him, refusing to stop unless Alexandros gives Him his word and becomes a priest! ' "

"And you listened to this foolishness?" said Origen.

"What else was there to do?"

"Why did you not summon me?"

She smiled weakly. "How could you have helped Alexandros?"

"We would have reasoned together. Nightmares are the works of fantasy, not God. Where is Alexandros? I must speak with him."

"He is not here."

"Not here?"

"He left by galley early yesterday morning . . . he said it was God's will."

"Where did he go?"

"To Palestine."

Origen stood up. "This is insane!"

"Are you saying he did wrongly?"

Origin's voice became bitter. "It is grievously wrong to do anything out of fear!"

He saw from her eyes that he had hurt her. She asked him to try one of the figs but he shook his head and walked to the door. Still in tears, she hurried after him. "Please do not be angry with Alexandros. He did not want to burden you with his problem. After he is settled in Palestine he will write to you and explain everything."

Origen opened the door. "What is there to explain?"

She came with him as far as the street. He begged her to return to the house but she stood there sadly, unable to speak. Confused and seething with rancor, he took her into his arms as he would his own mother and kissed her wet cheek. It was dark and she did not see the tears forming in his own eyes.

6.

Clement's words at class the next day passed faintly through his brain. " . . . thus man's salvation begins with faith, rises into love, and reaches its ultimate goal in perfect knowledge. Now we are all aware that men tend to shrink away from scholarly study. Greek philosophy terrifies them. Like those who passed the Sirens, they block up their ears because they fear if once they allow themselves to listen to Greek thought they will never be able to find their way home again. We are surrounded by such people here in Alexandria. They take fright at anything that concerns the mind, and continually scream out, 'We must engage ourselves only with what is necessary and bound in faith!' There are others who go even further and maintain that wisdom and knowledge were introduced into human life by some evil inventor for the destruction of mankind. 'Greek philosophy is a harlot!' they proclaim.

A mischievous grin flashed across Clement's face. "Perhaps she is. But we do not wish to marry her, only to linger with her a while and savor her beauty."

The class laughed.

Origen's uneasiness subsided when the students assembled around Clement's table at the close of the lecture. Someone asked, "If philosophy truly proceeds from God why then does it have so many contradictions?"

Clement did not have time to answer. Stepping boisterously forward, Heraclas asked, "What is your opinion of marriage?"

"The childless man falls short of nature's perfection," said Clement softly.

"Nevertheless I am to remain celibate," announced Heraclas.

Clement smiled. "This is understandable. You too wallow in the sands with Philimon's African hero. If Tertullian were permitted to have his way, life would be reduced to an asylum for idiots who forbid everyone from marriage."

"Christ did not marry, neither shall I!"

"But He was constantly in the company of women," Origen interjected.

"Are you implying that Christ had sexual desires?"

"He was a man was He not? You and Tertullian prefer to see Him as an immaculate little cloud tied to the Creator's toe."

Origen had clashed with Heraclas many times. Although Heraclas was shorter in stature, he was strong of body, with powerful shoulders and legs.

Sensing there would be another confrontation, the students fell silent but Clement intervened and lifted his hands in solemn admonition, "Let everything you do be done for virtue, both deeds and words. Learn gladly, teach ungrudgingly. Never hide wisdom from others by reason of a covetous heart, nor through false modesty stand aloof from instruction. Be first to practice humility. If you look for true knowledge and ask for it with importunity, you shall receive it."

After the last student had left the room, Origen said to Clement, "Alexandros is a priest."

"What?"

"Demetrius placed his hands upon his head two days ago."

"Who told you this?"

"His mother."

"I cannot believe it."

"He did it out of fear," said Origen.

"What do you mean?"

"He heard a voice in his sleep the night we returned from Natron and Demetrius told him it was God."

"Perhaps it was."

"God does not speak," said Origen flatly.

Clement gathered his scrolls together and walked into the courtyard. Origen joined him. "I am still waiting for your answer," said Clement.

Origen lifted his eyes to the tiled roofs of Alexandria. "Well?"

"There are many things to consider," snapped Origen. "We are a large family, a poor family."

Clement hunched his shoulders. "We will discuss it later. Your mother asked me to dine with you tonight."

Origen started to pull away.

"Where are you going?" asked Clement.

"To the Heptastadion."

Clement tossed him a smile. "As you sit on the rocks contemplating the pulse of the sea, please speak to God so that He might guide you into the proper decision."

Origen glared at him. "I speak only to my heart!"

After the meal, Origen joined Clement and his father in the front room. Little John clung to his sleeve. Cle-

37

ment was saying, "I enjoy coming to your house, Leonidas. It brings happy memories of my own home in Athens."

Origen's mother placed a bowl of oranges before Clement. He took one and began peeling it while little John watched intently. "Do you have a father, Master Clement?" the boy asked.

Clement took him into his lap. "Both my father and mother have found their eternal sleep, little John."

Leonidas gave his son an impatient pat on the head and asked him to leave the room. At first Little John rebelled but when he saw the austere look on his father's face he slid off Clement's knee and scurried to his mother who was busy near the oven. She tried to silence him but little John began whimpering and stomping his feet. Origen carried him to the upper chamber where the other boys had already snuggled under their covers and were waiting for their mother. It was her practice to chant from David in Hebrew each night.

When he returned downstairs Origen said to her, "Father is about to discuss my future with Master Clement. . . . "

She detected the tremor in his voice and answered soothingly, "Your future is already determined, Origen."

He wanted to remain with her but his father was calling him from the front room. Origen kissed her on the forehead and entered the room just as Leonidas rose to his feet. "Master Clement tells me that he asked you to teach at the college next year."

Origen gazed at the floor.

"Well, what is your answer?"

"I have not decided yet."

Leonidas frowned. "Indecision seems to plague you lately."

Clement tried to intercede. "God has gifted very few persons with your son's talent for looking behind words. . . . "

38

Leonidas responded heatedly, "And I tell you this, I see no point in looking *behind* words!"

Clement remained calm. "Leonidas, we must not let our minds be so naive as to suppose the manna which the Israelites ate was real food. If we are to take every word in Scripture as God-inspired we then become worshippers of the letter, not the spirit."

Leonidas returned to his seat. "I have no desire to enter into a theological dispute with you, Master Clement, but since you already raised the subject let me say that it is wrong to permit the wholesale interpretation of Scripture which you allow in your college. You are building another Tower of Babel. But now I am only concerned with my son. Are you certain that he can teach?"

"Origen is very capable."

"What about his age? Is it not an obstacle?"

Clement smiled. "We Greeks have a saying, '*As I teach, I learn.*' "

Leonidas was in no mood for Clement's pedantry. "Will my son be reimbursed for his labors at the college?"

"Eventually, yes."

"Eventually?"

"Bishop Demetrius does not believe that instructors should accept money."

"What has he to do with it?"

"The college falls under his jurisdiction," said Clement. "However, I am confident that Demetrius will make an exception in Origen's case."

"Did you know that Alexandros has become a priest?" Leonidas asked.

"Yes."

"He cannot read or write Hebrew. . . . "

"Nevertheless he will be a dedicated servant of God."

"My son is much better endowed," Leonidas ranted.

Clement struggled to his feet. "It is getting late, Leonidas. I can hardly keep my eyes open."

Still seething, Leonidas walked with him as far as the

39

door. "Did you also know that my son longs to go to Greece?"

Clement's eyes touched Origen. "Athens is eternal. She will wait for him."

After Clement was gone Leonidas pounced on Origen. "You are walking in circles. I warn you. Life has a strange way of turning everything around. Youth fades into wilting old age, friends become enemies, lofty ideals drown in a whirlpool of earthly anxieties. There is no escape. The priesthood can pull your heart away from a suffering and blundering humanity. It can sanctify your quest for wisdom."

"But I cannot stay in one place," said Origen. "My heart commands me to set out."

"Where?"

"I do not know."

"To find what?"

"I do not know."

Leonidas put on his sandals then fiercely began combing his beard. Origen's mother became alarmed. "Leonidas, you are not going to the agora again?"

"I am," he replied defiantly.

"But the streets are seething with animosity. It is not wise to speak openly of Christ."

Leonidas paid no attention to her. At the door he threw a despondent look toward Origen. "The world is a treacherous ocean. You cannot navigate it alone. I entreat you for the last time, let Christ be your Captain."

"I must steer my own vessel," said Origen.

"But you have no destination."

"I will find one."

Leonidas flung open the door. "Heed my words, you will be swallowed by oblivion!"

An hour later Origen went upstairs to his bed. He shut his eyes but could not lie still. Another hour passed. In the malignant darkness he heard his mother's soft steps, felt her warm hand on his head. In time he fell asleep.

40

## 7.

He was suddenly back in Natron, trapped on the high platform, the planks stripped away, the stench, the thunderous voice of Abouk, the torches, the acolytes chanting in unison, and far below, her hands flung high, Herais crying out his name, *Origen! Origen!* There were loud crashes, wild yells; now he was falling, reaching desperately for Herais' hand, discovering it was his mother's hand. . . .

"Origen, come quickly!"

He flung away the bed covers and followed her into the dark hallway. Below them, Roman soldiers had already broken down the front door and were dragging Leonidas into the street.

Origen chased after them and yelled, "What do you want with my father?"

The soldiers ignored him, clubbing Leonidas over the head until he lost consciousness. The sight of his father's blood enraged him and he ran back into the house for his sandals and robe.

His mother attempted to stop him but he cautioned her to remain in the house. Hurrying into the street, he looked for his father but no one was in sight. In a fit of despair, he ran to Clement's house and awoke him. "Roman soldiers broke into our house and dragged my father away!" he bellowed.

Clement tried to calm him. "Where did they take him?"

"I do not know."

"Was he at the agora last night?"

"Yes."

"That was unwise. But you must not be alarmed. Leonidas will not be harmed. A few questions perhaps, a flogging."

Origen started for the door.

"I am confident that your father will be released," Clement assured him.

Origen opened the door.

"This is not a persecution!" Clement shouted.

The word sent a dull blow into Origen's stomach. More than ten years had passed since his first encounter with bloodshed and death yet everything was still vivid in his mind . . . four Roman emperors within the short space of three weeks . . . Pertinax, Didius, Niger, Severus . . . each with his own method of violence, his own disdain for human life.

Clement's face had turned pale. "You must believe me. The Romans have no cause to start trouble."

"They do not need a cause."

"But your life will be in jeopardy. I beg you, remain here with me. Your father will be released in due time."

Origen was not listening to him. He pushed the door open and hurried toward the volcano of noise that had suddenly erupted over the Temple of Serapis.

He could not draw near the Temple. Cordons of soldiers had linked their arms together in one long chain, slicing Rhakotis Hill in two. Hundreds of shrieking faces tried to break through but the soldiers lashed at them with leather straps and clubs. Origen recognized one of his mother's friends and when she saw him she came sobbing into his arms. "They took Theodorus . . . they burst into our house and took him away!"

He tried to calm her but his words could not pierce her pain. She started mumbling and wringing her hands as the tears flowed down her face. He had always known her to be this way, even in happier days. His father once jokingly called her a jagged nerve. *His father!*

Pushing her aside, Origen confronted one of the soldiers and grabbed him by his copper wrist. A leather strap caught him on his face and when the blood began streaming down his cheek a frightening sensation overpowered him. *He was here once before, standing on this same plot of ground, among all these terrified faces, in front of this very Temple . . . sinking helplessly, drowning in his own grief.*

Clement's hand was suddenly on his shoulder. "Origen, I beg you. Return to your house."

Origen fixed his eyes on the blue body of Serapis. "I will not leave until I find my father."

"They are going to kill him," cried Clement.

Origen glared at the turbulent sky.

"They are going to kill everyone inside that Temple," Clement exclaimed, his voice clogged with tears. "There was a violent insurrection at the agora last night. Two Roman soldiers were slain."

The entire sky fell down upon him. Clement once more implored him to return home. He refused. Another hand touched his shoulder, vein-streaked, tender . . . his mother's hand. "You must come home with me right away!" she urged.

"They are going to kill my father!" he shouted hoarsely.

She took him into her arms and whispered childhood peace into his ear as a cancerous demon gnawed at his legs. Slumping to his knees, he succumbed to a direful darkness.

Several hours later, he found himself lying on the couch in the front room, still faint and nauseous. Clement entered the house. He went first to Origen's mother and took hold of her hand. "Leonidas is dead," he sighed.

Her only response was a despairing look as Origen's brothers started to weep. He felt that he should go to them and console them but he had no place to put his sorrow. His own voice sounded strange to his ears. "Where is he . . . where is my father?"

"In the Temple," said Clement, his mouth trembling.

"How did they kill him?"

Clement did not answer.

"I must know!"

"He was beheaded. . . . "

Origen put on his sandals and walked toward the shattered front door. When he reached the street he looked back and saw them all watching fearfully, their eyes filled with tears. Little John waved for a moment but his mother pulled down his hand and led him away.

The Temple was veiled in death. Most of the soldiers were gone. Only a small lamenting crowd remained. High above Alexandria an unsuspecting moon hung quietly in the sky, pouring a glaze of light through the porticoes of the Temple. Directly behind blue Serapis stood the figure of Isis, her pale skin shivering in the night. Origen pushed his way through the cluster of people and came to the great steps. The few soldiers who were present made no effort to stop him. At the top he moved through the maze of columns and entered the inner chamber where rows of torches burned. On the floor, in two large mounds, he saw the dead. Heads tossed into one heap, bodies into the other. The sight of his father's head brought him quickly to his knees. He picked it up with both hands and felt its coldness. His lips found their way through the blood-stained beard, to the cheek, to that same mouth which only yesterday had said, *'Life has a strange way of turning everything inside-out!'*

Holding it against his breast, he walked to the second pile and pulled free his father's body. He tried to attach the head to it but it kept rolling off to the side, leaving streaks of blood. He tried once more, carefully straightening the body until it lay perfectly flat. This time the head did not move away.

The Oratory of Blessed Mark was crammed with people that night. Throughout the long prayers Origen kept an anxious eye on his mother who for the first time was weeping freely and without shame. All around him, the wall torches flooded the Oratory with bouncing diagonals of light. Soon the testimonies began. First to speak was Linus who came to Origen's house each week with his fruit cart and mule. While Linus bargained with Origen's mother, the boys played with the mule, a docile beast who knew his name well, 'Themistocles! Themistocles!' Linus enjoyed watching them and before leaving he gave each of them a large orange.

Tonight he was not the same man. His face was ashen, his body trembled. "Not many of you knew my brother Michael. He was a shipman and traveled into many foreign lands. I stood at his side when sentence was pronounced upon him today. Michael looked his executioner in the face and blessed him . . . yes, blessed even the soldier's sword as he brought it down against Michael's neck in one blow."

There was a long silence.

Simon, the rug merchant, stepped forward and talked about his son Timotheos, who assisted him in his work. "I did not see Timotheos die. I am an old man and was unable to pass through the great crowds on Rhakotis Hill but

I did accompany Timotheos to the Eastern Cemetery to-night. I walked every inch of the way. . . . " He could not continue. Several hands came to his assistance and he was helped to a bench in the vestibule.

There was more silence.

A man unknown to Origen came to the front of the assembly and said, "My name is Ambrosius. Although I have lost no one dear to me, my heart commands me to speak. I am not a Christian. Like a leaf in the wind, I have alighted from one doctrine to another . . . Plato, Marcion, Montanus, Valentinian. This morning I stood on the top step of the Temple and saw a man go to his death without the slightest trace of fear. When the judges asked him to deny his faith and confess belief to the pagan gods he refused. The pro-consul then sentenced him to death. With my own ears I heard this man sigh peacefully and say, *'May the will of God be done!'* This is exactly what he said. I shall never forget his name. It was Leonidas. . . . "

Origen's heart leaped out of its pain. He quickly glanced toward his mother and brothers. They too had their eyes clamped on the stranger.

" . . . never before have I seen such courage," Ambrosius went on. Suddenly he was aware of himself and he began to stammer, "Let . . . let me add that, along with every other pagan in Alexandria, I have ridiculed you and mocked you but now I realize it is I who should be mocked and ridiculed . . . I . . . I have nothing further to say."

As soon as the testimonies ended Origen weaved his way through the assembly until he reached the stranger. He was a heavy-boned man, handsome in appearance, his hair and beard meticulously groomed.

"The man about whom you spoke," said Origen, "was my father."

Ambrosius' eyes lit up. "Indeed you must be very proud of him."

At this point Clement raised his hands from the pulpit. "Beloved brethren, every year on this day we shall

46

celebrate the memory of these glorious martyrs and we shall also visit their graves to read aloud the detailed accounts of their sacrifice. I say this unto you: these men and women have already achieved the blessedness of eternal joy. However, let me remind you that we must not fall into that error which still persists in the church of Smyrna today where the bones of blessed Polycarp are considered more precious than God, or in Antioch where equal veneration is paid to the remains of Ignatius, or in Carthage where the friends of Cyprian gathered up his blood in handkerchiefs and built an oratory over his tomb. I counsel you instead to follow the example of Peter when he beheld his own wife on her way to execution. He rejoiced and addressed her by name with words of good cheer, saying, 'Remember the Lord!' And so let it be. Our salvation comes only from the ageless spirit of truth, not from dead bones or dried-up blood."

While everyone filed slowly out of the Oratory, Origen remained at Ambrosius' side. They were soon joined by Clement. "I see that you two have already met," he remarked.

They proceeded down the granite steps, into the dark street. "Lord Ambrosius wishes to pursue some courses at the college," said Clement, shifting his eyes to Origen. "If you have no objection I shall assign him to you."

Ambrosius stopped walking. "This lad is a teacher?"

"As well as a brilliant interpreter of words," Clement added. "But more than that, he is now the son of a martyr!"

# II

On a sultry afternoon several weeks later, Clement took Origen aside and said, "There is a carpet of shade beneath the fig tree in the courtyard. Let us sit there a while." He had a platter filled with oranges and he placed it on a small marble table near the bench. As they sat, Clement sliced an orange and offered some to Origen but he had no desire for it. "Tonight I want you to come with me to a friend's house," said Clement.

"Who is it?"

"Her name is Paula."

"No, thank you."

"She expects us. I already told her that you would accompany me. Come now, wash your face and hands, smooth down your hair. In the name of the Father, I wish you would shave off that stunted beard. It does not become you."

49

Origen gave vent to his anger. "Why must you do this?"

"What?"

"I have not assented to teach here next fall yet you presume that I will. This is what you told Lord Ambrosius at the Oratory. And now you are making me go to this woman's house without having consulted me."

"Lady Paula desires to meet you very much."

"She does not even know me."

"We have discussed you many times," Clement persisted. "I am sure that you will enjoy her. She is a woman of great substance. Her house is like a lyceum, always bustling with activity."

"What kind of activity?"

"Lectures and discussions."

"What is the nature of the discussions?"

"Mostly philosophy," said Clement, a gleam flickering in his eye. He left the courtyard for a moment and returned with a pitcher of water, a basin, and a towel. Origen washed his face and smoothed down his hair.

"She expects us at dusk," said Clement.

"But it is dusk now."

"I had to wait until the last class. Come, we must not keep them from dinner."

"How old is this woman?"

"She has seventy-one years and is a widow," responded Clement. "Hurry, brush your robe . . . tie your sandals. Do you want these people to take you for a street urchin?"

They left the courtyard and entered the street. The Agora was deserted. Although it was almost dark, Alexandria still groaned from the stifling heat of the day. Moving under the shadowed porticoes along Canopic Way, they were afforded some relief, but Clement's robe was soon soaked with perspiration and he had to stop on several occasions to catch his breath. In time they passed the Gate

50

of the Sun and entered into the Jewish Quarter. It was somewhat cooler when they crossed the canal and walked past the Shrine of Pompey which was almost totally absorbed by the growing darkness.

As they turned into a wide street toward a large house of marble, Clement said, "Lady Paula lives there."

A large garden lay sprawled behind the house. Darting between the many trees, a swift-flowing stream emptied itself into a deep pool. Paved walks were guarded by statues adorned with crowns and garlands. In the very center of the garden, on a high pedestal of marble, stood an imposing bust of Epicurus. Pans of smoking incense were everywhere. Torches burned. Some of the guests sat on marble benches while others stolled leisurely along the walks. The men were dressed in rich tunics, the women in embroidered linen robes. They were in a festive mood. From out of their midst emerged a huge Nubian manservant. He walked directly toward Clement, bowed, then led them across a small wooden bridge to a long marble table that was laden with food. He bowed once again and walked away.

Clement straightened up and waved to a tall gray-haired woman who was conversing with several guests at the further side of the garden. She acknowledged Clement's greeting with a wide smile and hurried to meet him. Turning quickly, she beamed, "And this must be Origen. I have heard many wonderful things about you."

Origen bowed his head.

"Indeed you are more handsome than I imagined," she smiled. "The young maidens of Alexandria must constantly flock around you. And yet. . . . " She paused and stared at him.

"Is there anything wrong?" asked Origen.

"I detect something deeper in your eyes . . . a hunger perhaps for unattainable worlds."

"How can you say this? You hardly know me?"

51

She smiled again. "When I was your age I too had this hunger but now I believe only in what I can see and touch."

The heavy scent of food, the wine, the loud laughter ignited Origen and before he could stop himself the words had spilled out. "All Epicureans live solely for pleasure. What shall become of them after their senses grow dull?"

"They will die, as we all must die."

"Christ defeated death," chuckled Clement.

The smile left Lady Paula's face. "No one shall ever defeat death, Master Clement. In many ways I admire your Christ but he was a hopeless dreamer who sought goals that can never be reached."

"Did Epicurus reach them?" asked Origen.

Her face became warm again. "No."

The man-servant drew up to them nervously and whispered something to Lady Paula. She made a hasty apology to Origen and Clement, then followed the man-servant across the wooden bridge. Origen reached for a morsel of bread, tossed it into his mouth and blurted to Clement, "I have decided to teach at the college next fall."

Clement hunched his shoulders. "What decided you?"

Origen avoided the question. "But I will teach only academic subjects, not theological. Is this clear? And what is more, I will teach a course on Epicurus!"

Clement laughed. From across the pond, Lady Paula was calling to them . . . They joined her. She introduced them to her guests and Origen's brain caught fire at the first name. "Did you say Paul . . . Paul of Antioch?"

"I am pleased that you know of him."

Origen clasped the man's hand.

"I understand that you are a student at Clement's college," said Paul. He was a broad-chested man with warm penetrating eyes. Despite his massive strength, there was a gentleness in his nature, a mellow yet withdrawing spirit, the stigma of an ascetic. Before Origen could answer him, Lady Paula interrupted. "I have an important announcement to make," she said, placing her hand on Paul's wrist. "Paul is now my legally-adopted son. This is the reason for tonight's reception. Starting tomorrow evening, Paul will start delivering a series of lectures on various philosophers. You are all invited to attend."

"Who will be the subject of his first lecture?" asked Origen.

"The heretic, Marcion."

2.

He was disquieted by his father's presence, even into the last month of the college year. Clement noticed the change in his behavior and advised him to seek immediate release through a deeper pursuit of his studies. Alexandria also tried to help. She opened wide her womb allowing the earth's fulness to burst into resurrected beauty. Never before was the season of Sefi so enriched. Every corner of Alexandria was animated by the sweet scent of birth.

But all this had little meaning for Origen. Walking spiritlessly into the philosophy class one morning, he was about to go to his usual place when he discovered some-one else there. Brilliant chestnut hair, arms the color of ivory.

He sat behind her, half-listening to Clement, his eyes never leaving the chestnut hair. At one point she looked toward the courtyard but it was too fleeting a glance and he did not catch a clear view of her face. Just then he looked up and saw Clement staring at him. "You arrived late and were not introduced to our new student. She is the niece of a devoted friend to whom her care is entrusted, now that both of her parents have found their eternal sleep. Her name is. . . . "

Herais turned around and revealed her face to him.

Clumsily he whispered, "Abouk did not heal your father?"

She shook her head.

When the hour finally drew to an end he walked with her into the courtyard. They sat under the fig tree. "I cannot believe that you are in Alexandria. What brought you here?"

"It was my uncle's wish."

"But the college year is almost over."

"Master Clement suggested that I enroll now as a preparation for the coming year."

"I shall be teaching here next year," he said.

She gazed at him with astonishment. Students had crowded into the courtyard, casting inquisitive looks toward them. Nervously she said, "It is a beautiful day. . . . "

He asked, "Do you have any other classes today?"

"No."

"I walk to the Heptastadion every afternoon. Do you want to join me?"

She nooded.

After they left the courtyard he took hold of her hand. In his wildest fancies he never dreamed that he would walk boldly down Canopic Way in full view of Alexandria holding a girl's hand. At the Heptastadion, Herais asked, "Where are Cleopatra's Needles?"

He pointed toward the Caesarium but she cast only a quick look. "It is possible that I may be one of your students next year. . . . "

He helped her up the huge wall of granite that faced Pharos Torch. At the top, they sat and looked down. The sea was calm, not one sail in sight. For an instant the water cast a spell over him: he envisioned fleets of ships— Macedonian, Persian, Roman, Phoenician—all converging upon the harbor of Lochias, their splendid bows slicing the waves, the burning sun clashing against helmets and breastplates, the oars churning mightily over the face of the Great Sea. Thousands of centuries had already burned themselves out yet here she lay, this eternal woman, sleeping peacefully . . . dreaming of past glories, feeling the warmth of Alexandria's arms around her bosom.

"What are you thinking?" asked Herais.

He shook his head then noticed that she too had her eyes fastened on the sea. Edging closer, he cupped her face in his hands and kissed her on the forehead. She kept staring at the water. "My mother was only fourteen when she married. . . . "

"What made you say that?" he asked.

"She was sitting in her garden at Caesarea when my father asked for her hand."

The late afternoon breeze came to life and Herais stood up to allow its fingers on her hair. "The sun is falling," she said. "I must return to my uncle's house."

He helped her down.

Laborers and shoppers were crowded into the Street of the Soma while merchants hurriedly displayed their wares. Within moments the sun fell behind the red-tiled roofs and brought the first shadows of dusk into the city.

Herais moved away from him when they reached the Museum. She did not bid him farewell. Their eyes met but once and then she was gone. That night he tossed fitfully in his bed, one moment chained to his father's martyrdom, the other to a clear vision of Herais staring into the face of the Great Sea.

She did not attend classes during the last few days of the college year. Origen haltingly asked Clement if he knew the reason for her absence and was told that Herais had left for Caesarea with her uncle. "They will not return to Alexandria until the latter part of Sefi," Clement added.

Desperately he tried to forget about her, burying his mind in relentless study and shunning any person or place that might rekindle some memory of her.

It was futile.

One day, while sitting with Clement in the porous shade of the fig tree in the courtyard, he felt a sudden urge to go after her in Caesarea. Clement must have known what was going on in his turbulent heart. Raising his voice, he said, "If you desire to be a sincere teacher it is your first duty to instruct the world that the Creator is an intelligent nature which does not admit to direct connection with anything else; a pure source from which all natures take their growth."

They were in the heart of summer. Vapors of heat steamed from every corner of Alexandria. Dust was everywhere. Heaving an uncomfortable sigh, Clement added, "I am afraid the years have caught up with me. I must now call a halt and devote the rest of my days to the STROMATEIS."

"What does that mean?" asked Origen.

"It is quite simple. I am asking you to be Prefect of the college. I can think of no one else more qualified to succeed me."

"But I thought I was to be a teacher."

"I expect you to teach also."

"Master Clement, I am only seventeen years old. I cannot assume such a great responsibility. I must think about my family. I cannot allow them to suffer from want and neglect."

"Your family shall be looked after," said Clement.

"We refuse to accept charity!"

"Calm yourself. Alexandria shall always minister to the family of a martyr. This is not charity. It is mercy and kindness."

"No one shall minister unto me!"

"I have already made arrangements for you," said Clement, a tone of finality in his voice.

"What arrangements?"

"You are to stay with Lady Paula."

"What?"

"She has offered quarters at her house. You cannot refuse. Besides, I assured her that you would accept."

"You had no right to do this without asking me first!" exclaimed Origen.

"I had every right. My only concern was the college. Lady Paula has an abundant library which will be entirely at your disposal. You shall have the freedom to come and go as you please." Gazing at the sky, Clement continued, "You have serious work before you. Fortunately you are familiar with the basic structure of the college. You are also aware that Greek and mathematics must be thoroughly mastered before a student is allowed to investigate the philosophical sciences."

"I asked you never to do this!" Origen said.

"What?"

"I have not given you a definite answer nevertheless you assume that I am already Prefect of the college."

Clement rose to his feet as Origen began peeling the bark from the trunk of the fig tree. After a long silence, Origen said, "Do you honestly feel that I can do it . . . be the Prefect of this great college?"

"Yes," said Clement without turning around.

"Are you certain?"

"Indeed I am."

Origen's knees almost buckled when he stood up. "Then I will try. I cannot promise anything further than this—but I will try."

Clement faced him, his eyes moist. "I have great hopes for you, my son. Do you remember that day in class a few weeks ago when I asked you to define life? You answered by saying it was a grand symbolic drama, a mystery play directed by the Creator for the enlightenment of mankind. You said that behind every word we speak, behind every thought, lies a deeper and more profound meaning—and that you would dedicate your life toward finding it. You do remember?"

"Yes."

"Humanity is starving for knowledge but it should not listen to foolishness and narrow-minded hypocricies."

The sun was now unbearable and they had to seek refuge inside the house. Clement found a stiff sheet of parchment, made a fan of it, then sat on a wooden bench. There was a loud knock on the door. Ambrosius stepped inside, his face scarlet from the heat. Origen offered him his place on the bench but Ambrosius preferred to remain standing. "Do you have a little wine, Master Clement?" he asked.

"Of course."

"Is it cool . . . from the cask?"

While Clement went after the wine, Ambrosius asked Origen, "How is your family?"

"In good health," said Origen. "And yours?"

Ambrosius did not answer. Leaping to his feet, he exclaimed, "I must tell you how we buried our great king! Alexander had thirty-two years and eight months when he died. For a period of four weeks his body was left unattended while his generals fought and bickered over his throne. But we Romans were not idle, my young friend. To preserve the contours of his divine body, we bound him in malleable plates of gold then filled his coffin with the rarest spices in Egypt. . . . "

Origen looked toward the cellar door but Clement had yet to appear with the wine. Meanwhile Ambrosius plowed on, "The funeral chariot had two axles. Its wheels were shod of Persian iron and equipped with special devices to protect it from the poor Asiatic roads. The spokes were overlaid with gold. Sixty-four selected mules were strapped to the poles, each with gilded crowns and bells.

59

A trained staff of roadmenders, mechanics, architects and engineers walked beside the chariot. It required two whole years and a considerable amount of wealth to prepare for this funeral. Finally when everything was in order we set out from Babylon, then on to Mesopotamia, into Syria, Damascus, Lydia. We were about to proceed into our final lap before entering the ancient city of Aegae in Macedonia, when Ptolemy Soter intervened and brought the body to Alexandria. It was he who built the huge mausoleum that stands here to this day, calling it the Soma."

At last Clement returned.

Ambrosius drank alone, finishing two large cups before launching into another torrent of words. "On the night when I addressed the assembly I referred to myself as a leaf in the wind. This is true. I have never been able to satisfy my mind with ancient myths and fables. For this reason have I espoused almost every philosophy known to man. Is this wrong, Master Clement?"

"Of course not."

"My wife says that I can afford such pursuits because I am a very wealthy man. But this is not true. I am sincere in my quest for wisdom." Filling his cup once more, Ambrosius lifted his voice, "I am now obsessed with Valentinus, that same pupil of Theodas, who was a disciple of the apostle Paul."

Clement appeared to be enjoying this. "Are you aware that Valentinus withdrew from the body of the church after he was refused a bishopric?"

"A slanderous lie!" cried Ambrosius. "First hear what I have to say about his teachings and then tell me if such a person could fall into this human weakness."

Clement jokingly wrung his hands. "Both Origen and I are well-acquainted with Valentinus' doctrines."

Ambrosius was not listening. "My friends, I am not concerned with candidates for the bishopric. Valentinus begins with God, the First Absolute, the unfathomable

60

abyss locked within itself, without beginning or end. He is the original aeon who created other aeons until eventually they all formed the ideal world of fulness and perfection. You may ask, 'Whence then came evil?' My friends, evil exists only in the material world. It does not proceed from the Creator because He cannot be the author of evil. Valentinians do not lose themselves in groundless theories and theological debates. They place man in three categories: the spiritual, carnal, and psychical."

Origen cut in. "Which category is yours, Lord Ambrosius?"

"All Valentinians are spiritual."

"And I?" asked Clement, good-humoredly.

"Christians are less spiritual because they are unable to rise above blind belief. Too weak to attain virtue, too soft to do evil, they are thus caught between Scylla and Charybdis."

He motioned Origen to pick up the amphora and pour out more wine but before putting the cup to his lips he toyed with it awhile, shifting it from one hand to the other. "Yes, I am grateful to Valentinus for making everything vividly clear to me. We must resolve life into a new concept, tear away the flesh, suck out the blood until only the First Absolute remains. Of course, there are many who infer that Valentinians carry things too far at times. But as you can see, I am not one of those fanatics. I eat meat, drink wine, and still enjoy certain carnal pleasures. My wife expects me to outgrow Valentinus, as I outgrew Marcion, and Montanus, and Epicurus, and. . . . "

Suddenly he stopped. In a voice that overflowed with sobs, he threw himself at Clement's feet and cried, "Please help me, Master Clement. I am despicable and weak. Give me the strength and courage that I saw in this lad's father. Please!"

3.

For the next several weeks, Clement spent long hours with Ambrosius. Origen was invited to be present. Aware that Ambrosius had already investigated every known philosophical system in his quest for peace, Clement decided that he should now embark on a study of Scripture. Ambrosius rebelled from the outset but Clement was determined. "Since the Scriptures emanate from God we must conclude that they possess the distinctive characteristics of His works: truth, unity, fulness. . . . "

Ambrosius did not allow him to finish the statement. "And what about the imperfections of Scripture? I refer to the antilogies, the repetitions and unforgivable mistakes. For example, did Joshua not pray to God at Jericho and ask Him to hold the sun over the field of battle so that the Israelites could see their enemy far into the day and thus defeat him?"

"He did."

"But if God paid heed to such a foolish request the earth would have been destroyed by fire."

"Tell me," said Clement. "Does God throw his light over the entire world?"

"He does."

"And does He also enrich the universe with stars, planets, and glorious constellations?"

"Yes."

"Then perhaps it is possible that behind each ray of light that God threw over Jericho a deeper truth was hidden. Certainly if darkness represents ignorance, so light must symbolize wisdom. Thus when Joshua begged God to hold the sun over Jericho he was in truth asking for spiritual light and courage. Armed with these weapons, the Israelites could not fail but be victorious."

Ambrosius vigorously began rubbing his hands. "I can refer to more flagrant mistakes, blunders to which you cannot apply allegorical implications. Answer me this, can there be darkness without light?"

"I do not understand you." said Clement.

"Neither can I understand this nonsense, 'In the beginning, God created the heavens and earth, and darkness was upon the face of the deep. And God said, let there be light, and there was light. And God called the light day, and the darkness night.' "

"What point are you trying to make?" asked Clement.

"Moses was wrong. His account of the creation is entirely inaccurate. Darkness cannot exist before light."

Clement cleared his throat to answer but Ambrosius turned to Origen. "Little Teacher, what do you say about all this?"

Origen's first impulse was to strike back and remind Ambrosius that he was far from little, that he stood more than one head above Ambrosius.

"Well?" exclaimed Ambrosius impatiently.

"Time and creation began simultaneously," Origen replied. "We must remember that Moses spoke as a poet and refers to the existing world."

Ambrosius released a cynical laugh. "Are there other worlds?"

"The work of creation took place thousands of years before Moses, perhaps millions of years. There were infinite numbers of world orders before our world was created, and there will be an infinite number after ours comes to an end."

Origen stopped himself abruptly, for he could see that he was already entangled in a deep morass of concepts and ideas. Thoughts began to whirl inside his brain . . . did not the Stoics contend that every process in the world of time and space is but a circular movement which returns to its original state, that of periodical destruction, from where a new evolution begins? And did not Plato favor the brilliant hypothesis of Aristarchus the Samian, who claimed the earth and planets revolve around the sun? Aristotle nourished the firm conviction that the arts and sciences had been lost and discovered myriads of times during this circular movement, while Pythagoras asserted that each cycle had an exact recurrence of events. . . .

Clement got up from his cushion and stretched his arms high. "The day is fading swiftly. Perhaps we had better stop here."

They walked through the courtyard and stopped at the front gate. "I have one last question for both of you," said Ambrosius. "Will you dine at my house this evening?"

Clement shook his head. "I have dedicated myself to the STROMATEIS and must forego everything else until it is completed."

Ambrosius looked at Origen. "My wife and children have been very anxious to meet you. Please say that you will come."

Origen consented. They bade farewell to Clement and

entered the dusty street. After moving down Canopic Way for a short distance, Ambrosius halted before a large house of marble. To the right of the house extended a large courtyard with a huge garden of trees and flower beds. The left wall of the house bordered the Museum. Four huge Corinthian columns stood at the front entrance. At the gate, crouched on a slab of red granite, a marble lion with flaming red mane glared down at them. Ambrosius playfully patted its rump. They no sooner had climbed up the front steps when the door swung open and three young girls came dashing toward them, shouting a word that punctured Origen's heart, *"Father! Father!"*

Lady Marcella, a woman of gracious manner and noble carriage, met them inside. She wore a white Ionian robe that had two purple stripes running down its front, signifying her Roman citizenship. A gold net kept her glistening raven hair in place.

The three daughters of Ambrosius were little fireflies. They sputtered about the house and could not sit still even for one moment. Origen loved their names . . . Anastasia, Anthousa, Agathi. While Ambrosius washed his face and hands in a basin, he explained that they were given names beginning with alpha because he considered it to be the most important letter of the Greek alphabet. "Perhaps I should also tell you that I even changed my own name. It was formerly Orion. I shudder everytime I think of it because omega is the cruelest letter of all. It tells me there is nothing left in life, nothing for which to hope and dream."

Origen laughed. "In that case, I am doomed."

Ambrosius led him into the enormous front room that had a cool marble floor and walls emblazoned with bright tapestries. A large urn was placed between two marble benches. There was also a long walnut table with a half-dozen matching chairs. Origen preferred to sit on a bench. Ambrosius joined him then signalled to his Nubian man-servant who disappeared for a moment and returned with a two-handled amphora and two cups. Ambrosius took a long drink of the wine and leaned back. "Little Teacher, you will also observe that I live in a city whose name begins with alpha . . . furthermore, my street is named Academia."

"I observed one other thing," Origen remarked. "Your lion outside has a red mane."

"So?"

"Do you not know that red is the most detestable color in Egypt?"

Marcella had entered the room and seated herself in a chair. "I never heard of this," she said.

"It derives from Set, the god of drought and storm," Origen continued. "His hair was red."

Ambrosius scoffed. "Myth and nonsense!"

"Please continue," said Marcella.

Origen pushed aside his cup of wine. "Set haunted Egypt for many years, seeking the corpse of his brother Osiris whom he had murdered. The inhabitants of the Nile often saw him as he ran wildly along the river, his red hair scorching a trail behind him. For this reason did they abhor the color red, considering it evil and treacherous. They even forbade the presence of asses within their cities."

"Why?" asked Marcella.

"Because of their reddish coats."

"But what if a red ass strayed into a city?" sneered Ambrosius.

Origen laughed. "They would hurl it over a cliff!"

Ambrosius took more wine as Marcella changed her place to sit beside Origen. "Surely you do not believe all this?" she asked.

Origen's response was animated. "The seeds of truth are buried in mythology. We must not forget that Egypt's scholars were the most learned in the world. Moses was taught by them, Solomon also. These same scholars divided time into three hundred and sixty days, the left-over days being given to the gods to commemorate their birthdays. On the first extra day was born Osiris. . . . "

"The very thought of a black god is difficult to imagine." said Ambrosius.

"Yet black is the color of life," replied Origen.

"And white?" asked Marcella.

"Old age. Death."

Ambrosius leaped to his feet. "How did we fall into this gloomy subject? Is it not time for dinner?" he glared at his wife.

It was a lavish feast. After the dessert Ambrosius stretched out on the sofa-bed in the courtyard while Marcella watched the children at play with their huckle-bones. Marcella's hand-maiden started gathering the platters and cups. Origen caught the exotic scent of her perfume when she leaned over the table. "My name is Roxana," she declared. "From the moment you entered this house you have talked only about philosophy and religion. This is the season of Sefi. You should be thinking of other things."

He pulled his eyes away from her.

"I am speaking of love. Why do you blush so? Can it be that you have never known a woman?"

Origen walked to the window. Alexandria was sighing softly, preparing herself for sleep. He tried to put his thoughts elsewhere but his eyes kept coming back to Roxana. "And what about yourself?" he said. "Have you ever known a man?"

"Many times."

"Were you forced?" he stuttered. "I mean. . . . "

"It was done of my own choosing."

"Here, in Alexandria?"

She tossed back her head. "You ask many questions. In Assouan we have a saying, 'The hungry man sees mountains of rice in his sleep.' "

"You are from Assouan?"

"Yes."

Origen shifted his gaze toward the children.

"Are you angry at me?" Roxana asked, drawing near.

"Angry?"

"For speaking so freely to you."

"No harm was done," he said.

"You are not angry?"

"Of course not."

"Then kiss me."

"What?"

"It is a custom in Assouan. That way I will know for certain you are not angry."

He leaned forward to put his lips on her forehead but she gave him her moist mouth. Her soft embrace tortured him. It was as though he had entered a mysterious room, each wall covered with mirrors. Everywhere he looked there was a startling image of himself, unfamiliar and bewildering.

## 4.

He walked to the Heptastadion the next day with
Ambrosius. They took off their sandals and lowered their
feet into the tepid water. Ambrosius had been quiet most
of the afternoon and many minutes passed before he finally broke the spell. "What do you think of Roxana?"

Origen began thrashing his feet in the water.

"Let me tell you how I first met her," Ambrosius continued. "She was dancing at the Great Temple on
Elephantine Island near Assouan during a pagan festival
honoring Osiris. You know of course that the Egyptians
identify Dionysus with Osiris, and since they love to com-
pound everything, they soon attached to Osiris their
bull-god Apis who is the incarnated god of the Upper
World. Now if you repeat both names in rapid succession,
Osiris . . . Apis. Osiris . . . Apis, you will understandably
arrive at Serapis, the Egyptian god of the Lower World."

69

"I want to hear about the dance," said Origen.

"I am coming to that but first let me explain about Erasistratus."

Origen could fathom no connection between an Egyptian dance and a physician who lived more than five hundred years ago. Ambrosius was eager to explain: "Erasistratus was the first to detect a sexual cause in nervous afflictions. As a result of his studies, sexual rites became powerful symbols in Egyptian religion. Everyone was initiated into these mysteries at an early age. Indeed I saw this drama reenacted in a dance performed by Roxana when she was only sixteen, on Elephantine Island in full view of thousands."

"Did she dance alone?" asked Origen.

Ambrosius winced with impatience. "Little Teacher, she performed the sexual act. The complete act!"

"Who was her partner?"

"A professional dancer from Assouan, and black as the night. As they lay on the platform in the midst of that aroused crowd, I felt my own desires boiling. The foreplay took ages. He enticed her with his hands, his serpentine tongue, enormous penis . . . then finally he gave out a savage cry and fell upon her as the wild cheers from the crowd deafened me. It was at this precise moment that I decided to purchase this girl, not only for my own pleasure but also because Marcella wished to have a handmaiden."

Ambrosius stopped when he looked up and saw young Barnabas racing toward them, his face streaked with tears. "Origen, come quickly," he cried. "Roman soldiers are taking away all our belongings!"

Origen grabbed his sandals. "Has anyone been harmed?"

"No," Barnabas sobbed. "But they forced us into the street. What is to become of us, Origen?"

Origen told him to stop crying then tenderly brushed the tears from his eyes. All three hurried down the Hep-

70

tastadion together. When they reached the house Origen saw his mother standing dejectedly in the middle of the street while a half dozen soldiers bobbed in and out of the door carrying furniture and clothing toward a waiting cart. Her eyes moistened when she saw Origen. She took hold of his hand and did not release it until the soldiers had finally gone.

He embraced her, kissed her on the cheek, then slowly walked into the house. His eyes lingered on the place where his bed once lay, where his mother sat to read from David each night . . . on the empty floor and bare walls that once echoed with the joyful sounds of love. Here his father crawled beside him one night, kissed him on the breast, and stamped his heart forever with the indelible words, 'I thank Thee for enshrining this human temple with Thy divine spirit!'

His mother was staring at him from the threshold. He pulled her gently away and brought her into the street where Ambrosius had gathered the six boys together, joking with them and trying to make them forget their pain.

"We are all going to Clement's house," said Origen.

They moved down the street while inquisitive faces peered at them from windows and doorways. Children and dogs chased after them as though they were a family of freaks and idiots. Barnabas lunged at one of the taunters but his mother pulled him back and warned him to walk with his head upright.

Clement was relieved to see them, and when little John tried to recount everything that had happened, Clement touched him lightly on the head and said that he had already heard about the soldiers. To encourage everyone's appetite he brought out a large amphora of wine. He then asked Origen's mother to help him prepare a meal. Little John refused to eat despite his mother's firm pleas. His fast was soon broken when Barnabas put aside his own platter to amuse little John by walking on his hands and making clownish faces.

After the meal Clement cleared his throat and said, "You will all sleep here tonight, and tomorrow we shall make arrangements for your new home."

"Where?" asked Origen's mother.

Clement stroked his beard. "Of course, it will be difficult to put you all under one roof, nevertheless Origen is to reside with Lady Paula."

"Who is she?"

"An elderly widow and very wealthy."

"You are welcome to stay at my house," interjected Ambrosius. "I have ample chambers for all of you." Suddenly his eyes flashed. "In the name of Serapis, why did I not think of this sooner? I have a brother in Assouan who is married but childless. He operates a large granite quarry. Whenever I visit with him he begs me to send him a reliable family with growing sons who can assist him and then inherit his business. He will be overjoyed if I write to him and say I have found the ideal family. His name is Chrysanthus."

Origen's mother appeared grateful but she remained quiet. Ambrosius did not press any further. Meanwhile a blanket of darkness had covered the courtyard. Clement lit a wall torch and several hand lamps. "Origen and I will make our beds in this classroom. The rest of you shall sleep in the upper chamber."

Origen's mother objected. "It is not proper for us to take your sleeping quarters."

Clement hunched his shoulders. "I have learned one lesson from life, to accept any dwelling place without complaint."

Origen swept little John into his arms and carried him up the stairs. The others followed. Little John's eyelids hung limp and sad as he snuggled under the covers. When Origen turned to leave, his mother whispered, "I am happy that you will be staying with the wealthy lady."

"I think you should accept Lord Ambrosius' offer and go to Assouan," he replied.

She stiffened. "I will speak to God about it tonight. If it is His will then we shall do so."

Every nerve in his body rebelled.

"Origen. . . . "

There was a long silence.

"Do you still speak to God?"

He retreated into dark silence.

"When you were but a boy of seven," she murmured, coming close to him, "you had already committed all the psalms of David to memory. How it warmed my heart to see you at prayer each night, reciting them one after the other. . . . "

"I am not a boy any longer," he said.

She kissed him tearfully on the cheek and walked away. Clement was already asleep on the bed he had made for himself. Moving quietly so as not to awaken him, Origen pulled off his sandals and slid under the covers. Like a sparrow on a grapevine, he flitted from one thought to another. Suddenly Roxana appeared with her huge black partner on Elephantine Island. They performed for his pleasure alone, again and again, until he finally and exhaustedly closed his eyes in sleep.

5.

Nili!

The season of rain and floods. Sullen winds from the heart of Africa funneling through the streets of Alexandria like the angry breath of Set. Chrysanthus responded immediately to Ambrosius' message and sent money for clothes, passage, and whatever Origen's family would require for the long journey four hundred miles by barge up the Nile. On the day of their departure, Origen and Clement went to the docks near the Gate of the Moon to see them off. Origen kept assuring everyone that he would visit with them in Assouan before summer but little John did not want to hear this. With tears the size of hailstones, he whimpered, "Come with us now, Origen. Now!"

"But you must try to understand, little John. I am Prefect of a college. Stop crying. I promise that I will come to Assouan this summer."

Barnabas stepped in and tugged little John away. In the heavy silence Origen caught his mother looking at him mournfully, trying to conceal her grief.

"Goodbye," he said.

She embraced him, kissed his cheeks with muffled sobs. Origen looked the other way when Clement lifted his hand to bless them. He blessed the barge, the captain and crew, even the swirling brown waters of the Nile that soon pulled them out of sight.

Lady Paula was like a mother to him during this trying period, and especially after her adopted son Paul was called to Antioch on an urgent matter of business. Her library was even more bountiful than he expected. It included the entire works of Plato, Philo, Euripides, Aeschylus, Sophocles, and Aristotle. He was given the choicest rooms of her house, the complete east wing which faced the Great Sea. He still never missed a day at the Heptastadion, always sitting on the same slab of granite that had felt the warmth of Herais.

On the day before college was to resume, he was startled to see her walking alone near the Museum. He called out to her but she did not hear. His heart pounding, he ran after her and grabbed hold of her arm. She looked wan and troubled. When he asked her if she had been ill, she replied: "I feel fine, thank you."

"Herais, what is it? Why are you acting this way?"

"I am in a hurry. . . . "

"But I must speak to you."

"Please, not now."

He let her go.

At supper that evening, although he tried to eat, he was without appetite. The thought of standing before a class terrified him. Would he stammer and make a fool of himself? Would the students laugh? Just before the midnight hour he fell into a deep sleep. Roxana appeared.

75

This time she had no partner and danced for him alone. He awoke at daybreak, his passion swollen and throbbing with lust.

After washing his face and combing his beard, he put on his robe and sandals, and came downstairs. Lady Paula's man-servant was waiting for him near the dining table. "Is the Master hungry this morning?"

Origen's mouth felt sour.

"Perhaps a cup of asses' milk? You will find it very settling."

"I am not unsettled, Euergetes."

"You seem to be, Master."

"Stop calling me Master," said Origen, walking to the front door. Euergetes rushed to open it for him. "Do you fear something, Master?"

"No!"

"Are you certain, Master?"

"Quite certain,"

"Nevertheless I see a disquietude in your eyes."

Origen hastily tied the sash of the robe which Ambrosius had presented to him only yesterday. His stomach rumbled as he walked down the front steps. Euergetes followed him into the street. "Master, you should try to eat something otherwise you will faint in the classroom."

Origen feebly waved him back.

Euergetes' face beamed. "I will go to the Temple this morning, Master and make a sacrifice in your name. Serapis will sustain you throughout the day!"

The class in Greek was tyranny. As he ground his way through the Anabasis he felt more exhausted than Cyrus after the long trek across Asia Minor. In the short recess that followed, he remained in the classroom, struggling to calm himself. He was so immersed in misery he did not hear Herais come into the room. "Origen, what is wrong with you?" she asked.

Through the open doorway he saw students huddled

together in the courtyard. Surely they were laughing at him.

"Origen, your face is pale. Are you ill?"

"No."

She lowered her eyes. "I did not speak to you yesterday because it was not proper."

"Not proper?"

"You are Prefect of the college and. . . . "

He arranged his notes on the table, thinking about the next class. He had temporarily lost his battle with Clement and was now committed to devote the second hour to theology. He had absolutely nothing to say to the students. But when Herais put her hand on his and kept it there even after the students began to file into the room, his discomfort miraculously disappeared. "The seeker of wisdom is like a field about to be tilled," he began. "The oxen he drives are his thoughts and desires. Under the plowshare of knowledge, he receives the seed of wisdom but he must be watchful and not plant it along the wayside where false teachers lurk, nor must he cast it among the stones of deceit and vanity. The sincere philosopher places his seed in the fertile ground of science where it endures and bears the richest fruit."

The words poured from his mouth with such ease he lost all sense of time until he saw Clement standing at the door, waiting for the class to be dismissed. After the last student left the room Origen went to him and said, "I cannot endure another day like this."

Clement laughed. "We must not measure life by its first breath. Have courage. It will be less painful tomorrow."

They walked out of the classroom and into the courtyard. "I did not see Lord Ambrosius," said Origen, his eyes darting toward several students who had just left his class. He now felt that he had achieved a victory and they were speaking well of him.

"I am afraid that Lord Ambrosius has his mind on too many things," Clement replied. "I shall be calling on him this evening."

Origen fell silent.

Clement looked up at the cloudless sky. "It is not at all like the season of Nili. There is no promise of rain in sight."

"Perhaps it is raining in Assouan."

Clement gave him a compassionate smile. "Time passes swiftly. Sefi will be upon us before we realize it. You will be reunited with your family in a few months."

Origen was not paying attention to him. "I must tell you again that I prefer not to teach theology. . . . "

Clement stiffened. "We have gone over this enough. As Prefect of the college, you have to offer the subject."

"Then I will teach it my way!"

"Of course."

"Without any interference."

"Agreed."

"I mean it. I will not permit you or anyone else to censure what I have to say."

Clement laughed.

"What is the joke?" cried Origen.

"I said precisely the same thing to Pantaenus on my first day as Prefect."

He had hardly enough strength to sustain himself through the last hour. Leaving his notes and scrolls on the table, he hurried out of the college before Clement could show his face. At the Heptastadion he threw off his robe and sandals then dove into the water, swimming for almost an hour before coming out. The sun dried him instantly. He put on his robe and walked barefoot as far as Pharos Light. Herais was sitting on a slab of granite.

"How long have you been here?" he exclaimed.

"A few minutes."

"You saw me swimming?"

"Yes. I have been waiting for you."

"Herais, I am asking you for the last time . . . why did you leave Alexandria without saying a word?"

"It was my uncle's wish."

"Is this all you can say?"

"He was summoned to Caesarea on a business trip."

"What did this have to do with you?"

She started to weep. "Forgive me, Origen. I am not speaking the truth. My uncle saw us that day when we walked together along the Street of the Soma. He does not want me to get involved with you."

"Involved?"

"I am promised to another."

"Herais. . . . "

She rose to her feet, sobbing. He tried to take her into his arms but she wrestled free.

"Herais, I missed you. . . . "

"Please, you must not talk like this."

"I cannot help it. I missed you very much."

She moved away from him. Putting on his sandals, he hurried down the Heptastadion after her but she turned sharply around and begged him to go back. Soon she was lost in the shadows of Canopic Way. He stopped a moment to look back at Pharos. Scores of fishermen and merchants had crammed into the Heptastadion. They jostled him, shoved him aside, dug their elbows into his body but he felt nothing.

Euergetes was waiting for him outside the front door of Lady Paula's house. "Master, I have food on the table for you."

He stepped inside. "Before I forget, you must go to Serapis tomorrow and thank him."

"He helped you, Master . . . Serapis helped you?"

"Did you not expect him to help me?"

That night it was Herais who crept into his sleep. She danced in the same manner as Roxana, revealing her nakedness, and permitting him to kiss and fondle her. At his highest moment of desire he was aware of a penetra-

79

ting brilliance pressing down on his loins. At first he thought it might be the sun but after its flames had ignited his passion he realized that he was being consumed by the holocaust of Herais' body . . . burning him, melting him down, disintegrating him until nothing remained but an inaudible gasp.

## 6.

He found Clement pacing impatiently in the class-room the next morning. Origen's greeting was dismissed with a brisk sweep of the hand and the sombre announcement that Ambrosius had departed for Athens with Marcella.

"What about the children?" asked Origen.

"They are in Roxana's care."

Origen placed his notes and scrolls on the marble bench near the fig tree and sat down. "You are troubled," he said to Clement. "What is wrong?"

"Bishop Demetrius wants to see you."

"For what reason?"

"I do not know."

"Did he come here personally?"

"No. He sent his scribe, Theophanis. Demetrius expects you at his residence this morning."

81

"But I have my classes."

"Heraclas can take them," said Clement, walking toward the fig tree. His presence did not disturb the many sparrows on the branches. A few even perched themselves directly above his head and filled the morning with their chattering voices.

"Will you feel better if I come with you?" asked Clement.

Origen nodded. He waited until Clement had scribbled a note for Heraclas and then followed him through the courtyard into the street. A sudden windstorm unleashed itself, sending great gusts of sand over the city. The sky darkened. Canopic Way was deserted except for a handful of beggars trying to seek shelter from the storm.

The bishop's residence was a full mile into the Greek Quarter. When they passed the Gate of the Moon Origen noticed the old Arab woman at her usual place, fighting desperately to protect her hyacinths from the fierce wind. He helped her into an enclosed courtyard then went back into the street to gather up the flowers that had been blown away by the wind.

"I have seen you almost every day for years," said Origen, "Yet I do not know your name."

"Huldah," she responded hoarsely.

"Do you have a family?"

"Three sons and a daughter."

"And your husband?"

"He is dead."

"Where do you get these flowers?"

"In the Western Cemetery."

"You take them from the dead?"

Her tired eyes opened wide. "Flowers are for the living!"

Clement was making impatient signs. As Origen turned to bid the woman goodbye, she reached into her basket and handed him a bunch of hyacinths. "I cannot take them," he said. "I have no money."

She thrust them into his hands. "Does it not move your heart," she muttered, "to know that a graveyard can give birth to such beauty?"

He brought the flowers up to his nose. Behind him, Clement had already started walking. When Origen caught up to him, Clement asked, "What were you saying to that old woman?"

He did not answer.

They came into a narrow street which ran parallel with the docks. A foul scent permeated the air. The houses looked squalid, ragged children ran barefoot in the street.

"Does the bishop live here?" asked Origen incredulously.

Clement's reply was tinged with bitterness. "Demetrius thrives on a false sense of humility."

A young bearded monk answered the door. He was of delicate body and voice. With a gesture of his fragile hand, he invited them inside then softly closed the door. After escorting them to a wooden bench in a shabby room, he asked them to be seated. The place had a rank odor that reminded Origen of the last judgment . . . decaying flesh, gnashing of teeth, the earth opening her bowels and disgorging the stale breath of the dead.

Another door opened. An obese man of short stature came stomping toward them. His forked white beard was unkempt and covered with food stains. His soiled and wrinkled brown robe trailed behind him, picking up the dust from the floor. Clement took his hand and kissed it.

"And this is the new Prefect of my college," Demetrius puffed. "I have heard many praises heaped upon him. I trust that he will live up to them."

Origen felt a coldness in the room.

83

"Since the college of Alexandria falls entirely under my jurisdiction," added Demetrius, raising his voice, "I have the sole authority of appointing or dismissing anyone connected with it, whether he is a teacher or the Prefect himself."

Origen glanced toward Clement who was squirming with uneasiness. All this time Theophanis was seated at the far end of the room, reading from a scroll.

Demetrius continued, "Another thing, Master Clement has proposed that you should be reimbursed, perhaps twenty obols a day."

"Twenty obols?"

"Do you find this inadequate?"

"It is more than enough," said Origen.

Demetrius raised his hands. "Do not leap so swiftly. Before I give final approval and accept you as Prefect of the college, there are several questions I must put to you. . . ."

"Of course."

Demetrius studied him severely. "Do you believe in God?"

"I do."

"In one God alone?"

"Yes."

"And in His Son Jesus Christ?"

There was a silence.

" . . . and in His Son Jesus Christ?"

Origen looked at Clement.

"For the last time . . . do you believe in Jesus Christ?"

"In what way?"

"As God."

"I cannot find sufficient proof to support such a belief," said Origen.

"Then let me refresh your memory," Demetrius declared. "Did not blessed Peter say, 'Thou art Christ, the Son of the living God?' "

84

"But this only proves that He was the Son of God . . . as we all are."

The bishop paled. "Do you believe in Satan?"

"I believe that an angel of God indeed fell from grace. . . . "

"Do you believe in Satan?"

" . . . and that there exists a spirit of evil as well as a spirit of virtue."

Demetrius separated each word carefully, "Do you believe in Satan?"

"I believe there is a satanic spirit in all of us which can be saved."

"What?"

"God's ultimate purpose cannot be thwarted," said Origen. "It is His nature to want the restoration of all beings, and for this reason each spirit must return to Him, even Satan."

Demetrius left his chair and paced around the room. "Are you prepared to enter into the priesthood?"

"No," exclaimed Origen.

"Why not?"

"I am a teacher."

"I cannot permit a layman to continue as Prefect of my college. Either you become a priest before the year is done or I shall have to replace you. Is this clear?"

Origen rose to his feet. "Allow me to cite from the Apostolic Constitution. . . . "

"I refuse to hear it!"

" . . . though a man be a layman, if experienced in the delivery of instruction, and morally worthy . . . he can teach."

Demetrius drew back, his face quivering. Before he could say another word, Origen unburdened himself, "Furthermore, I believe in eternal creation. God's work never ceases. It extends even to those inhabitants of the stars and planets, and is not confined to the See of

Alexandria, or to Rome. I believe that man needs God—but God needs man also, otherwise His grand scheme of universal love could never be fulfilled. I believe that man is not pompous flesh, nor is he saved by long-winded prayers and ablutions but through his own victory over evil. I believe. . . . "

"Enough!" bellowed Demetrius, flinging both hands into the air. He motioned Theophanis to show them out. When they reached the street Clement looked back at the closed door and exclaimed, "He who sits in the principal seat of the church should do so with dread in his heart knowing that God can overturn his chair at any moment!"

Origen kept walking.

"If Christ wept with due cause over Jerusalem," Clement's voice pounded on, "how much more does He weep now when He sees wolves devouring His flock . . . gluttonous, lecherous wolves!"

A great throng was massed along Canopic Way near the Temple of Isis . . . pagan youths holding palm branches in their hands and singing hymns to the goddess. He edged his way toward them but Clement warned that they should proceed into another street.

Origen did not heed his words. Moving forward, he reached the bottom step of the Temple and was immediately surrounded by the frenzied students. One tried to grab him but he struck him on the face with the back of his hand. This incensed the students. They closed in on him and seized him by the arms. He kicked them. Suddenly he was lifted off his feet and carried to the top step of the Temple. With raucous gaiety, the students tugged off his robe and attired him in the vestments of a pagan priest. Laughing and cheering, they bound his wrists together, and although he squirmed and tried to break free, they held him down long enough to shave the top of his head.

At last they untied his wrists and ordered him to distribute the palms to the students around him. Feeling helpless and giddy, he decided to enter into their festive spirit. Holding the palms up high, he shouted, "Come, receive the palms . . . not of the graven image Isis, but of the universal God and Father of us all!"

A dead silence fell on the students. The laughter stopped. One by one they started moving away until he was left alone. Slowly he walked down the steps and joined Clement who was waiting in the street. He proudly displayed his pagan vestments and broke into laughter. If only Demetrius could see him now . . . a pagan priest! In his exultation, he felt his heart heave with joy, take wing and depart altogether from his body.

# III

The months flew.

He did not alter Clement's routine at the college. Classes began at daybreak and ended at dusk. A brief respite was allowed at the middle of the day. Unlike Clement, he set a free goal for his students and permitted them to examine all teachings: Greek, mystical, profane. True to his word, the atheistic works of Epicurus were investigated. His method was direct, reading first from a text then comparing it with various translations. They took key words and explored them further until a deeper meaning was found, however remote or symbolic. The universe too was examined in this same manner. "It is not a narrow prison," he reminded them, "But immense—both in magnitude and meaning—world following world in endless sequence, new stars being born each day, new planets and constellations. Man is but one letter in the stream of words pouring from the mouth of time."

Even though the ominous threat of Demetrius prevailed, he poured all of his energies into the college whose fame had now circulated into every corner of the world. Among the hundreds of students, several dozen were pagans. A young negro named Beryllus enrolled from far off Arabia. Many came from Athens and Rome.

One day in December, he received a message from Alexandros.

*Alexandros to Origen*

*Cappadocia, 24 November 205*

*Forgive me for not writing sooner but my duties as presbyter here in Cappadocia have kept me very much occupied. However, I think of you always. Pilgrims from Alexandria constantly bring me news about you. I understand that your family now resides in Assouan. I learned with great joy that you are now Prefect of the college. Alas, I also weep with you over the loss of your beloved father.*

*Please convey my love to Master Clement and tell him I shall write soon. Remember me to your mother and brothers when you write to them in Assouan. If it is at all possible, please come and visit with me this summer. There is much to see . . . many things for your soul to absorb.*

His thoughts clung to Alexandros for weeks. Although Herais continually shunned him, after the last class he would run to the Heptastadion and wait there until nightfall hoping she might appear. During Paul's absence Lady Paula kept busy with visits and receptions during the day but she devoted each evening to him, making certain that he finish his dinner, then sitting with him in the library until the early hours of morning, discussing Greek philosophers or reading from Greek poets.

Paul returned from Antioch in the middle of January. At first Origen had no desire to hear the lectures on Marcion but Lady Paula insisted that he attend out of courtesy to her son. After the invited guests had seated themselves, Paul's opening remarks pleased Origen . . . " A man can consider himself wise only after he has first examined each of the many schools of philosophical thought. Marcion lived in Rome during the days of Antoninus. He was the son of a bishop and came originally from Pontus in Asia Minor.

"The fundamental point of difference between Marcion and the Church centers around his doctrine of the First Principle in which a belief in two gods is affirmed, the god of the Old Testament whose law embodies the precept, 'An eye for an eye, and a tooth for a tooth!' and the New Testament god who commands, 'If someone smites thee on one cheek, turn to him the other also.' "

Origen's mind flitted to Elephantine Island . . . to Roxana . . . Herais.

" . . . for this reason, Marcion did not consider the god of the Jews to be the god of the New Testament. The Hebrew prophets foretold the coming of a Messiah who would deliver only the Jewish nation from bondage, whereas the New Testament god delivers the entire human race."

Paul's voice was strong and magnetic, his arguments interesting and convincing. After another hour, he brought the lecture to a close with a detailed discussion of Marcion's theory of the three heavens.

"You neglected to tell us," shouted an old man, "that Marcion once seduced a virgin and was excommunicated from the church by his own father!"

There was a wave of laughter.

Chuckling, Paul replied, "That is an allegorical statement. Its meaning is quite clear: *Marcion corrupted the virgin church*. This should not be difficult for you to comprehend. After all, the whole world knows that allegory was invented by the Alexandrians."

There was more laughter. "In truth," Paul continued, "Marcion was an ascetic of the highest degree who denied himself not only carnal pleasures but the use of meat and wine as well."

The following day Clement did not make his usual visit to the classroom. After the final hour Origen went to the upper chamber of the house and found him in his bed coughing and flushed with fever. He placed a woolen cover over the bed then carefully tucked it around him. "Do you want me to bring you a little broth?" he asked.

Clement shook his head.

"Perhaps I should summon the physician."

A frightful coughing seizure attacked Clement once more and Origen hurried out of the room. He went directly to Lady Paula's house. She was alarmed at the news and sent Euergetes immediately to the residence of Arsenius the physician. After a long examination, Arsenius made the pronouncement that Clement was suffering from a severe attack of pleurisy that would require several weeks of rest in bed.

Origen remained at Clement's side throughout the long recuperation, caring for him and attending to all his needs. His nights were racked by the recurring nightmare of Herais' presence. In the deep silence of the dreary days he found the time to re-examine his own life and decided that he must leave Lady Paula's and support himself. Now certain that Demetrius would never reimburse him, he negotiated with a literary collector on the Street of the Soma who was willing to pay him four obols a day to copy manuscripts from the Greek poets.

When Clement heard of it, he lashed out at him, "How can you possibly live on four obols a day?"

"I will manage."

"What about the college?"

"It will not be neglected."

"There is Demetrius also," Clement reminded him. "You have less than two weeks to meet his ultimatum."

Origen prepared his bed for sleep.

"If you are not a priest before the end of the month he will make you resign as Prefect. He means every word."

Origen slid under the cover. "You should know more

than anyone else that I cannot bear the thought of becoming a priest."

"Why?"

"Because all priests look to avarice and greed. . . . "

"Can you say this of Alexandros?"

Origen clamped shut his eyes.

"Or myself?" exclaimed Clement.

He was taken back. He had never regarded Clement as a priest. He did not think like a priest, nor act like one. A man of Clement's stature should never have allowed the seal of Melchizedek to be stamped forever in his heart like a branding iron on a sheep.

Within moments Clement's snores filled the chamber. Origen came closer and tapped him on the shoulder. "I have something to discuss with you."

"What is it?"

"I am troubled by a dream. . . . "

Clement yawned.

" . . . the same dream, night after night." Little by little, he exposed himself to Clement and told him everything, Herais drawing open the curtain of his sleep each night, scorching his brain, tormenting him, racking his soul with pangs of wretchedness and despair, draining every ounce of strength from his body.

Clement started to snore again.

Origen woke him up. "What must I do?"

"It is only a dream," Clement mumbled. "You are giving it too much credence. Fill your mind with God. . . . "

Origen flung away his cover and walked out of the bed chamber. He lit one of the wall torches in the courtyard and sat on a bench. The night felt cold. Toward the western sky he discerned the glow of lights from the porticoes along Canopic Way. Pharos seemed close enough to touch. He leaned back and shut his eyes for a moment. *Herais!* He should have known that Clement would respond the way he did. 'Fill your mind with God!'

A loud knock on the front door startled him. It was Paul, his whole body trembling, his face ashen. "Where is Master Clement?" he asked.

"Upstairs in his chamber."

"Please summon him."

"But he has been ill with pleurisy."

"Is he sleeping?"

"Yes."

"Then you must waken him. Lady Paula has suffered a severe attack. She is dying!"

They ran upstairs together. Clement had overheard them and was already out of his bed, struggling with his robe. "After you woke me up," he said to Origen, "I could not sleep."

Origen helped him with his robe. When they came into the dark street Paul explained between sharp breaths that Lady Paula was just about to retire for the night when suddenly she clutched at her breast and fell to the floor. Paul and Euergetes carried her to her bed chamber and then Euergetes went to summon Arsenius.

"What did the physician say?" asked Clement.

"He holds no hope for her life."

"Was the Rabbi Joshua summoned?"

"Yes."

They had to stop near the Caesareum when Clement started faltering. Origen assisted him the rest of the way. They were met on the front steps by Euergetes. He was weeping. He gripped Origen's hand before guiding him through the torch-lit courtyard and up the dark stairs that led to Lady Paula's bed chamber. Arsenius and the Rabbi Joshua were leaning over her. When the physician saw Clement he reproached him for having left his bed but Clement brushed by him and greeted the Rabbi Joshua with a warm embrace. He was a stooped little man of many years, his long gray beard half the size of his frail body. While he and Clement remained at the bedside, Euergetes again took hold of Origen's hand and whispered, "Master, what is to become of me when my lady dies?"

"I am certain that she has provided for you," Origen assured him.

"I am not speaking of her riches, Master."

Lady Paula's lips started to move. "Where . . . where is my son?"

Paul knelt at her side and put his face close to hers. She nodded her head feebly. "Is my other son here also?"

Origen knelt beside Paul as the Rabbi Joshua began to chant in Hebrew:

" ' *Unto Thee oh Lord do I lift up my soul.*
*Oh my God I trust in Thee.*
*Let me not be ashamed;*
*Let not mine enemies triumph over me.*' "

Origen felt a calm sense of peace when Paul gave him his hand, when everyone was linked together. Only Arsenius remained alone, his arms folded, his eyes measuring the last few breaths that trickled from Lady Paula's lips.

On the day of Lady Paula's entombment Origen invited Paul to stay with him at the college. After they had prepared their beds in one of the classrooms they talked far into the night. Paul told him about his mother and father, his two younger brothers. He wept when he described how his parents met their martyrdom, hung upside down on a cross for three days.

"Were they also followers of Marcion?" asked Origen.

"Yes."

After a long silence, Origen said, "Tell me about Antioch."

Paul's words became spirited, explaining that one must approach Antioch from the Gulf of Alexandretta which lies just to the north of the city. "At this time of the year the bay is a deep blue from the cold sky. Alexander fought the Battle of Issus here and with his victory opened

95

the gates to the East. The Apostle Paul was born on the western shore. From the heights that surround Tarsus one can look toward the west on a clear morning and see the island of Cyprus. Every day the gulf is choking with vessels that journey to Mersine for currants, or to Cyprus for mules. It is a full-day's climb from Alexandretta to Antioch, across great mountain slopes whose northern walls are covered with snow and ice. But it is a rewarding sight to pass through the Gates of Syria and look down at the Plain of Antioch. In the month of January the lake is swollen by floods. Thousands of wild birds spread their wings over the entire surface of the water. Streets and houses are chalk-white, the people hospitable and peaceful. Antioch has no enemies. In the season of Sefi the finest wheat in all the world grows along the eastern shore of the lake where the earth is vibrant with life. Toward the north, the Amanus River flows into Asia Minor while to the south rises the enormous peak of Casius whose shoulders once braced the great temples of Greece and Rome. And across the wide desert to the east lies the ancient and beautiful city of Aleppo. . . . "

"I have heard strange tales about the pillar hermits of Syria," said Origen.

"Syria is indeed the land of the pillar hermits. They perch themselves everywhere like crows. It is said that during the days of Commodus a great wind blew over the land, uprooting all the trees and throwing the holy men down from their platforms."

Origen laughed but stopped quickly when he heard the rise in Paul's voice. "The world is entwined in materialism. It is our duty to free it!"

"How?" asked Origen.

"By setting the soul at war against the body."

"Surely you are not suggesting that we too perch ourselves on trees?"

"No, on the arm of God."

Origen wished that he had not said that. How could

he sit on the arm of God while his veins swelled with desire! Like Marcion, Paul no doubt had never known a woman, nor touched one. He could easily perch himself on God's arm.

He quietly drew the cover over his shoulders then asked Paul, "What are your plans now?"

"I am sailing for Antioch tomorrow."

"But you have other responsibilities. You are Lady Paula's son. . . . "

"And you also," smiled Paul.

"I mean her legally-adopted son. Her entire estate is in your hands."

"I have already instructed the Rabbi Joshua to transfer some of it to Euergetes, and the residue will be distributed to the poor of the city."

Sleep possessed them.

At daybreak he walked with Paul to the docks. He was eager to converse with him further but Paul was anxious to climb on board the waiting galley. They clasped arms and bade each other farewell. When the ship finally set sail he began waving at Paul and did not stop until there was nothing left but sea and sky.

2.

The month of March found him immersed in abysmal gloom. Herais still avoided any private meeting with him and even looked the other way whenever he tried to speak to her. But at night she continually haunted him. He was tempted to go to her uncle's house, demand that she marry him right away, no matter what her uncle's plans were, but he could not find the courage. All this time, Alexandria was drenched by a seven-day rain. Many students caught chills and fever, and he had to postpone all classes.

Sitting alone one evening at his desk while working on some poetry translations, he heard the soft patter of feet in the courtyard. Hoping it might be Herais, he ran to greet her but instead discovered Anastasia, her little oval face blanched with fear. "Master Origen, you must come quickly!" she cried. "Roxana is ill!"

"Where is your father?"

"They are still in Athens. Please hurry!"

By the time they arrived at Ambrosius' house the rain was coming down in torrents. Every room was damp and cold. Anthousa and Agathi sat at a place near the oven, toying with their platters of food. When they saw him, they leaped to their feet and ran into his arms. "Roxana is sick!" Agathi shouted.

Anastasia pressed her hands against her hips and commanded them to finish their supper. They obeyed and took their places again near the oven. Origen asked Anastasia to direct him to Roxana's bed chamber. She pointed toward the furthest door off the courtyard. It was half-open. Roxana's soft invitation echoed in his brain when he knocked. "Come in, Master Origen."

He entered.

She was lying on a bed of clean linens, her room scented with perfume. Rain-drenched leaves from a sycamore tree brushed against the window. He placed his hand over her forehead but did not find it feverish. She sighed when he drew it away.

"What is wrong with you?" he asked.

"I have a terrible pain in my stomach."

"Do you want me to summon a physician?"

"No."

"You may be seriously ill."

"I have had the same pain before. It will go away. Please sit here beside me and hold my hand."

Just as he sat down, the three girls came bursting into the room. He asked them to keep their voices down but Agathi pulled at his hand and cried, "Did you make Roxana's pain go away?"

Anthousa started to giggle. Roxana turned to Anastasia and said, "Take your sisters back into the kitchen. It is warm there and free of the wind."

After they left, Origen asked her again. "Are you sure you do not want me to go after a physician?"

She shook her head.

"Can you take a little broth?"

"No," she moaned, reaching for his hand. She turned his palm over and stared at it for a long time. "I see much happiness for you. You will be married and have five children . . . all from one wife."

He withdrew his hand and walked to the window. Darkness was lurking outside, the sycamore tree was now barely visible. "Did you actually allow that man to violate you?" he asked.

"What man?"

"The dancer . . . on Elephantine Island."

"Yes."

"Before all those people?"

"Of course."

"But why?"

"Because my religion commanded it."

"That is preposterous."

"Christians do similar things," she declared.

"What do you mean?"

"They eat the body of their god, drink his blood."

"But that is done symbolically."

"Our dance of love is symbolic also."

"It is fornication!" he exploded, walking to the door. Before opening it, he looked back and saw her trembling under the covers. Her eyes were stained with tears. He stopped. Every nerve in his body rebelled. For eighteen years he had stood vigilant over his brain, striking down every invading desire that dared enter. And for what? To please a strong-willed father, an immaculate mother, a dead god, a commandment written on stone!

Ambrosius at last returned from Athens. He appeared at the college one afternoon shortly after classes had ended, leveling curses on the government for detaining him all this time, then in the very next breath remarking how much he and Marcella had enjoyed their stay in Greece.

"How is Lady Marcella's health?" asked Origen.

100

"Excellent."

"And the children?"

"All well, praise Osiris. They complain that they have not seen much of you." Ambrosius gave him a close look. "Little Teacher, are you ill?"

"Of course not."

"Perhaps you are working too hard. This college will be here long after Osiris calls you." A wry grin crept over Ambrosius' face. "I must tell you what happened to me in Athens one day. Along with every other good thing that has come into the world, the Athenians have also put their claim on Christ."

The rain clouds that had hovered over Alexandria were finally disappearing. Wide expanses of blue filled the sky. "Yes," Ambrosius went on, "I challenged one of these haughty Athenians one morning, and with a pompous flick of his wrist, he responded *'I am amazed you did not know that Christ paid a visit to Athens.'* I tried to tell him that Christ never left Palestine but he threw me a defiant glare and shouted, *'He came here to study philosophy. How else could He have been so wise?'* "

Origen fell into laughter.

"We shall be expecting you to dine with us this evening," Ambrosius said, rising to his feet.

Origen stiffened. "I must decline. I have much work to do."

Ambrosius came closer. "Clement tells me you have moved your belongings away from here."

"That is correct."

"Where do you live?"

"Under the stars."

"What does that mean?"

"I make my bed in the sand along the Heptastadion."

"Have you taken leave of your senses?"

"I cannot go through life borrowing from others."

"This is insane," cried Ambrosius. "Only beasts sleep on the ground!"

101

"I will not be dissuaded."

"In the name of Serapis, what are you trying to prove?"

"That I am a free man, accountable to no one."

"I insist that you come home with me."

Origen made no reply.

"Are you not ashamed, living like this?"

"It does not bother me."

"But you are Prefect of a college."

"So?"

"How do you support yourself?" Ambrosius fumed.

"I copy manuscripts for a literary collector who has a small shop near the Caesarium. He pays me four obols a day."

"Outrageous! I urge you to come to my house immediately. You will have your own room where you can do your work with dignity and respect."

Origen remained silent.

"When I was your age," shouted Ambrosius, "I made no attempt to run away from life. Open your eyes before it is too late. You have a body that craves food and drink . . . and a woman's embrace. If you continue to deny these things you will end up in the desert, a raving maniac!"

## 3.

The dream persisted. Awakening from a deep stupor one night, he fell upon his aroused manhood and grappled with it fiercely until at last it succumbed. With its hideous froth still clinging to his fingers, he raced to the edge of the sea and scrubbed his hands with sand until they bled. In utter despair, he walked out of the water and threw himself on the sand. Hours later, he was awakened by the sharp rays of the sun. Again he washed his hands and noticed they had begun to bleed once more. He buried them in the sand until the bleeding stopped then dragged himself to the college.

Throughout the morning classes he hardly knew what he was saying or doing. He could not keep his eyes off Herais. Time was reluctant to unwind itself. By midafternoon his voice had faded into a mere whisper. His whole body ached. When he returned to the Heptastadion he plunged immediately into the sea and swam for several hours, unmindful that his hands had started to bleed again. He returned to the rocks and put on his robe. The sun quickly dried his body. As he leaned back and closed his eyes, Herais' voice startled him. "Origen, I must speak with you."

He was too numb to reply. She came beside him and sat, her lips twitching. "I refuse to abide by my uncle's wishes!"

"Herais. . . . "

"I am of age. He has no right to control my life with his primitive beliefs and customs! I will see anyone I want, go where I want."

Below them a large cargo vessel heavy with wheat churned slowly through the harbor, her bow pointed toward Crete. On their right hand the sun was sinking into Eunostos Bay.

"I must leave now," she whispered. "I have several things to do."

He started to help her down the rocks but she pushed him tenderly away. A radiant smile possessed her. "Someday I will live in my own house near Lochias. I will marry and have four children, all boys, tall and brazen-bodied like you. . . . "

She waved to him. His eyes never left her, following every step she took until the darkness engulfed her. That evening he ate smoked fish which he purchased for two obols from a fisherman on the docks. After drinking from the fountain at the Museum, he walked along the shore then returned to the Heptastadion and prepared himself for sleep. During the early morning hours he was awakened by strange sounds reverberating over Alexandria . . . loud cries, songs and cheering. He left the sand and climbed to the highest rock near Pharos. Flames were gushing over Rhakotis Hill. The Temple of Serapis was aglow. He could make out throngs of people milling about the steps, dancing, singing, defying the black sky with pagan hymns. Soon the flames died down and he returned to his place in the sand. He waited for the sun to rise then threw himself into the sea. The cold water refreshed him. Running all the way to the college, he remembered a Hebrew prayer his mother often sang to him:

' I am God's garden.
I will lift up my eyes to Him
And let His fingers pluck the weeds
From my face.
I will let His rain forgive me.'

Clement was not in his chambers. He looked for him in the courtyard, the classrooms. Nothing. As he came into the courtyard again, he saw Heraclas rushing toward him, his face the color of wax. "What are you doing here?" he yelled. "All your students are on Rhakotis Hill!"

"Why?"

Heraclas fell into sobs. "Ninety-two of our brethren were executed last night. They were tied to poles and set on fire."

"For what reason?"

"A Roman centurian was slain near Pompey's Pillar. Two brothers of the faith were blamed. Soon after it got dark, bands of soldiers prowled the streets and grabbed every Christian they could find. My brother was among the first. . . . "

"Plutarchus?"

"They also took Minas, Theognostus, Zacharias, Didymus, Aristides. All were coming from the Mother Library when the pagans fell upon them. Philimon saw them from inside and tried to hide but they went in after him." Suddenly Heraclas stopped. Turning his eyes away from Origen, he stammered: "They seized the maiden Herais also. . . . "

He grabbed Heraclas by the shoulders. "What are you saying?"

105

"She was walking alone on the Heptastadion at dusk. First they defiled her . . . three pagans. They took turns."

"You are mistaken," Origen cried. "It was not Herais!"

"She was seen by many eyes."

"It was not Herais! Do you hear me? It was not Herais!"

Heraclas questioned him with his eyes then moved quickly away. Origen raced out of the courtyard, past the Mother Library, the Palace. The streets were barren. Curtains were drawn over windows, doors closed shut. Not one child was in sight.

Everything on Rhakotis Hill had a ghostly appearance . . . the Temple, the ugly poles jabbed into the earth like spears in a wounded beast, the smouldering ashes, hundreds of wailing faces moving from pole to pole, their tearful eyes fixed on the charred remains . . . men digging graves, women unloosening their hair and baring their breasts in mourning, exorcists droning out their incantations, young boys competing with one another in a search for the largest stones to place over the graves.

As he approached the first pole his mother's voice still rang in his ears. He blocked them with both fists and yelled back at her, "Where is your Great God and Gardener now? Where is He?"

Someone handed him a spade. He glued his eyes on a black-red body slumped against the base of the pole, blistered beyond all recognition . . . a chunk of burned flesh that might easily have been Herais but he would never know. With an agonized groan, he tossed the spade away and lifted the monstrous thing into his arms, carried it to a freshly-dug grave, held it there for a torturous moment and then set it down.

## 4.

That same night Herais appeared to him again, whole and beautiful as ever, inflaming his desire, igniting his passion, driving him into a fit of lust. Confused and dazed, he leaped from his bed in the sand and ran frantically through the dark streets, all the way to Clement's house. He threw his fists against the front door and when Clement did not answer, he raced down the long row of marble busts, into the courtyard. He flailed at his chest with heavy blows, sank to the marble floor and clawed at it until his fingers bled.

There was no release.

With a hoarse cry, he begged the awakening sky to throw a mantle of mercy over his brain. He put his thoughts on the college, his work, on his mother and brothers in Assouan, on Alexandros in Jerusalem. He invoked the spirit of his martyred father to come quickly to his assistance and when he heard a distant cry, *'Whosoever will save his life shall lose it!'* a ravenous guilt gnawed at his soul. Then from the deepest veins of his memory a second echo reached his ears, *'There are eunuchs who have made themselves eunuchs!'*

He called upon his mother's Hebrew voice to comfort him. But it was too faint and inaudible.

Suddenly he discovered himself in Clement's bed chamber. His eyes fell on Clement's razor. Distraught and numb, he picked it up, stared at it, then threw off his robe and sat cross-legged on the floor. His hand shook as he brought the razor down to his groin.

One frightening stroke. Now another.

He was free.

*5.*

Soft words drifted into his ears, "Can you hear me, little Teacher . . . ?" It pained him to open his eyes. He was in an unfamiliar room, lying on a soft bed of linen. Through a wide window he could make out the bare branches of a tree. Birds were chirping. Angry flames lashed at his groin. His body was on fire.

"Little Teacher, can you hear me?"

He nodded weakly.

"Lie still," Ambrosius whispered. "You need not be alarmed. No one else knows about this, except for Arsenius the physician and Heraclas. . . . "

"Heraclas?"

"He was the one who found you in Clement's bed chamber. All three of us carried you here."

"Where . . . where is Clement?"

"He just returned from Antioch. . . . "

"Antioch?"

"He went there to attend a Synod."

"How long was he gone?"

"Almost a month."

He felt a wave of nausea. "Have I been ill all this time?"

"Yes," said Ambrosius, drawing near the bed. "Little Teacher, what drove you to do such a terrible thing?"

He closed his eyes.

"Can you take a little nourishment?" Ambrosius asked.

He shook his head.

"Perhaps I should leave you alone for a while," said Ambrosius. "You may feel like eating when I return."

He managed to sleep for a short time but was awakened by Arsenius' hand on his forehead. "How do you feel?" the physician asked.

He was too ashamed to speak.

Arsenius frowned. "The fever has almost abated. I am afraid that you will recover and regret this rash act for the rest of your life."

There was a long silence.

"You realize of course that you made a clumsy mess of it," Arsenius scowled. "I am confounded that you survived. You should thank God for endowing you with a strong constitution. Any other man would have died."

He squirmed with uneasiness while Arsenius leaned over the bed to put an ear on his heart. With a disgusted grunt, the physician finally left the room. The birds had stopped their singing and thick black clouds were moving stealthily across the sky. He heard the soft sound of approaching feet. Marcella entered the room, followed by her three children. Agathi was the first to speak, "Are you feeling better, Master Origen?"

Anthousa came around the bed and kissed him shyly on the cheek while Anastasia watched from her mother's side. There were more footsteps in the corridor. When

110

Roxana showed her face, he turned his eyes toward the blackening sky.

Clement called on him later that afternoon. He looked tired and very old. Peering intently into Origen's eyes, he sighed, "Do you expect to find peace now?"

When Origen did not answer, he shook his head sadly. "Surely you realize that you committed a grave error . . . that you will continue to have bodily desires?"

Origen tried not to listen to him.

" . . . that in fact your passions will become even more acute . . . and worst of all, that you will never be able to fulfill them. Never!"

Clement's face mellowed. He took a few steps toward the door and said, "I have decided to take leave of Alexandria. There is a deep longing in my heart for Athens and I must see her before I die. My house shall be your house. From this moment on, you will have no excuse for sleeping in the sand."

He was too weak to argue with him.

Clement muttered on, "We must learn to look upon life not as a wall but a door which leads into new horizons." Before leaving the room, he hunched his shoulders. "I almost forgot, Demetrius is anxious to see you."

On his first day back at the college he had the dreadful fear that his students knew the real reason for his month's absence. He thought he discerned it in their eyes and the guarded manner in which they listened to his words. He was afraid to look at the place where Herais always sat. After dragging his body and mind through the last hour, he decided to call upon Demetrius. The bishop was unusually cordial and even touched him on the forehead with his fingers. "Never before have I known such firmness of will, such powerful faith. I praise you and bless you, my son."

Origen squirmed with discomfort.

"There is no point in hiding it," said Demetrius, seating himself. "I know what you did. I am aware of every detail. I have my little angel who tells me everything that goes on in Alexandria." Abruptly the bishop's attitude changed. His tone became austere. "I also know that you teach far more philosophy than theology. This must cease. The science of God should be foremost in your mind."

"My Lord, I realize that you are awaiting my decision."

"What decision?"

"About the priesthood."

Demetrius rose to his feet. "I summoned you here to commend you. Nothing else. Now then, return to your college. I must prepare myself for evening prayers."

"Does this mean that you have rescinded your demand that I become a priest?" Origen inquired.

Demetrius escorted him to the door. "We can talk about that some other time. For the present, it is sufficient that you conduct yourself properly as Prefect of the college. And remember what I said, there shall be no more emphasis on profane philosophy!"

He dined with Clement that evening after arriving there with his one possession, the sheep skin blanket given to him by Lady Marcella the time she had learned that the government had confiscated all his belongings. Clement was quiet throughout the meal but when Origen recounted his episode with Demetrius, Clement sat back and laughed. "I cannot believe it. Demetrius must be approaching senility."

It was very mild for winter, the cold blasts having lost most of their vigor. In a few weeks Sefi would be upon them, but what promise could the season of birth have for him now? As a child he yearned for its first sounds, its first breath, waiting for Egypt to burst forth once again and show her reborn face. But now after a very short time all this had changed, and even Sefi could not fill the deep void in his heart.

He helped Clement with the platters, washing them in the basin and drying them with a coarse towel. Clement was not sleepy. He went to the bench beneath the fig tree. "Tell me," he said, breathing deeply. "How did Demetrius know?"

"About what?"

"Your . . . castration."

Origen's reply was cold. "I suspect that Heraclas is his angel."

Clement pointed to a platter of oranges on the bench. Origen took one and slowly began peeling it. "In God's name," said Clement, scowling. "You must learn to eat again. I shudder every time I think of your hoveling in the sand all these months, destitute, living like a hermit. Another thing, the world does not look kindly upon a sombre face. Laugh a little. Go to the theatre, the games. It is not right to sever yourself from everything!"

6.

April fell upon them. Unceasing winds howling over
Alexandria like deranged gods, causing Clement to delay
his departure for Greece and spend long days on visits to
Ambrosius, and to the classrooms. Origen still felt uneasy
with his students, and although he tried to dismiss it from
his mind, the thought prevailed that Heraclas had injected
a deadly venom into their ears.

Herais continually troubled him. In a desperate effort
to erase her from his mind, he thrust himself into a deeper
dedication to study. New life took form in his brain, new
beliefs. He became obsessed with the idea that some beings advanced in spiritual development while others
failed.

One day he brought these thoughts to the attention of
his students, and as he anticipated, Heraclas was the first
to object. "This notion is derived from Plato. It holds no
truth because it closes the door to redemption!"

"Is the Creator responsible for evil?" asked Origen.
"No."
"Then where did it originate?"
"Some people are born good, others evil."

Origen left the table and walked to the open window. "Only by our free choice do we acknowledge evil. Our lives are not victimized by irrational fate, as Heraclas would have us believe. Many years ago there was a man from Syria who claimed to be a prophet and went about the countryside preaching a doctrine of fate. One day as he entered a certain village, the chief elder asked him his name. 'Benjamin,' came the curt reply. 'I am a prophet of God!' 'And what do you prophesy?' asked the elder. 'This,' cried Benjamin. 'Fate has brought me into your village today so that I might preach expressly into your ears!' 'Fate has decreed this?' cried the elder, and without another word, he turned sharply about and walked away. Similarly fate should hold no terror over us unless we cower at its sight and fall victims to it."

There was muffled laughter but Origen continued, "The agents of wisdom are the five senses. If a man is deprived the use of one, or two, or even four . . . he can still attain to knowledge. But when all five are twisted into knots of religious fantacism how can he ever deem himself worthy of learning?"

That evening as he sat with Clement by the warmth of the oven there was a loud knock on the front door. Ambrosius came briskly in and seated himself beside Clement. Origen lit one of the wall torches.

"You Athenians indeed have odd customs," Ambrosius addressed Clement. "As I was about to cross the agora one morning, I saw a long procession heading my way. Soon a large gathering formed along both sides of the street. I asked a tall youth what the occasion was and he said a funeral was passing through. Within a few moments bearers appeared, each straining under the weight of a huge bronze coffin. Just then the crowd began to cheer and applaud. I tried to silence them but someone tapped me firmly on the arm and warned, 'Be quiet. The man in that coffin was an esteemed actor. We are giving him his due acclaim.' "

Clement beamed. "Of course, they were applauding his last performance."

"Pagan nonsense," Ambrosius scoffed. He started rubbing his hands with agitation.

"Is anything wrong?" Clement asked him.

"Marcella is leaving me. . . . "

"I do not understand."

"She is taking the children with her."

"But why?"

Ambrosius avoided Clement's eyes. "We made plans to attend a comedy of Aristophanes last night at the Amphitheatre but because I felt tired and not up to it Marcella went along with Arsenius and his wife. Soon after they left, I reclined on the couch in the front room and drank a whole amphora of wine. I was feeling depressed. Things did not go well at court yesterday. Within an hour I was drowsy. I started for my bed and passed Roxana's room. I went in. Unfortunately Marcella returned home much earlier than I expected and she found us together."

"Why are you telling me all this?" said Clement.

"Because I want you to go to her and make her understand."

"Understand what?"

"That it was the wine . . . that she should forgive me."

"But she caught you in the act of fornication."

"Yes, but I did not know what I was doing."

"Is this the first time?" Clement asked.

Ambrosius did not answer.

Clement threw a cloak over his shoulders and asked Ambrosius to follow him outside.

"Where are we going?"

"To the Oratory."

116

"Why?"

Clement peered into his eyes. "Are you prepared to enter into a new life?"

"What do you mean?"

"To willingly accept Christ in your heart?"

"I am," Ambrosius sputtered.

"More faithfully and more lastingly than you accepted Montanus, Marcion, Valentinus, Epicurus?"

"Yes."

"Then you must do it right away."

"Do what?" Origen stepped between them.

Clement grabbed Ambrosius by the arm and walked with him across the courtyard. Origen angrily followed. The street was deserted, only a few lamps were burning in the Greek Quarter, the night had turned unusually cold. Ambrosius tried to stop when they reached the steps of the Oratory but Clement shoved him inside. He lit a small hand lamp, touched its flame to one of the torches on the wall then ordered Ambrosius to take off his robe and sandals. Ambrosius again tried to protest but Clement refused to listen. He went to the two large ewers that were filled with water, emptied them into the baptismal font and commanded Ambrosius to step inside. Scooping up some water with a silver pan, he began pouring it over Ambrosius' shivering body.

"The slave of God, Ambrosius, is hereby baptized in the name of the Father, and of the Son, and of the Holy Spirit. . . . "

From a small marble table near the font, Clement picked up a silver phial and emptied its oil over Ambrosius' head.

"The slave of God, Ambrosius, is now anointed in the name of the Father, and of the Son, and of the Holy Spirit."

He intoned a hurried prayer then stepped back, his face covered with perspiration. Slowly Ambrosius climbed out of the font. He was trembling. Clement snuffed out

117

the torch on the wall with a damp cloth, waited for Ambrosius to dress, then followed him out of the Oratory. When they reached the college Ambrosius walked away without a word.

Origen was furious. "Is this how we combat evil?" he shouted at Clement. "Two ewers of water, a phial of oil, a Kyrie eleison!"

"It had to be done," said Clement stiffly.

"You cannot pour God over a person's head!"

Clement kicked off his sandals and started for his bed chamber. At the top of the stairs he stopped, and without turning around, addressed himself to the dark wall, "It had to be done."

Demetrius came to the college with Theophanis the next day. Origen left the front of the room to greet him but the bishop motioned him back and sat with the students. The hour slipped by. After the students left the room Demetrius came forward and spoke to him. "That was an inspiring discussion but tell me, must you repudiate the literal meaning of all written words?"

"My Lord, there is a hidden explanation for everything . . . including your visit here today."

The bishop smiled. "I am not about to ask for your resignation if that is what you are implying. Indeed as long as I am bishop of Alexandria you shall remain Prefect of this college."

A few students still lingered at the door but Demetrius' icy stare sent them away. He cleared his throat and made a sign to Theophanis. "Tell him, Theophanis . . . tell Master Origen what you have been doing these past months."

Theophanis' voice was hardly above a whisper. "I am copying the scrolls of John."

"They were loaned to me by the bishop of Pontus," Demetrius explained. "Do you want to see them?"

"You have them with you?" Origen asked.

"They never leave my sight." Demetrius motioned to Theophanis and the monk pulled out a thick package that was wrapped carefully in oilskin. He handed it to Origen.

"Do you admire John?" Demetrius asked.

"He has come closest to the truth," said Origen.

"What truth?"

"That God is a spirit and those who worship Him must do so in spirit."

Theophanis stared at him. "Can God truly be found?"

Demetrius gave him a sharp look. "What kind of question is that? Of course He can be found!"

Theophanis was waiting for Origen's answer.

"Well, tell him," cried Demetrius impatiently.

"Those who seek God already have the promise of finding him," said Origen.

Demetrius immediately pounced on him. "Of course, you are suggesting that He be sought through allegory and symbolism?"

Origen nodded.

"There are too many instances where the literal meaning cannot be adulterated by mystical interpretation," refuted Demetrius. "For example, the apostle Paul indeed was blinded by God's light on the road to Damascus."

"He was going there to persecute Christians, my Lord. It was his guilt that really blinded him, not God."

Demetrius threw up his hands in disgust. "We can discuss this some other time. Now I must disclose the real purpose of my visit. I want you to prepare yourself for several journeys."

"Where?"

"Wherever I designate. You will be called upon to teach and instruct. At times you will be questioned, nay attacked, by eloquent heretics and pseudo-philosophers mired up to their necks in earthly theories. They revel only in argument but you will be armed with the powerful

119

shield of truth. It will be your duty to seek out these false prophets and bring them back into the bosom of the church."

Origen rebelled at the words but he remained silent.

"I want it perfectly understood that you shall undertake these journeys willingly and without reservation."

Origen had no time to answer. Demetrius had already spun around and was walking out of the room. Theophanis trotted after him, cradling the scrolls of John in his arms.

The seas at last calmed themselves and Clement's passage to Piraeus was arranged through Ambrosius. On the evening before his departure they gathered at Ambrosius' house for supper. Origen's mind was still chained to Demetrius' request, and although he was anxious to visit the places his heart had always desired, he felt a growing sense of fear and trepidation. Who would listen to him in a foreign land? What right had he to confront other men with his own thoughts and ideas?

Clement must have guessed what was going on in his mind. "You are a full-grown man with one of the most enviable positions in the world. When are you going to stop regarding yourself as an infant?"

Origen toyed with his food.

Ambrosius poured more wine into their cups then said to Origen, "You are enjoying your work at the college, are you not?"

"Yes."

"Then why are you troubled?"

Origen seized a morsel of fish and shoved it into his mouth.

"Tell me," said Ambrosius. "What was the subject of your lectures today?"

"Knowledge."

"And how did you define it?"

"It is essentially a recollection of those fundamental

truths that have been imprinted in the human mind from the beginning of time."

"Are you saying that man must learn what he once knew but forgot?"

"Yes."

"Does God enter into this?" Clement interjected.

Origen ignited. "Must we have God in our hair every minute of the day? We are speaking about knowledge, not religion!"

Clement offered his apologies to Ambrosius, saying he could no longer keep his eyes open. Origen helped him to his feet. As Ambrosius bade them goodnight he reminded Clement that he would accompany him to the docks in the morning. Tearfully Clement embraced Marcella and then kissed each of the children before blessing them.

At daybreak Origen left the house before Clement awoke. He ran to the docks and climbed the high knoll that overlooked the harbor. An hour passed. Two. After a while Clement appeared. Ambrosius was walking at his side. He helped Clement into the waiting galley then stood on the dock while Clement absorbed Alexandria for the last time.

Origen fought back his tears. He wanted to yell out his name, run after him, implore him not to leave . . . but the galley was pulling away from the docks and gliding past Pharos Torch. In one hour it was swallowed by the Great Sea.

7.

The months dragged on, without hope, without joy. On the last day of classes he spoke at length on the subject of Tertullian. "This man's prime target is now the Emperor Severus under whose reign the world has enjoyed a time of peace. There still remains a large group of hostile pagans in Alexandria who hate not only the new religion but everything new. Their motives are selfish and based on a sagging Egyptian trade that suffers seriously under foreign influence. Many of these pagans still cling to ancient superstitions while others nourish deep-rooted ancestral fears. A small spark can ignite this hostility into a terrible conflagration. I am convinced that Tertullian is that spark. His writings have goaded the Emperor to the point of possible vengeance, especially his most recent work, DE CORONA MILITIS.

"This display of imprudent zeal brings no profit to

humanity since those who were already hostile to Christianity now oppose it with even greater hatred and look upon all Christians as enemies of the State. One passage of Tertullian's treatise is particularly indiscreet, *'During these days the Emperor Severus and his son Caracalla directed that a gift be distributed to all the soldiers of a North African Legion who had performed heroically in one of the frontier wars. On such occasions it is customary for the soldiers to appear wearing crowns of laurel on their heads. One soldier refused to conform with this and instead held it in his hand. When the Tribune heard of it he summoned the soldier and inquired why he chose to be different from the others in his attire. 'I cannot wear the laurel crown because I am a Christian!'' the soldier replied.' "*

He stopped here. Several students attempted to speak but Heraclas overpowered them. "I must remind the class that this same soldier was subsequently crowned with the perfect gift of martyrdom. If one is to call himself a Christian he must look upon the wearing of laurel crowns as a concession to pagan worship. Nowhere in scripture does it say that a patriarch or prophet, apostle or disciple ever wore crowns. Christ was the only Crowned One, and His diadem was made of thorns!"

Beryllus of the black face stood up. "How can you and Tertullian condemn a harmless sprig of laurel?"

There was a burst of laughter. Heraclas shifted his wrath to the class. "The flower dies but he who conquers shall receive the crown of life!"

"Conquers what?" asked Beryllus.

"Sin!"

"And what is sin?"

"Wrong-doing."

"But who is wrong . . . the Romans, whose custom it is to receive an Emperor's gift wearing a crown of laurel on their heads, or that soldier who debased this custom and carried the laurel in his hand?"

123

Heraclas fumed.

"Tertullian praises the soldier's action," continued Beryllus. "Do you also praise it?"

"I do," cried Heraclas.

"Knowing that such action could bring violent death to others?"

"Yes!"

"Then this makes you and Tertullian parties to wrong-doing."

The class erupted with applause but Heraclas stood his ground. "Christianity is no longer an innocuous little sect. We have gained our way into the Roman army, the courts, the government, trade and industry. Our days of persecution are ended!"

Origen lifted his hand. "Perhaps Heraclas speaks the truth. Severus may very well indeed close his eyes to Egypt's disdain of Rome. For all we know, he may even allow Tertullian to rant on. Let us not forget that they are countrymen. However I lean upon history, also on the Roman mind. Yes, Christians have effected their position in every city of the Empire but Rome cannot stomach this much longer. It is unfortunate that Tertullian must boast so vociferously. He should bear in mind that over-confidence ultimately leads to destruction. But time is pulling us to new destinations. And so, we must bid each other farewell. Let us remember that all paths lead to one inescapable goal, the kingdom of love which we should seek with swiftness of heart and sincerity of purpose."

The students filed jubilantly from the room, leaving him alone with Beryllus. "I fear that I shall never see you again," said Beryllus.

"What makes you so certain?" asked Origen.

"Arabia is another country, another world."

After he put aside his notes he saw a tear trickling down Beryllus' face. "What is wrong?" he asked.

Beryllus kept looking at the floor. "I did not intend to be cruel to Heraclas. . . . "

"I saw no cruelty in your words," said Origen.

"They call me black savage. . . . "

"Who?"

"Some of the students. I try not to get angry but it is difficult."

Origen came beside him. "We should never pay heed to what others say of us, whether it be good or evil. Many delude themselves into thinking they are better than others but their claims rest precariously on the color of their skin, the size of their tents, the sparkle of their jewels, the abundance of food in their coffers. These are the real savages."

Beryllus stopped weeping. "My father wants me to go to Rome and study law."

"After your performance here today I would concur."

"I am not going to do it," said Beryllus.

"Why not?"

"Because it is my desire to become a priest."

Origen went back to his table. He gathered his notes under his arm and asked Beryllus to walk with him into the courtyard but Beryllus took his hand to bid him farewell.

"What is your hurry?" asked Origen.

"I must go to Heraclas and apologize to him before I leave Alexandria."

Origen made no comment. With a smile, he said, "Perhaps some day I will come to Arabia and visit with you."

Beryllus clasped his arm once again then walked away without another word.

That night he sat down and wrote a long letter to his mother, explaining that he would be unable to visit Assouan as he had promised. He tried to justify his decision by telling her about his many responsibilities as Prefect. He also told her about Demetrius' request that he undertake several important journeys. A whole week passed before he could find the courage to dispatch the letter. Once he

125

had handed it to the master of a barge at the docks he sank into deep melancholy. To lift himself from his misery, he decided to enroll in the School of Ammonius Saccas for the summer.

He had known about Saccas for a long time and was intrigued by tales of his reputation and method of teaching. Ambrosius also knew about him. "He is called Saccas because he formerly earned his livelihood carrying sacks on the docks of Alexandria. His fame has travelled throughout the world. He calls himself a Neo-Platonist, whatever that means. He is secretive about his methods and very selective in choosing his students. You should feel flattered that he accepted you, and with such short notice. Of course, he will expect you to wear a philosopher's cloak and keep secret everything you learn . . . I suspect that you will get along with him."

"Why do you say this?"

"You too are secretive. Your one hand never knows what the other is doing."

"I still do not understand you."

"Whenever I look for you I can never find you."

Origen did not reply.

"It has been months since you last visited with us."

"The college has kept me busy."

"You cannot use that as an excuse any longer," Ambrosius snorted. "We are in the heart of summer. The college is closed. I shall expect to see you soon. Do you hear?"

On the opening day at the School of Ammonius Saccas, he indeed was given a cloak and was asked to take an oath of secrecy. Feeling ill-at-ease and very conspicuous, he followed the other students into the great hall of the Mother Library. Not long after this, Ammonius made his entrance. The class measured each step he took, each breath, and then they began applauding.

He lifted his hand to quiet them and carefully unwound the scrolls he had been carrying under his arm. Origen was immediately awed by the depth of his knowledge. After the lecture ended, he heard someone behind him say, "Is your name Origen?"

He turned to see a slight body, gaunt bony face, penetrating brown eyes. "Yes," he replied.

"And mine is Plotinus."

He was at a loss for words.

"I said my name is Plotinus!"

"What . . . what brings you to Ammonius?"

Plotinus nervously shifted his eyes around the room. "Ammonius is the one man I have been seeking from eternity."

Origen could not believe that he was face-to-face with the great Plotinus. Remembering that he had Clement's house entirely to himself, he invited Plotinus to lodge with him. Plotinus accepted.

They ate bread and cheese that night and talked for hours in the dimly-lit courtyard. Time had little meaning. Their spirits cleaved to each other like earth to sky and did not release themselves even after the first rays of sunlight streaked through the windows. Origen wanted to know everything about him and began by asking where he was born. When he received no answer, he pressed on, "How many years do you have, Plotinus?"

Plotinus frowned. "The descent of my soul into this fragile body is an event so insignificant I do not care to discuss it."

Origen was aware that every person in Alexandria, Christian as well as pagan, wallowed in fatalism. Charlatans cast long looks toward the stars and foretold detailed events to gullible ears. Vendors of horoscopes stood on every street corner. Sooth-sayers flourished. He asked Plotinus what he thought about all this.

"My friend, we must convince man that the stars do not cause human events. They merely announce them, as the birth of Christ was announced to the wise men."

127

"What is your opinion of Christ?" asked Origen.

"We will take one question at a time." Plotinus responded briskly. "Is it possible to say the stars can determine the course of our lives when this has already been determined by the Creator? Do we dare admit there is another force pulling against that which He has already decreed, or that the arrangement of the stars today is responsible for events that occurred many years ago?"

He did not wait for Origen's answer. "Indeed the stars exercise a mysterious influence over the powers that maintain order in the universe but the very thought of expecting a sign or glimpse into the future reeks to me of delusion and sorcery." He stopped a moment then asked, "If one truly seeks to understand the language of the heavens how should he go about it?"

"By the method of analogy," said Origen.

"Explain yourself."

"When I see a dove soaring high in the sky this should indicate to me man's lofty aspirations and goals."

"Go on."

"And the brilliance of the sun is in effect the eye of wisdom whose warmth and love we all should cherish."

"Continue."

"When clouds fill the sky with darkness mankind must derive the lesson that life is not all happiness and that it should learn to live with sorrow."

Plotinus sighed. "You actually believe that everything in life has a symbolic meaning?"

"Everything in life, everything in death."

"But if such were the case the Creator would be a mere puzzle-maker who puts us here on earth and then proceeds to cut us into tiny particles. After scattering the pieces over the universe, He then enjoins us to find them."

"He is not a puzzle-maker," said Origen firmly. "He is the highest intelligence and since we too are believed to be made in His image it follows that we must also learn to look at things intelligently. A tree is not merely branch and leaf. It is creation, life giving birth in the season of Sefi and dying in autumn splendor. The Creator does not place us on earth to stare at the four walls of a universe. He asks us instead to take each moment and hold it tenderly in our hands, compare it with other moments, with earth and sky, planets and constellations . . . examine what other meaning it may hold, what other purpose or end."

A wide smile stretched across Plotinus' face. "I think I perceive now why Alexandria has your name on her lips. From this moment on, I shall call you 'Master Allegory.' "

The first cock crowed, the sun began pouring its warmth into the courtyard. Plotinus stretched his arms and said, "Tell me, why did you castrate yourself?"

Every muscle in Origen's body became paralyzed.

"If we are to submit entirely to your allegorical theories, can we conclude that it was done to separate yourself from the physical world?"

Origen did not reply.

"Do you feel that you have succeeded?" The smile disappeared from Plotinus' face.

"Surely you must be aware that many young maidens attend the college," said Origen in a faltering voice. "It is also great sport in Alexandria to accuse celibates of immorality."

Plotinus smirked. "Some say that you never did castrate yourself . . . that this was a rumor planted by yourself to conceal your homosexuality."

Origen laughed.

"Others say that you sustain yourself on exotic drugs from the East . . . otherwise you would go mad."

Origen waited for a long moment. "And what do you say, Plotinus?"

Plotinus rose to his feet. "I refuse to look for signs. If your body, by allowing itself to grow fat and slovenly, reveals indeed that you are a eunuch, it matters little to me. I am drawn to your mind and to your thoughts."

"And I to you in like manner," said Origen.

Plotinus released a muffled laugh. "Then we shall march into heaven together, dressed in these foolish cloaks!"

They ate, then after several hours of sleep, walked to the sea. The sun lay heavy on their backs. The air felt sultry and laden with moisture. When they reached Pharos a soft breeze awoke and brushed against their faces. They climbed to the top of a great wall and sat. Origen said, "What are your thoughts about the Creator?"

"He is not one but three," replied Plotinus. "I do not refer to a trinity similar to which Christians believe. As humans we are all imprisoned with feelings of frustration that originate solely from the body and its passions. As long as the mind is held captive inside such a material body it must of necessity be subjected to evil and suffering. Thus the body becomes a tomb for the mind. A far greater tomb is the world. Since the mind earnestly desires to escape from its imprisonment but cannot, tension is the subsequent result. This tension between the mind's existence in a material world and its deep yearning for the eternal is like a man plunged in mud from head to foot, causing his original beauty to be marred by ugliness. In order to become beautiful again he must undertake to cleanse himself."

"How?"

"He must accomplish this himself, by the gradual ascent of his mind from *Here* to *There*."

"I do not understand you."

"From the lower region into which the mind descended, to the higher region . . . the fulfillment of its spiritual destiny."

"You have yet to explain what you meant when you said the Creator is three."

"I am coming to that. First let me say that the ultimate cause of the universe is the One. He is the *Agathon* which transcends all being, and since He is the source of life, He must consequently be beyond the material as well as the spiritual. He is absolutely One and absolutely Good. For this reason He has nothing whatsoever to do with the creation of the existing world."

"How then did the universe come into being?"

"It was not created. It proceeds from the One like water pouring out of a fountain. From this overflow is generated the second stage of the creative process, the intelligible world of thought which alone created the third stage, that of the mind. Everything we comprehend through our senses comes from this mind. It creates animals, trees, stones, oceans, the prophets of Israel, the gods of Greece and Rome. I repeat: the Creator is Good. He is Divine. He is Mind. Three in One. He is the goal of creation. Not only do all things overflow from Him but they also strive to return to Him, for we are potentially divine and can never be happy in our material state."

Plotinus stopped to wipe his forehead with the sleeve of his cloak as several fishing barges drifted past them toward the open sea. Origen stared at him questioningly. "Are you trying to say that humanity can actually strive for this goal?"

"I am speaking of a spiritual journey," exclaimed Plotinus. "This goal cannot be found by that inane practice of taking God into one's mouth, or worshipping the bones of martyrs. Such atrocious customs must be set aside and looked upon as ignorant manifestations of a material existence. If you are to be sincere you must withdraw into your own mind and see yourself as beautiful, act as a sculptor who plans to create a statue. He cuts away, smoothes down, carves deeply until a lovely face is formed. When you too realize that you are a perfect work, that your being is wrapped in purity, that nothing can shatter its inner strength . . . when you discern yourself abiding in perfection then you must take still another step. Be not afraid. Now another. If your eyes have not been blurred by vice, if you are whole and strong, if your mind is beautiful, if it is pure . . . you shall behold a sight never before envisioned by man. You will see yourself as God!"

Origen detected the shadow of Plato hovering behind each word, for it was he who first saw the material world as an imperfect copy of the intelligible. There were also marked footprints of Eastern theology running parallel with Plotinus' concept of the One. Whereas the prophets and Christ promised that man might eventually see God, Plotinus was claiming that man can *be* God. His theories seemed to contradict one another . . . Greek philosophy and Eastern mysticism seasoned with blends of Christian dogma and Hebrew theosophy. And they failed to answer one important question.

"What is that?" declared Plotinus.

"The existence of evil."

Plotinus became irritated. "Sooner or later we must all realize that evil is a deficiency of good. Poverty, disease, and crime cannot disturb the man of virtue. Moreover war among animals and men is not entirely evil since both multiply so rapidly they would perish if they did not destroy each other. Nor should the death of men in battle terrify us. I believe that even the most wicked have their place within the cosmos, for in the universal drama the bad as well as the good are called upon to play the roles assigned to them. We must stop viewing the world as a tiny corner of earth made expressly for humans. This is false. It is immense and overflowing with competing minds which of necessity are evil because they are chained to bodies, minds which must eventually separate themselves from material bondage."

"But how can this be accomplished?"

Plotinus sighed impatiently. "By attaining the Highest Vision."

Origen stood up. "It is almost midday. Ammonius will start lecturing soon. We can continue this later."

They hurried down the sun-splashed promontory and turned into Canopic Way. At the Museum Origen

132

said, "Plotinus, God is much more than a Vision. He is an intelligible sphere whose center is everywhere, whose circumference is nowhere. There are no bounds to his love. It is deeply lodged in our hearts. From the beginning of time man has believed in gods of punishment and vengeance. Love has freed us from this. It has lifted our hearts into the glorious light of God's forgiveness. This is what your god is unable to do."

"But what is there to forgive?" cried Plotinus. "If you open your mind you will discover that my god asks only one thing, to see yourself as He sees Himself."

Moments after they had seated themselves in the great hall, Ammonius made his appearance. Everyone arose. Sweeping out his powerful sun-tanned arms, he motioned them to sit. "Today," he said, "we shall discuss the nature of God."

Throughout the following weeks Plotinus' words burned inside Origen's brain. *'Your body, by allowing itself to grow fat and slovenly, will indeed reveal whether you are a eunuch or not.'* Fearful of this, he began to watch over his flesh with the eyes of Argus. He ate more sparingly than ever, and early each morning while Alexandria slept he ran through her deserted streets to the point of exhaustion. Not only was he determined that no one would recognize him as a eunuch but he had no other way of striking back at his vexations. One morning as he stood before the large metal mirror in Clement's bed chamber he discovered that he was winning his battle. Plotinus too noticed it as they sat to eat. "Are you ill?" he cried.

"Of course not."

"You look frightful."

Origen nibbled at a morsel of dark bread. "Perhaps my soul is attempting to escape its imprisonment."

"This is no joke," exclaimed Plotinus. "Everyone at the Mother Library is talking about you."

"What are they saying?"

133

Plotinus smoothed down a few unruly strands of hair on his head. He had the features of a Roman statesman who had prematurely aged, cheek bones jutting out from a pointed beard, forehead and chin carved out of granite.

"What is everyone saying about me?" asked Origen.

"That you are deliberately starving yourself just to prove you are not a eunuch. Master Allegory, you are waging a hopeless battle. The meddlesome world already has its eye on you. Now then start eating. Your soul will find its own way of escape. It needs no prodding from you."

Origen took some cheese. "Plotinus, have you noticed any change in the sound of my voice since first we met?"

Plotinus lost his patience. "The voice changes only if one is castrated as a child. Eat your food!"

"I cannot understand why virtue is so difficult to achieve. . . . "

"Nothing can be achieved under the eye of scrutiny," said Plotinus, his voice mellowing. "If you truly seek to be virtuous you must close your eyes to all things and look only to your mind. It is here that you will find enduring peace."

Origen finished the cheese and bread then took a cup of goat's milk. "Above all," Plotinus continued, "stop regarding your body as something evil which must be punished into submission. Remember that it was created by the Mind and therefore it should offer you a vision of truth."

Origen took more cheese and bread. Between mouthfuls he told Plotinus about Herais. Plotinus showed no emotion. "Your true nature is not lodged in your genitals. You must renounce all worldly thought. There are diverse ways through which you can accomplish this. The first is by the use of dialectic which helps you attain knowledge of the mind's structure and achieve unity through con-

134

templation. A second way is through virtue which produces likeness unto God in your own mind. Lastly there is the path of beauty which will lead you from the love of the temporal to that of the eternal. This is exactly what this young maiden should mean to you, for while she had life you saw only the smallest fraction of her beauty. You must not linger at fractions. Continue your climb. Do not stop until you come face-to-face with the One, until you have emptied yourself of all thoughts and desires anchored in flesh. Then only will you behold the true beauty of Herais."

They walked leisurely toward the Mother Library. Origen was sorry that he had brought up Herais because now he was struggling desperately to erase her from his mind. He asked Plotinus what plans he had for the future.

"I shall travel into Persia."

"Why?"

"To take part in a military expedition."

Origen suppressed a laugh. He could not envision this delicate vessel as a soldier.

"It is the only way in which I can learn more about Eastern culture," Plotinus went on. "Naturally I shall do my utmost to avoid killing or being killed."

"I wish you would not leave," said Origen.

"I shall be ascending, not leaving."

"Plotinus. . . . "

"Yes?"

"If only I could believe that your answers hold the true key. . . . "

Plotinus raised his voice in anger. "There can be no key because there is no door. Life consists only of Here and There!"

"This is precisely what I mean. Is it possible for me to pass from Here to There solely on my own effort?"

"There is no other way," answered Plotinus icily.

Three days after Ammonius' last lecture Plotinus left

135

Alexandria and once again Origen's spirits sank. When it seemed that his life was utterly void and meaningless a new sky showed its face. Spurred by his reawakened hunger to see where its sun arose and where it descended, he accepted Ambrosius' invitation to accompany him on a voyage to Rome.

*8.*

Taking passage on a large wheat-ship of the Imperial Service, they sailed out of Alexandria in the month of August. Although she was a large vessel she did not reach Myra on the Asia Minor coast for seven days. Half of her cargo was unloaded there and in its place several hundred sacks of choice barley from the fertile soil of Lycia were brought on board. The ship was commanded by a savage-looking captain whose only concern was to convey the cargo to hungry Rome in great haste because delay could result in serious political consequences. Ambrosius told Origen that Claudius was once mobbed by a starving crowd outside his palace. He went on to say that an identical food crisis occurred in the days of Nero, when the Emperor had to dole out bushels of wheat every month to several thousand citizens at the expense of the Treasury.

Another week passed before they were able to enter

137

the harbor at Cnidus on the western coast of Asia Minor. A sleepless Zephyrus assailed the ship daily, sending frightening gales that swelled the seas to ominous heights. When they finally put into the docks, the ship's company passed cables beneath the hull and tightened them over a windlass to save the strain on her timbers. Early the next morning they set sail once more through gigantic waves and howling winds, running under the lee of Crete, and hugging the shore until they were blown into the harbor of Fair Haven where they waited for the storm to abate. Unfriendly mountains surrounded them and they dared not leave the ship even to search for a fresh supply of water. Two days later they were at sea again, plowing onward through massive waves and driving rain. Dreading a disaster, the captain ordered the crew to be strapped to the oars, and although the men pleaded with him to return to Fair Haven, he commanded them to keep the ship on her course.

Ambrosius remained on deck all this time, ill with nausea, cursing every Egyptian god that came to his mind. For twenty-one days they had seen neither sun nor stars. Food became so scarce they had to gnaw on raw wheat. Origen refused to let the sea conquer him but he felt himself growing weaker by the day. The grumbling crew was hourly put to task by the captain yet Ambrosius never interfered even though his position gave him the authority to do so. Instead he found a place near the stern and lay there under the warmth of two sheepskin covers.

One morning, when it seemed certain they would be trapped in an under-current of shifting sands off the coast of Africa, the wind veered and sent them northward past Malta. Soon they were enwrapped in the bosom of the Tuscan Sea. The sun finally appeared through broken clouds. The winds died. The rest of the voyage into Puteoli was without further disturbance and Ambrosius at last crawled out of the stern. Within an hour they approached the long mole protecting the harbor. Hundreds of hungry faces rushed to meet them, and once the vessel was moored, they zealously joined in to help the ship's company unload the cargo.

A strange sensation gushed through Origen's blood when his feet touched Italian soil. Before him stood a busy market place. A temple to Serapis rose from a large rectangular court. Marble columns were everywhere. On his left hand, less than a hundred yards away, soared a massive amphitheatre. Ambrosius explained that two aqueducts had supplied water to the city. "Many merchants from the dye factories at Tyre maintain their residence here," he said. "Puteoli is rich with heritage. Cicero had a house in this city, and also kept a villa on the edge of Lucrine Lake near Cumae. During the Civil War Puteoli sided with Pompey, then later with Brutus and Cassius. The apostle Paul set foot here. . . . "

Ambrosius shifted his gaze to the small square off the docks where a long line of carriages waited. He hailed one and ordered the driver to pick up the two canvas bags. They were whisked away by a panting white mare and as they proceeded toward Rome, Ambrosius shouted out the names of Appia, Pontine Marshes, Lanuvium, Aricia, Bovillae. Toward the west, the Alban Hills had already turned purple. Torches became more evident, their glare bouncing against the tall porticoes of painted marble that lined both sides of the wide street. In less than an hour they entered Rome through Porta Capena whose shadowed stones glistened from a leaking aqueduct overhead. Hordes of people swarmed around the gate, dodging the carriages and wagons.

"You had better get off here," advised Ambrosius. "I must continue to Palatine Hill."

"When will I see you again?" Origen asked.

"In two hours, at the Arch of Titus."

"Where is that?"

"Ask anyone. Most Romans converse in Greek."

"What about the bags?"

"They shall remain with me," said Ambrosius. He ordered the driver to move on. Although it was rapidly getting dark, much of Rome's beauty was still visible. Pompous and proud, she reflected a regal countenance, a queen who deplored the wind because it might disarrange her hair.

He came into a wide street that was paved in red granite. An old man, his face and hands grooved with many lines, sat on the first step of a magnificent temple. Origen addressed him in Greek. "Can you please direct me to the house of Hippolytus?"

The man did not understand and he swept his hand aside gruffly. Origen then tried Hebrew and instantly the man's face beamed. "Of course, everyone in Rome knows where Hippolytus resides. You are not too distant from his house. Continue down this street for another hundred yards, then turn eastward to the Forum. His house will be the fourth structure on your left hand."

Before Origen could thank him, the old man plunged into a long monologue, droning out that he was once a prosperous merchant in Antioch with a sizable shop near the North Gate, just under the shadows of Mount Silpius. In great detail, he described his house . . . a fine villa on the southern slope with a large orchard of fruit trees and flowers. He had a panoramic view of the sea. Origen asked him why he left. "I had no other choice, my son. The entire city had lost her head over Christ. But Rome too is accepting the new religion. Why must things change? Our lives were so much better without Christ."

"Where do you worship?" said Origen.

"Are you blind?" cried the old man. "I come to this Greek temple every day."

"But you speak Hebrew."

"Of course. It is the spoken tongue in Antioch."

"What is your ancestry?"

"I am Greek."

"But you cannot speak Greek."

140

"One need not speak Greek to worship in a Greek temple."

"How do you pray to Athena?"

"In Hebrew."

"And she hears you?"

"Of course. She has heard me for seventy years."

Origen laughed then bade him farewell. After passing the Forum, he reached Hippolytus' house and knocked on the front door. A man of many years and kind face answered.

"May I speak with your master?" said Origen.

"Do you seek Hippolytus?"

"Yes."

"He is my son, not my master. He left early this morning but did not say where he was bound. If you are anxious to see him he will be at evening prayers in a short while."

"Where does he worship?"

"At the house of Zephyrinus. To find it you must walk down this street for half a mile until you come before the Basilica Ulpia. Directly across the street stands Zephyrinus' house. It has four marble columns guarding the door, two on each side."

Origen thanked him.

"You are a stranger to Rome?"

"I am from Alexandria."

"You have come to our city at a good time," said Hippolytus' father. "Although Septimius Severus is being kept busy with the Parthians, we are grateful that his religious sympathies are wide, permitting us to worship openly. It was not so with the former wearers of the purple."

Origen started to move away.

"You must ask Hippolytus to show you the cemeteries before you leave Rome."

He had no trouble locating the house of Zephyrinus. An old priest in a brown robe opened the door but did not permit him to enter. "You are too early. Evening prayers have not started."

"I came to see Zephyrinus," said Origen.

"The bishop is reclining in his bed chamber."

"It is urgent that I speak to him."

"What is your name?"

"Origen."

"You traveled here, all the way from Alexandria?"

It was incredible that a fragile old man in a foreign land should know his name. "Please remain here in the courtyard, Master Origen. I will summon his Lordship."

An expansive garden flourished in the center of the courtyard. It was surrounded by statues and busts of stern Caesars, philosophers and statesmen. When the priest reappeared he beckoned him to follow. They passed through a long corridor of white columns and stopped before a large walnut door. The priest stepped aside while Origen entered. The walls were covered with paintings, portraits of ancestors, and numerous scenes of biblical events, Jonah thrown to the whale, Christ and the Woman of Samaria, lambs, fish, birds, Moses striking the rock. . . .

At the extreme end of the room, within a circle of attendants, sat an obese man in a long-flowing red robe. His elaborately-carved throne was elevated several steps above the floor. When he saw Origen he ordered the attendants to move away then said, "You are much younger than I imagined. What brings you to Rome?"

"I came with a friend who is in the service of the Empire," said Origen.

Zephyrinus labored with his breath. "How long do you plan to stay here?"

"Only a short while."

"But Rome cannot be savored in just a few days. You must implore your friend to stay longer."

"My Lord, is this the only house of worship in Rome?"

142

"It is."

"Does Hippolytus attend here?"

"Yes."

One of the chamberlains handed Zephyrinus a silk cloth. His face was beaded with perspiration. The arm pits and neck of his robe were drenched. Sucking in a harsh breath, he said, "I expect you to address the gathering at prayers tonight."

Origen nodded. Ambrosius had alerted him about the bitter dispute that had been raging here, Zephyrinus and Hippolytus clawing at each other, hurling anathemas and excommunications, both of them laying claim to the bishopric.

Origen walked out of the room when Zephyrinus allowed his attendants to swarm over him once more. After he stepped outside he did not know where to put himself. His stomach had not touched food in days. Moving away from the basilicas and temples, he found himself in a neighborhood of squalid houses, starved children, emaciated animals. Nearby there was a small field of grass that was cloaked with patches of wild dandelions. He gathered a bunch, the most tender, than sat on the ground and ate. Further down the road he came upon a cistern. Children had assembled around it and were playfully tossing water at each other. When they saw him they moved courteously away and permitted him to take water.

In the gray distance the walls of an arena climbed over the horizon and for one agonizing moment he heard crowds shouting, lions roaring. Painfully he turned around and headed back for Zephyrinus' house. The old priest led him through the torch-lit courtyard, past a long vestibulum leading to the atrium, a huge room that was open to the sky at the center. Here too the walls were decorated with many paintings. The most prominent, although it was faded and beginning to crack, was the Good Shepherd. Origen seated himself on a wooden bench and soon the room was filled with people, most of them finely-attired and of prominent station. There was much jabbering which continued even after Zephyrinus entered, borne on a chair covered in red silk that was supported on the shoulders of four men. He turned to the right and left, blessing the bowing heads. He was transported thrice around the hall and then put down beside the painting of the Good Shepherd.

The prayers were sung in Greek.

Before the Benediction, Zephyrinus rose to his feet. "Among us today, beloved brethren, is a visitor from a foreign country, a man whose name and work are known throughout the world. We are all awed by his youth, his important position as Prefect of the great college at Alexandria, the blessed sacrifice of his martyred father. I speak of Origen. . . . "

The assembly stood up and politely applauded. Ignoring Zephyrinus' sign to come forward and speak from the ambon, Origen remained at his place and waited until everyone was seated. He struggled to calm the tremors in his voice. "From the time I was a child I felt a great veneration for the church of Rome and have always believed her to be the most ancient and honorable seat of Christendom. I have also yearned to witness her rich worship and traditions. Consequently I am moved to speak of the true essence of the universal church, a structure not visible but eternal . . . one great family born of the cosmos and bound together by the warm hands of love. I do not see such a union in Rome. Among you, there is much envy and strife. Some say '*I am with Hippolytus,*' others '*with Zephyrinus.*' But who is Hippolytus and who is Zephyrinus? Are they not children of the universal God? When Christ entered into Jerusalem He did so in a lowly manner, riding on the back of an ass, and wearing not a king's crown but a plain garment of burlap which His disciples had borrowed, nor was He lifted up by human hands but by the unseen hand of humility. . . . "

His body was still trembling when at last he finished.

144

He looked squarely at Zephyrinus but the bishop turned the other way. No one spoke to him as he walked out of the atrium. In the courtyard a stranger approached. "I understand that you have been looking for me. My name is Hippolytus."

Ambrosius suddenly appeared. He stared at Hippolytus and asked: "Who are you?"

Hippolytus again introduced himself as Origen turned his eyes toward the atrium. Through the open door he saw Zephyrinus being borne once again by the four men and conveyed through the assembly.

"What are you thinking?" Hippolytus asked him.

"I fear that I have made an enemy," Origen murmured. He looked at Ambrosius. "How did you know that I was at Zephyrinus' house?"

Ambrosius laughed. "I suspected that you would be about your father's business."

They walked out of the courtyard. In the street, Hippolytus said to them, "I want you both to join me. There is to be a discussion at the house of Sextus the philosopher."

Ambrosius protested. "I have had my fill of philosophy, Brother Hippolytus. My bones ache, my body needs washing, my stomach craves food."

"Of course, how can I be so thoughtless?" said Hippolytus. "We shall dine at my house. But first I will take you to the baths. They are on this very street." He peered at Origen who was deep in thought. "My young friend, Rome is still an adolescent maiden. She cannot yet make up her mind between the old and the new. Many of us have tried to pull her away from her former lover but we are voices in the wind. Only the birds and trees hear us."

Origen was amazed when they entered the baths. It was a huge place, lavish and ornate. Hippolytus paid their fee then led them through a world of subterranean corridors that were bordered on both sides by storerooms and heating chambers. Hippolytus explained that the building and the hot-water pools were heated by a system of hot air circulation which passed through brick tubes beneath the floors and within the walls. The main source of water was supplied by a great aqueduct high above a vaulting. A splendid garden encircled the pools. There were also many shops, libraries, lecture halls, dressing rooms, lounges, and exercise rooms. Hippolytus suggested that they go first into a circular hot-water pool which was enclosed within a domed rotunda. Origen followed Ambrosius into the pool and as the hot water swirled over his body he remembered what Seneca had said about such wasteful ostentation: 'We think ourselves poor and mean if our baths are not resplendent with large and costly mirrors, if our marbles from Alexandria are not set off by mosaics of Numidian stone, if their borders are not faced over on all sides with difficult patterns, if our vaulted ceilings are not buried in glass, if our pools are not lined with Thasian marble. What a vast number of statues, of columns that support nothing! And what masses of water that fall crashing from level to level!'

After a brief stay in the cold-water pool, they dried their bodies in a heated chamber then put on their robes. Ambrosius vigorously began rubbing his hands. "Brother Hippolytus, I am hungry enough to devour six Roman lions in one sitting!"

## 9.

After they had dined, Hippolytus' father bade them goodnight and retired to his bed chamber. More wine was brought out. "Brother Hippolytus," said Ambrosius frowning, "do you truly believe that God knows everything?"

Hippolytus came back to the table and sat down. "Indeed He does."

"If I were planning to commit a crime would He know of this before the deed was done?"

"Certainly."

"Then this makes Him an accomplice."

Hippolytus smiled. "You forget one thing. He endowed you with a free will. The choice between evil and good is entirely up to you."

Ambrosius slammed his fist on the table. "I shall never be able to understand why God does not prevent evil before it happens!"

"Because He feels that we should prevent it ourselves."

Ambrosius was not convinced. "Although I am clothed in Christ, I am not ashamed to admit that whenever Satan makes his move and places a beautiful woman in my sight I am powerless to resist."

"But God gives you the strength to overcome such temptations."

"He also gives me passion, Brother Hippolytus. What do you say to that? I remember as a small boy I often watched my mother when she baked many batches of delicious biscuits and then smothered them with honey. She would place them on the kitchen table to cool, right before my very eyes. My mouth drooled, my hand itched to grab hold of them. But she warned me not touch them. This is how God works. He tickles us under the armpits but forbids us from scratching!"

Ambrosius wanted to say more but Origen interrupted him. Without looking at Hippolytus, he asked, "How long do you intend to carry on this feud with Zephyrinus?"

Hippolytus stood up. "I alone hold the episcopal office in Rome. This honor was bestowed upon me in the proper manner."

"Zephyrinus claims to hold the same office. Who bestowed it upon him?"

"Rome has always looked to the practical side," answered Hippolytus. He left his chair and started pacing around the room. "Zephyrinus is an administrator, not a theologian. It was the bankers and tradesmen who chose him."

"And so, we slice God in two . . . one portion for Zephyrinus, the other for you?"

Hippolytus sat down again. "You are young. Someday you will realize that the affairs of mankind have very little to do with God. I have publicly accused Zephyrinus

148

of favoring the heresies of the Monarchians. He has also been warned not to close his eyes to gross offenses which threaten to undermine the structure of the church. But Zephyrinus concerns himself only with material glories."

Ambrosius yawned.

"You cannot leave now," said Hippolytus, his voice suddenly apologetic.

"We must. It is past the midnight hour."

"But where can you find quarters this late?"

"The Empire takes good care of me, Brother Hippolytus. We have been provided with suitable accomodations at Palatine Hill."

"Shall we meet again tomorrow?"

"Of course."

Ambrosius waited for Hippolytus to open the front door. "I just had a strange thought," he said. There was a grin on his face.

"What kind of thought?"

"It was like a white cloud passing over my head. For a moment it seemed that it would disappear behind the mountains in the north but then it started to descend. . . . "

"Can you not describe it more fully?"

"It is difficult."

"Surely it had some form?"

Ambrosius slapped Hippolytus on the shoulder. "I will tell you what form it had. It looked exactly like Zephyrinus . . . white and puffed-up . . . and floating over Rome on four pillars of salt!"

They dined again with Hippolytus the following evening. Throughout the meal Hippolytus governed the conversation. "No, my friends, Utopias do not exist. We must arrive swiftly and soundly at the core of truth. Unfortunately there still remains in Rome a tendency to minimize the mind of God and stress instead mysterious

149

revelation. Christ is regarded not as the Logos but more as a magician who was able to walk on the sea and turn water into wine. Such idolatry must cease."

Origen wanted to know more about Zephyrinus.

"What can I add to that which has already been stated? He is a man of little education, ignorant of ecclesiastical law, and even covetous. I am surprised you did not ask about Callistus."

"Who is he?"

"Let me start from the beginning. Callistus was a Christian slave during the reign of Commodus. His master was a certain Carpophorus, an important official in the Imperial Palace, who was also a Christian. Callistus possessed a keen business mind and for this reason Carpophorus entrusted him with large amounts of money. In due time he launched Callistus into a business venture as a money-changer and banker. Christians and Romans began depositing money with him and his fortune grew. But soon there came a period of financial difficulty and Callistus lost all his capital. Fearing his master's wrath, he fled from the city but was captured in Portus and brought back to Rome where Carpophorus indignantly dispatched him to prison. A good friend of mine, Apuleius by name, visited the prison and was appalled by the treatment accorded Callistus. His skin was lacerated with daily lashes from a whip and marked so badly Apuleius could not bear to look at him. Callistus wore only a small girdle around his loins. His forehead was branded, his hair shorn, enormous iron rings were clamped to his feet. After a long stay in prison, he was finally released, but only on the condition that he regain his losses from the parties who were in debt to him. Several of these were Jews. They became annoyed with Callistus' cruel methods of collection and accused him before the Prefect of Rome, claiming that he had created many disturbances in their synagogues. The Prefect needed no urging since he was already ill-disposed toward Christians, and thus he condemned Callistus to the malaria-infested Isle of Sardinia. After much suffering, he was set free and he dwelt for a time in Antium until Zephyrinus recalled him to Rome and conferred upon him his present office."

"And what is that?"

"Overseer of Cemeteries."

Ambrosius roared with laughter.

"This must not be taken lightly," warned Hippolytus. "Callistus has already won the favor of the presbyters, deacons, and sub-deacons. I predict that when Zephyrinus closes his eyes Callistus will succeed him."

"The bishop of Rome . . . a grave-digger!" Despite his amusement, Ambrosius could not keep his eyes open. "Now that we have solved your city's problems, Brother Hippolytus, we must bid you goodnight."

Hippolytus brought up his hands in protest. "Tonight I insist that you stay here with me. I have already asked my father to prepare your beds."

Ambrosius was too tired to object. "Brother Hippolytus, will you permit me this last question?"

"Of course."

"Have you never given thought to marriage?"

Hippolytus smiled nervously. "A man cannot be considered whole unless he nourishes such thoughts."

"Yet you have eluded them."

"I dare not ask a woman to share my anomalous way of life. I keep irregular hours, and am never in one place for a long period of time."

"Do you have an aversion toward women?"

"I can think of none, unless perhaps. . . . "

"Perhaps what?"

"There lurks a hidden scar beneath the surface of my mind. I have never been able to forget that my mother died in her struggle to give me life. I would never want my wife to suffer the same fate."

"I have no further questions, Brother Hippolytus." He beckoned to Origen.

"I am not sleepy yet."

Ambrosius gave them both a wry look. "Of course, you want to continue your theological debates. But you are wasting your time. God is no fool. He never divulges His secrets!"

Soon after he was gone, Hippolytus brought up another subject. "I am in the midst of a book that deals with Sabellius. What do you know of him?"

"Only that he was born in Libya and was for a time associated with Epigonus. . . . "

" . . . who in turn was the disciple of Noetus of Smyrna, the founder of Sabellius' abominable heresies!"

"Does he not claim that God the Father was also born of a Virgin?"

"Can you not see what Sabellius has done? He has clothed the Father in flesh and has made a nonentity of Christ. Both Zephyrinus and Callistus espouse these errors!"

Origen made no reply.

"Tell me," said Hippolytus, with a searching look, "how do you regard the Father?"

"He is a limitless ocean of love, a kingdom of mercy whose subjects require no redemption, no forgiveness or atonement," said Origen.

"And no Christ!" snapped Hippolytus. Without another word, he went about the house, snuffing all the lamps and torches. Origen followed him to the upper chambers. He bade him goodnight but Hippolytus remained silent. Crawling into his bed, he listened to Ambrosius' loud snores. His brain was still spinning. He could not believe that he was in Rome, that he had encountered Zephyrinus in his own house . . . discussed God with the great Hippolytus.

He fell asleep only after he had caught a clear vision of Herais.

Ambrosius left the house early the next morning. Hippolytus and his father prepared a light meal and later

Hippolytus offered to show Origen several sites. They began with the Arch of Titus and Vespasian. The sculptured reliefs depicted a triumphal procession of Titus in a chariot and soldiers in armor bearing the golden candlestick, trumpets, and the table of prothesis taken from the Temple of Solomon in Jerusalem. From there they walked to the north hill of Campus Martius near the banks of the Tiber where the Mausoleum of Augustus towered over the city. Its massive walls were faced with newly-whitened stone while inside were radiating chambers in the plan of a wheel. On the top of the Mausoleum was a great mound of earth with growing trees, flowers, and shrubs.

A more magnificent work was the Mausoleum of Hadrian, a large circular building on a square podium. Its walls were of enormous thickness and lined with marble. The entire structure was enclosed by a colonnade with rows of statues. At the Circus Maximus, which was wedged between Palatine Hill and Aventine Hill, he listened intently to Hippolytus as he explained that each successive emperor kept restoring the Circus until it eventually reached its present appearance . . . first the Tarquins, then Julius Caesar, Augustus, Claudius, Domitian, Trajan. "It held two hundred thousand spectators. The sun clashed against its marble facade and external tiers. Even the upper tiers were constructed of marble."

"On my first day in Rome," said Origen. "I came upon several children playing at a cistern. They had a starved look on their faces. Their clothes were tattered . . . and the cistern was only a stone's throw from Zephyrinus' house."

Hippolytus did not respond. They swung around the subterranean walls of Tiberius' Castle and approached Basilica Julia. Inside, Origen passed down the marble aisles to the clerestory which was surrounded on three sides by marble statues that stood two storeys high. The nave was surfaced with oriental marble, the aisles inlaid with mosaics. Hippolytus placed his hand on one of the columns and said: "This Basilica holds four law courts. In important cases, all four conduct joint sessions."

Origen's mind was still on the children at the cistern. "It is getting late," he said. "Lord Ambrosius must be waiting for us."

Hippolytus pointed to a bridge connecting Palatine Hill and Capitolium. "This was constructed by Caligula so that he could climb there daily and toss coins to crowds of screaming people below. He did it for amusement."

"Which road do we take to your house?" asked Origen.

Hippolytus' face clouded. "But we have yet to see the deep sandpits and graveyards that extend for miles under Appian Way, also the Forum, and that place on Ostian Road where the Apostle Paul was martyred."

"Another time," said Origen.

"But you will be leaving in a few days."

They entered into a street called Nova, and after passing the Temples of Lares and Jupiter, they arrived at Hippolytus' house. Before opening the door, Hippolytus said, "What is it, my young friend? Why are you upset? Surely you are not still thinking about Zephyrinus? How can one man alleviate the poverty of an entire city?"

Two days later Hippolytus accompanied them on the carriage journey to Brundisium. It rained hard throughout the three-day trip. Hippolytus remained silent most of the way but when it came time for them to board the galley for Alexandria he put his hand on Origen's shoulder and said, "I plan to leave Rome within a few weeks."

"Where are you going?"

"Arabia."

"For what reason?"

"I really do not know. To search for something . . . something that has eluded me all my life."

"Marriage?" exclaimed Ambrosius with a loud laugh.

"I am afraid it goes much deeper than that," replied

Hippolytus. There was weariness in his voice. "It is my real self. . . . "

Origen clasped his arm and held it warmly. "We shall meet again, Hippolytus."

"I pray."

Ambrosius was first up the plank. Origen carried the two canvas bags and placed them near the stern of the ship. They both waved to Hippolytus. By this time a heavy darkness had fallen over Brundisium. At last the anchor was lifted. One loud command from the master and the oars were put into the sea. He issued a second order and slowly they pulled away from the harbor.

# IV

*Origen to Clement:*                    *Alexandria, 4 April, 215*
    *The years seem to lose themselves like water sinking into sand. New faces are constantly revealed to me but they disappear even before I can fully know their dreams or hopes. I find it impossible to believe that you have been gone for one decade.*
    *Demetrius has kept me diligently occupied. In addition to my duties as Prefect, I have also undertaken many journeys, the last of which was to Arabia where I was called in compliance with a request brought to Demetrius by a soldier of an Arabian Prince, asking that I be permitted to visit that country and deliver a series of philosophical lectures in the presence of the Prince. While there, I had the good fortune to meet with Hippolytus. He had lost much of his antagonism and not once did he mention Callistus, the successor of Zephyrinus to the bishopric of Rome.*
    *Alexandros now lives in Jerusalem and is the new*

bishop there. He repeatedly urges me to visit with him but I can foresee no respite from the many demands Demetrius places upon me. Aside from this, the increasing multitude of students at the college has induced me to ask Demetrius for an assistant. Heraclas was chosen.

Even as I write to you, my conscience leans over my shoulder and whispers, 'Pick up your quill immediately and send word to your mother; tell her that you will go to Assouan for certain this summer!' But I cannot put myself to do it, nor can I accept the weak justification that four hundred miles is too great a distance. You are the only person to whom I can reveal the true reason: I dread that she and my brothers would see me as half a man.

Herais never leaves my thoughts. I often wonder what we might be doing if she were here beside me. I imagine myself walking down the Street of the Soma or along the Heptastadion, holding her hand with a firm grasp, fearful that she will slip away. Sometimes when I come before a handsome house on Lochias I look at it admiringly and say, 'This shall be our home, Herais. We will have our children here . . . and listen to them grow.'

My anguish is relieved only by intense study. If Demetrius should question me again on the nature of God I will reply that the Father and the Son are two distinct essences, two substances and beings. Christ should not be the object of supreme worship. Prayer must never be addressed to Him. It should be offered only to the God of the universe, to whom Christ also prayed. I place Christ at an immense distance from the Father. It is profane even to suppose an equality or union between the Father and any other being.

I cannot dislodge myself from the inclination that all beings are endowed with reason and were produced long before the foundation of the visible world. At first they were pure intelligences glowing with love toward their Maker but since they were entirely free they also had to possess the capacity of virtue and vice. These choices estranged them *from the Creator and caused their original love for Him to grow cold. In time they were reduced to varying ranks of beings. Some were placed in the bodies of the stars and were appointed to the noble task of enlightening and adorning the universe.*

*It is my strong conviction that all beings will be restored to virtue and happiness. Tertullian maintains they shall first be subjected to a trial of fire before they attain this goal but I say the only fire that can burn vice is the flame of conscience. The wrongs of the wicked will be vividly presented to their thoughts, and their evil will be spread out before them like a red carpet in the desert. In this manner all will be chastised. But our sufferings will have an end because we must all be restored to purity and to love.*

*These are my thoughts.*

*I must now close this lengthy epistle on a sad note. A barbarous persecution has broken out in Alexandria. Incensed over an accusation that he murdered his brother, Caracalla pointed his finger at Alexandria and converged upon us with several legions. Thousands have already been slain. . . .*

He dispatched the message early the next morning, assigning it to the Master of a galley that was about to set sail for Piraeus. After returning from the docks, he found Ambrosius waiting for him in one of the classrooms. He was distraught. "You must leave Alexandria immediately!" he cried.

"Why?"

"Stop asking questions. Heed my words!"

"I cannot abandon the college."

"You must. Caracalla intends to seize you."

"For what reason?"

"Undermining the State religion."

"That is absurd."

"He has accused you of ensnaring Roman students into this college."

159

"They come of their own free choice," said Origen. "I close the door to no one."

"In the name of Serapis, you do not have to convince me. I am only trying to warn you. Caracalla follows every step you take."

"Will he not follow me if I attempt to escape?"

Ambrosius desparingly flung his hands into the air. "This is no time for philosophical debate. I want you to come to my house immediately. As soon as it is dark you will leave through the garden. A carriage will be waiting for you. . . ."

He was gone before Origen could say another word. With mounting reluctance, he scribbled a message to Heraclas, asking him to assume the duties of Prefect during his absence.

When he reached the street, he was suddenly besieged by a huge throng of citizens. They came rushing toward him. A stone caught him on the head, another thumped against his chest. Blood began streaming down his face. He was shocked when he discovered they were his own people and not Romans.

"We die but the great Origen lives on!" a poisonous voice bellowed. "He is a friend of the Romans . . . a traitor!"

A hail of stones struck him on face and body. He tried to push his way past them but they formed a thick circle and started pummeling him with fists and clubs.

"You are making a terrible mistake," he cried.

"Eunuch! Eunuch!"

Someone kicked him in the groin, flooding his brain with darkness. When he recovered, he found himself alone on the street, bleeding from his nose and mouth, his whole body numb with pain. He managed to crawl back into Clement's house but before he could reach his bed he crumpled on the floor under a second wave of darkness.

It was night when he opened his eyes. He groped his way to the water basin and feebly washed his face. The

160

blood started to flow again and he wrapped a cloth around his head. Gathering a few belongings into a small canvas bag, he came downstairs. From the closet behind the oven, he took bread and raisins, filled two goatskins with water, and put everything into the canvas bag.

The street was black. Alexandria slept. A shaft of light had penetrated the eastern sky and he summoned his heart to take him there.

By late afternoon of the next day he was in sight of the desert. The heat of the sun scorched his face and he had to stop many times to rest his body. His wounds no longer bled but they still throbbed. He walked almost twenty miles before falling on the burning sand, exhausted. At dusk, hordes of sand flies attacked him. After beating them off, he munched on some bread and raisins, then took a few swallows of water from the goatskin. His head started to pound again. Using the canvas bag for a pillow, he sprawled on the sand and slept.

It was dark when he awoke. The night had turned bitter cold and he trembled. Picking up the canvas bag, he walked another six or seven miles until he saw a hut in the distance. A faint light burned inside. He hurried toward it and heard a dog bark. The door opened and an old man showed his face. He grimaced when he saw the bloodied cloth, the blistered cheeks and arms. Attending first to Origen's wounds, he washed them carefully with water then anointed them with oil. He brought out food and wine. The friendly black dog wagged its tail while Origen ate.

His name was Theophilus. He said that he had eighty-two years but his eyes looked young and alive. Origen asked him if he were a Christian.

"No!"

"You have a Christian name, a friend of God."

Theophilus snorted. "God and I have never been on friendly terms. He goes His way, I go mine. Besides, why

161

should He befriend me? I have nothing to my name but eight scrawny sheep and this old dog. . . . "

Origen patted the dog. "What is his name?"

"Name? He is a dog!"

"Surely you call him something."

Theophilus narrowed his eyes. "When I am angry with life I call him vile names. I spit on him. I curse him."

"And when you are happy?"

"That rarely happens," Theophilus grunted. "But when it does, I call him *dog*. 'Hey, dog,' I say. 'You are my only friend. You eat with me and sleep with me. You are my eyes, my ears, my nose. . . . "

"Where do you keep them?" asked Origen.

"Who?"

"Your eight sheep?"

"Can you not smell them? They are under our feet!"

Origen finished with his food then squatted on the the floor near the dog. After a long silence, Theophilus said: "It is not true what I told you moments ago about God. We are the best of friends . . . only I do not call Him God."

"What do you call Him?"

"Dog."

Origen helped him with the cups and bowls. The sheep started a commotion and Theophilus went into the cellar to quiet them. While he was gone Origen stepped outside. The night engulfed him. A cold blanket had enshrouded the sky. Somewhere the four winds had congregated and were listening to the gray complaints of still another year. He could not understand what mad power was pulling at him, scraping him over the face of the universe. Only yesterday he was in Alexandria. In Rome. Moments ago he was looking into the face of Herais, his father, his mother and brothers, Clement . . . but now he was buried in this desert of loneliness, cast out of his beloved city, confused, hated by his own people, cut off from his college and his work.

162

He felt something moist on his hand. He bent over, lifted the dog into his arms and carried it back into the hut. Theophilus was reclining on his bed. "From what place have you come?" he asked.

"Alexandria."

The old man scratched his ribs. "You are unusually tall of body." Soon he was snoring. Origen threw a sheep skin cover over him then took the canvas bag and propped himself against it. The dog came and snuggled beside him. They slept.

He was awakened early in the morning by Theophilus who already had prepared a breakfast of millet cakes, cheese and milk. Origen hardly touched the food. Shaking his head, Theophilus stuffed a large portion of cheese into the canvas bag, along with a supply of millet cakes. He accompanied Origen to the crest of a sloping hill of sand as the dog pranced between them, stopping every so often to snap at a sand fly that buzzed near its ear. Origen patted it many times before embracing Theophilus. He was skin and bone, and his body smelled of sheep. Not one word was exchanged.

Origen did not look back until he had walked almost one mile. Man and dog were still on the crest of the hill, two tiny specks of gray against the brightening sky. He moved eastward once more, holding his course until midday when he came upon a cluster of palm trees. A vein of water, protected by a small wall of red tiles, coursed through the trees. Nearby stood a fallen tomb whose defaced inscription was written in Aramaic. Several palm-leaf stalks were stuck in the sand to indicate the site of more graves.

The long trek had improved his appetite and he ate a few millet cakes even though they were soft and soggy. He washed his head in the cool water then took a long drink. It was salty but he continued drinking until he had his fill. There was some shade under the palm trees. He lay down and was about to shut his eyes when he saw a

163

group of dark-skinned women drawing near. They were carrying jars on their shoulders and heads. After filling the jars with water, they moved off.

He awoke with a start. Clouds of sand had engulfed him. He waited until the air started clearing and then he opened his eyes. He saw an army of fierce-looking men, all of them as dark-skinned as the women at the spring. They were wearing headbands of red cloth and holding long wooden spears in their hands. They did not dismount from their dromedaries. Their leader, a man of advanced years with a bright green turban around his head, yelled down at him. "Where are you bound?"

Origen pointed toward the east.

"From where have you come?" The old chieftain spoke in coarse Aramaic.

"Alexandria," said Origen.

"Who gave you permission to drink from this spring?"

"There was no one here and I was very thirsty."

"This spring is ours. We demand that you pay a tribute!"

"I have no money."

The chieftain motioned to one of the tribesmen who leaped from his dromedary and seized the canvas bag. He searched through it wildly but found nothing except the two goatskins. The chieftain commanded Origen to take off his robe. At first he refused but when the tribesmen made a threatening move, he obeyed.

"I ask you again, where are you bound?" the chieftain said.

"I truly do not know."

"You drank from my spring without permission. You must pay!"

"But I have nothing to my name . . . only these millet cakes."

"I want money!"

"I have none."

164

The chieftain tried to gather his tribesmen together but they started yelling and cursing. He silenced them quickly and came back to Origen. "The nearest spring is a full day's journey from here. For your safety, we will accompany you but first you must pay a tribute."

Suddenly one of the tribesmen rushed toward Origen and ordered him to open his mouth. With dirty fingers, he groped under Origen's tongue then turned him sharply around and shoved his fingers between Origen's buttocks. Origen struck him on the cheek with his fist, knocking him to the sand. Cursing the sky, the tribesman spat at him and went back to his beast. There were more heated words between the tribesmen and the old chieftain, more thrashing of arms. Finally they all mounted their dromedaries and bolted off, disappearing behind a hill of yellow sand.

Feeling weak and dazed, he picked up the canvas bag and started walking. Darkness fell but he did not stop until he found a shallow valley between two sharp peaks of sand. From the canvas bag he took out a goatskin and drank. Sleep possessed him.

He was awakened by the piercing howl of a desert wind. A new world seemed to be forming before his eyes. Hills and plateaus were swept away, sky and earth assumed one color, clouds of deranged sand lashed at his face. Suddenly he was racked by a coughing fit. Nausea.

After this, he remembered nothing else.

2.

He was lying on a soft woolen carpet under a great
tent of black goat-skins that were spread over six high
poles. A woman of dark face, wearing a loose yellow garment under a blue over-cloak, leaned over him and began
washing his face and body with a cloth. Bracelets of red
glass hung from her wrists and ankles. A copper necklace
circled her neck. She was pleasing in appearance and
when she caught him staring at her she quickly narrowed
the folds of her cloak.

The tent was at least fifteen yards long and equally as
wide. A partition of goatskins separated it into two sec-
tions. The first contained the carpet on which he lay, some
camel-saddles, rope, and a sharply pointed spear whose
stem was made of cane. This was sticking into the ground
beside the door of the tent. In the other section were several cooking pots, some platters, wooden drinking bowls,
and earthen vessels of various sizes and shapes.

Outside, he could hear the happy sound of children at play. One curly-haired boy poked his head through the tent and peered at him with long curiosity. He was completely unclothed and very brown of body. After flashing a wide smile, he disappeared. By this time, the woman had finished bathing him. She pulled the hood of her cloak over her head and quietly left the tent.

Moments later the man with the green turban entered. In his gnarled hand he held a long staff made of almond wood. He leaned over, and in a compassionate voice, said, "We found you covered in sand several miles south of here. We returned to the spring and looked for you but you were not there. However one of the women saw you and told us that you had just left and were traveling eastward. My name is Ahsen. I am leader of our tribe."

Origen lowered his head.

"You must forgive us for what happened at the spring," said Ahsen. "We are people of the tent. The desert is our home. Many regard us as plunderers but we only seek what is just. Water is precious. This is why we ask all trespassers to pay a tribute. But in your case, this will not be necessary. From this moment on, I promise that you shall have my personal attention. I make this vow in the name of the desert wind: as soon as you are well, two of my most trustworthy tribesmen will accompany you to your destination."

Origen was speechless.

"Now then, you must tell me where you are bound."

"In truth, I do not know."

"Surely you do not expect me to believe that you traveled all this distance without knowing your destination?"

"I left Alexandria because she is being persecuted."

"By whom?"

"The Emperor Caracalla."

"What crime did Alexandria commit?"

"She has accepted the new religion."

167

Ahsen shrugged. "The new . . . the old. What is the difference? Are we not all children of one Father?"

Origen tried to stand up but Ahsen pushed him down. "You are still weak, my son. It is best that you stay with us for a few days."

"How far is the nearest village?"

Ahsen pointed eastward. "Twenty-five miles from this tent lies Succoth. Its fertile valley and many springs afford an ideal resting place for caravans. It is also a military camp."

"For Romans?"

Ahsen laughed. "No, my tall one. For Arabians."

"Can I reach it in one day?"

"Of course. I will supply you with our best dromedary . . . and as I promised earlier, two of my most trustworthy tribesmen."

Origen tried to tell him there was no necessity for all this but Ahsen would not hear of it. "Tonight we are having a feast in your honor. The women have been busy all morning with the preparations. . . . "

Again Origen protested.

Soon after Ahsen had left the tent, he fell into a tranquil sleep. He was awakened several hours later by the sound of singing voices. Through the slitted opening of the tent, he saw a great fire burning in a sandy hollow. Dancers circled around it and a strong scent of roasting meat saturated the chill night air. Suddenly he felt a hand on his shoulder. Ahsen said, "Now that you have opened your eyes, my tall one, we can start eating." He clapped his hands and the dancing stopped. Everyone came and sat around Ahsen. The women brought out bowls of food and placed them in the center of the circle. They ate. Origen drank freely of the wine. It was heavy and tasted very sweet.

One of the men started playing on a lyre. Feeling giddy, Origen said to Ahsen, "I shall sing you a verse that my mother taught me. . . . "

Ahsen straightened up. "Is it a sad song?"

"No."

"Ah then, a song of love?"

Origen shook his head and began.

*"Whither shall I go from Thy spirit?*
*If I ascend into heaven,*
*Thou art there.*
*If I make my bed in Hell,*
*Behold Thou art there also.*
*If I take wings of the morning*
*And dwell in the uttermost parts of the sea,*
*Even there shall Thy hand find me."*

Ahsen sighed. "You see, my tall one, it is just as I told you. We are all children of one Father."

"You comprehended the words?"

"Of course. We speak Hebrew as well as Aramaic." Ahsen wiped his eyes with the back of his hand then clapped his hands. The man with the lyre started to play once again and a young maiden of bronze skin came forward. First she gave a reckless toss of her head and then flung away her garment. Swaying before the flames, she taunted everyone with her naked dance. Ahsen was very proud. He leaned toward Origen and said, "That is Zaega, the youngest of my many daughters. Does her beauty please you?"

"She is very lovely," said Origen.

"Zaega has fourteen years. Upon my solemn word, she is untouched."

The girl now turned from the fire and slid to her knees. Bending back, she stretched her supple arms and body toward the flames as the crowd roared its approval. This was Roxana offering her maidenhood on Elephantine Island. He could hear the lewd cries of the multitude, feel the blood pounding through their veins.

Ahsen was staring at him. "If it is your desire, my tall one, I shall command Zaega to come to your bed tonight."

169

A sudden turbulence lashed at his brain.

"I swear, she has not known a man!" cried Ahsen.

He tried to get up but Ahsen seized his arm. "I have chosen you because you are of handsome appearance and very tall. You must not refuse me."

With a firm pull, Origen freed his arm and slowly walked away. When he reached the black tent he stopped and looked back. Ahsen had the wine cup to his mouth, intently watching his daughter. In the frenetic commotion of song and dance that went on, he picked up his canvas bag then crept quietly out of the tent, past the herd of sleeping dromedaries. Remembering Ahsen's directions to Succoth, he turned his face toward the east and began dragging his feet over the sand.

He was inside the village two days later. Tents of black and white goatskins were spread over the fertile valley. In the very center of the encampment he came upon tall palms and a spring of water. Several young maidens were about to fill their earthen vessels but when he drew near they stood aside and waited until he drank. He asked if a caravan would be leaving the village but they smiled and lowered their eyes. Then one of them came forward and pointed toward a small tent just behind the spring. He bowed his head and started walking there as a chorus of giggles fell on his ears. It seemed incredible that he was in Succoth, that place of tents, the first camp of the Israelites in their flight from Egypt.

A man named Etham lived in the small tent. A robust caravan-leader with hairy arms and legs, he glared at Origen suspiciously. A white turban was wound around his head.

"When do you leave on your next journey?" asked Origen.

"Tomorrow morning."

"Where are you bound?"

"I am bringing a herd of mules to Antioch."

170

"May I join you?"

"Do you have money?"

"No."

Etham growled at the sky.

"I can work for you," said Origen. "I will feed and water the mules, put up the tents, help prepare all the meals. . . ."

Etham rubbed his chin. "Your speech sounds foreign. Where is your home?"

"Alexandria."

"If you work for me you must obey all my commands."

"Yes."

"Very well. You can eat with us now then sleep in our tent. I expect you to arise at daybreak."

Origen nodded.

"Well, why are you standing there? Step inside. My woman is about to serve the evening meal."

"My name is Origen."

Etham grunted.

"Is not Etham the name of a nearby town?" Origen asked.

The caravan-leader frowned. "I was born there, and so everyone calls me Etham." He stepped aside and asked Origen to pass into the tent. It was smaller than that of Ahsen and had no partition separating it. Everything was scattered about . . . cooking pots, platters, camel-saddles, rope, and waterskins. Three children sat quietly on a small red carpet, two boys and a girl. The boys gave Origen a warm smile but the girl kept her eyes fastened on her mother who sat beside them. Sitting alone at the far corner of the tent, was a paunchy old man in a long dirty garment.

"These are my children," said Etham without a trace of pride. "And she is my woman. The old man is her protector. . . ."

"Protector?"

Etham reprimanded his sons for snickering. "We of Succoth," he explained, "are jealous of our women, it is true, but we do not prevent them from speaking to strangers, nor do we insist that they wear veils. Occasionally I lose my temper and strike her. When this happens, our laws permit her to call upon her protector to pacify me and enlighten me with reason. But she is a good woman. She and her daughter grind wheat with the handmill and then pound it into powder. They prepare meals, bake bread, fetch water, work at the loom, mend the tent, and wash clothes."

"And what are your duties?" asked Origen with a smile.

Etham inflated his chest. "I sit here and watch them as I smoke my hemp. . . . "

"Hemp?"

A look of distress flashed across Etham's face. "In the name of the desert wind, I have forgotten my manners!"

"What do you mean?" said Origen.

"You are a guest in my tent. It is necessary that we smoke before we eat."

"Smoke?"

Etham brought out a small walnut chest and pulled free several stalks of dry leaves. They were brownish-green in color. He rolled them between his palms, spat into them until a firm strand was formed. Now he struck flint, and with the hemp stick in his mouth, he began sucking at the tiny flame. Soon clouds of smoke filled the tent. He sighed deeply then handed it to Origen who guardedly put it to his lips.

"Suck!" cried Etham.

He took a nibbling breath.

"Like this!" bellowed Etham, grabbing the hemp and gulping from it savagely. Origen started to pull back but Etham's piercing yell halted him. "In the name of the holy prophets, it cannot kill you. It is only hemp!"

Etham's wife came to his rescue. She placed a wooden

bowl before him and invited him to eat. The wheat soup was barely warm but he was hungry and filled his bowl twice. After the meal Etham reclined on his side and began smoking again. Origen could not endure the smell. He walked out of the tent and took a deep gulp of air as Etham's voice fell on his ears, "Remember my words. We are leaving at daybreak. If you are not ready we will depart without you!"

He defeated the sun and was up even before Etham. They ate bread, honey, a sweetmeat made of sesame seeds, and drank goat's milk. He helped Etham pull down the tent and strap it to a camel. Etham led the mules to the spring while his sons filled all the water-skins. Etham's wife and daughter looked after the food and the cooking utensils. All this time, the protector squatted in the sand and watched. Just then a stranger appeared and began counting the mules. He was dressed in a long woolen overcloak that touched the sand. Origen whispered to Etham, "Who is he?"

"His name is Nousan. He will accompany us."

"Why is he counting the mules?"

"They belong to him, all twenty-six."

"Does he live in Succoth?"

"No. He is from Heliopolis. We have transacted together for many years. Nousan is wealthy but honest." Etham patiently waited for Nousan to count the mules before introducing him to Origen.

"You have come a long distance from Alexandria," said Nousan. He closed his huge brown eyes for a moment. "I traveled there often in my younger days. Tell me, how did you learn to speak our language?"

"I had a student from Arabia who taught me."

"You are a teacher?"

"Yes."

"What do you teach?"

"Mathematics, history, philosophy, Greek."

Nousan wanted to continue the discussion but Etham cut him off. "It is getting late. We must set out."

The mules were laced together to form a single line behind the camels. Etham mounted the first camel. His wife and children followed behind him, each on a separate camel. Origen's beast strode behind that of Nousan which trailed the last mule. Several children from the encampment came chasing after them, shouting and teasing the camels, but Nousan made a gentle plea and they walked away.

The caravan moved northward, along the sandy shore of a dry river. The sun had now gained full stature and was beating heavily upon them as desert flies swarmed over the sweating backs of the mules. Nousan leaned toward Origen and said, "We should arrive at a place called the Bridge before sundown. Beyond that lies the great desert of Sinai."

"Have you made this journey often?" asked Origen.

The mule-merchant took off his turban and tousled the gray hairs of his head. "Count them," he laughed.

"Do you breed these mules yourself?"

"No. They come from Cyprus."

"But would it not have been easier to transport them to Alexandretta by ship and from there to Antioch?"

Nousan shook his head. "Antioch is guarded by impenetrable mountains. Her only approach is from the southwest. Our route will carry us into Heliopolis. I have a very active market there. Yes, my mules have found homes in many cities . . . Memphis, Alexandria, Paraetonium, Assouan . . . even the deepest parts of Nubia." He clicked his teeth. "It is a pity that you chose to be a teacher. You should look to the world. There are boundless opportunities in commerce and trade for someone who knows many languages."

They proceeded in silence for several hours. At midday they stopped to eat, and although Nousan wanted to rest a while, Etham insisted they move on. Before mount-

174

ing his beast, Origen said to Etham's wife, "Your protector did not accompany you on this journey?"

Etham overheard him and pounded his fist against his chest proudly. "Her protector is here. Climb your camel. We are losing time."

They wound their way across a wide sandy plain covered with thorn bushes and desert grass. The mules started to eat but Etham lashed at them with his leather strap. Soon Origen was in the midst of an odd phenomenon. The world of sand was transformed into an illusionary lake whose ruffled surface of blue seemed to sparkle with wondrous clarity. Nousan was suddenly concerned about him. "How do you feel?"

"The heat has never bothered me before," said Origen, shaking his head.

"Your discomfort will pass once we reach Gaza. We shall then have the Great Sea on our left hand throughout the rest of the journey. Ah, I cannot wait to embrace those delicious breezes!"

They climbed a hill for some distance, over wearisome plateaus of sand, and at the crest they came upon carcasses and skeletons of camels that were scattered about like leaves in a storm. One of the carcasses still reeked with a foul odor and the mules scurried to escape it. A great raven circled impatiently over their heads, waiting for them to pass.

As they edged their way cautiously down the slope, they saw several dozen Bedouins approaching. Etham spurted ahead and confronted them, thrashing his arms and cursing. After a while, he returned to the caravan and reported to Nousan, "They want water!"

"Give it to them," said Origen.

Etham cursed the sky. "No!"

Four of the Bedouins, a man, woman, and two young boys clasped their hands over their faces and fell to their knees before Etham. He spat at them, swore at them.

Origen leaped from his beast and grabbed hold of

175

Etham's arm. "You cannot ignore them like this. We have plenty of water."

"No!"

"But they will die."

Nousan calmly stepped between them. "Etham is doing the proper thing. If we give water to these people the word will swiftly circulate and whole tribes will come screaming at our feet. In the desert, each man must learn to look after himself."

The younger boy appeared emaciated. He was perched on bony legs, his tiny body weaving and swaying in the soft sand. Origen gathered him into his arms and carried him to one of the pack-camels. He unstrapped a water-skin.

"What are you doing?" cried Etham.

"This boy is burning with fever. He needs water."

"Stop. I command you!"

"I shall not deprive the caravan," said Origen. "He can have my share of water, his family also."

"I swear . . . if you come begging to me!"

The boy grasped the water-skin from Origen's hand and gulped from it. Origen cautioned him to drink slowly and was touched by the affectionate eyes. After a while he took the water away from the boy and passed it to his mother.

"You will regret this!" bellowed Etham.

Origen paid no attention to him. He patted the sick boy on the head and waited for the others to finish drinking. The mother threw herself at his feet but he turned and mounted his camel. Etham was shaking with rage. As they moved off, the Bedouins pressed their hands together as though in prayer and fell to their knees in gratitude.

Shortly before dusk the caravan pulled into a tent-filled valley. Scores of camp fires reflected against the horizon. The scent of food filled the air. Nousan got off his camel and said, "We have finally reached the Bridge."

"Where is it?" asked Origen.

Nousan pointed toward some nearby palms. "There, just beyond that last row of tents. Now we can replenish our water-skins. The spring here is deep and cold."

Etham did not speak throughout the evening meal. After the others had fallen asleep, Nousan crept up to Origen and whispered, "Are you going into the village?"

"At this time?"

Nousan smacked his lips. "Does not the aroma stir your blood?"

"What aroma?"

"That of young maidens. When I was your age I had seven wives, not to mention the countless women who catered to my needs throughout my many travels. In the name of the holy prophets, where do the years go?"

"How many wives do you have now?" asked Origen.

"Alas, only two . . . both of them as hard as granite. But it is a sin to abandon them. I am destined to spend the rest of my days shivering in a cold bed."

"How far is Gaza from here?"

"Why do you ask?"

"Just curious."

"Four or five days . . . but first we must pass through the Place of the Camels.

"Etham is a very exciteable man."

"The mill that makes the most noise grinds the least," said Nousan, coming close beside him. "Are you certain you cannot catch that aroma? In the name of the prophets, how my soul yearns for a soft woman!"

The Place of the Camels was a small village situated on the very edge of the Great Sea. On its outer perimeter were tents of many colors; several caravans had already stationed themselves there. Within the inner camp were rows of mud huts flanked by herds of sheep and goats. Patches of green grass splattered the brown earth while flocks of gulls circled lazily overhead. A great wall of granite protected the inner encampment from the sea. As they passed through its only gate Nousan said, "This village has almost three thousand inhabitants. There are also five hundred camels, sixty dromedaries, two hundred and eight goats, ninety-seven sheep, and twenty-six cows. I must not forget the six thousand palm trees whose sap produces the sweetest sugar in the East . . . nor those delicious black and red dates, the juicy white grapes, figs, melons, oranges, lemons, garlic, barley, and maize. This indeed is a heavenly spot!"

Origen unfolded the tent. Nousan helped him lift it into place over the six poles which Etham had driven into the ground. Meanwhile Etham's wife started cooking. The caravan-leader was still sullen. He ordered Origen to the spring with the water-skins. When he returned, he was commanded to water the mules and camels. Nousan came with him. The sun had now disappeared in the western hills and a cold chill swept over the village. As the mules and camels fought for a place at the spring, Origen muttered, "I once knew someone from Heliopolis. . . . "

"Who?" asked Nousan.

"Her name was Herais."

"What was her father's name?"

"I do not know. We met at Natron more than ten years ago."

Nousan shook his head. "Heliopolis is a large city."

"Her father died of palsy."

"Why did you go to Natron?" asked Nousan with curiosity.

"A pillar-hermit resided there. Herais brought her father to him for healing."

"Was he cured?" Nousan sneered.

"No."

Nousan picked at his teeth with a stiff blade of desert grass. "I have yet to see it happen."

"What?"

"God correcting His mistakes."

178

After the beasts finished drinking, Origen tied them together and returned to the camp. Etham and his family were waiting with impatience. Nousan seated himself next to the caravan-leader's wife while Origen sat between the two boys. They ate morsels of roasted meat blended with sesame seeds, and after the meal Etham brought out his small wooden chest and rolled a stick of hemp.

Six days later, after they passed through Gaza, Origen decided to leave the caravan. Etham got angry and kept reminding him that they had desperate need of his help and could never reach Antioch without him. But Origen had already made up his mind.

Nousan was disappointed. "You cannot turn back now. We are only ten days from Antioch."

"I am not turning back," said Origen.

"Then where are you going?"

"Eastward."

Nousan snorted. "That endless desert which you see before you belongs to the Bedouins. They are treacherous thieves and murderers. If they do not put an end to you, the burning sun will."

Origen clasped his arm and bade him farewell. Tears invaded Nousan's eyes. He squirmed off his camel and began untying one of the mules.

"What are you doing?" asked Origen.

"You cannot cross that vile desert on two feet. I am giving you this mule."

"But you have already transacted for twenty-six."

"So? One perished along the way."

"Thank you, but I cannot accept it," said Origen. Again he bade Nousan farewell.

"Where are your two water-skins?" Nousan exclaimed.

"I do not know. I lost them."

"In the name of the desert wind, do you expect to

walk into that inferno without an ounce of water? Wait here!" Nousan ran to the pack-camels, unstrapped two water-skins, and brought them to him.

"Etham will be angry," said Origen.

"I will pay for them," Nousan replied. He reached under his overcloak and drew out two loaves of bread. "Etham's wife baked them for you late last night while Etham slept."

"How did she know that I would be leaving?"

Nousan hunched his shoulders. "Women know everything!"

Origen laced the two water-skins together and slung them over his shoulder. He shoved the bread under his arm. "I shall miss you, Nousan."

"Perhaps we will meet again," said Nousan, his eyes moist.

Three days after parting from the caravan, he reached a small village. He stayed the night in a dung-filled stable and left at daybreak before anyone awoke. As in Gaza, he noticed skulls of camels attached to the doors of all the houses. He had asked Nousan what this meant and the mule-merchant sadly responded, "This is how these unfortunate creatures protect themselves from evil spirits."

Just before nightfall he reached Marissa where he found water and a small grove of almond trees. Their fruit hung heavy on the branches and as he satisfied his hunger he remembered that it was in Marissa that the God of the Jews smote thousands of Ethiopian invaders. He slept. In the morning he filled his robe pocket with almonds then went to the spring and refilled the water-skins. By midday he was in Eleutheropolis, and at dusk he stood on a high ridge overlooking the Valley of Elah where David slew Goliath.

Throughout the next day he struggled feverishly across bleached hillsides and through burning sand while ravens kept a vigilant watch overhead. The night turned bitterly cold. He awoke the following morning, hungry and numb with pain, but he set out once more, his eyes pointed toward the east. When it seemed that the world was but a huge log on a lake, spinning furiously and without purpose under his feet, he came upon a magnificent sight: rising high above him on a golden plateau, loomed the table of God, *Jerusalem*.

3.

On his long climb to the city, the Jewish historian
Josephus flooded his mind. It was from Caesarea that
Vespasian was proclaimed emperor. Although he had already conquered most of Palestine, he assigned the task of
destroying Jerusalem to his thirty-year old son Titus who
assembled a force of seventy-five thousand soldiers before
the walls of the city. Along with this army came hordes of
cavalry and auxiliary troops. Knowing that the Jews inside
the old walls were embroiled in a fierce civil war, Titus
gave orders to keep a close watch on the east wall. He then
stationed the Tenth Legion on the Mount of Olives. The
remainder of his force encircled the city and when the
battering rams could do nothing against the powerful
walls he himself entered the outskirts of Jerusalem and
warned the Jews they must surrender or die. They refused. Enraged, Titus constructed a second wall around
the city and made each of his four Legions responsible for

a particular section, leaving strict orders that not one Jew was to escape alive.

Famine set in. The Jews tossed hundreds of corpses over the wall daily, and to prevent anyone from deserting, they enforced the penalty of death by crucifixion. Some did manage to flee. They were puffed up and swollen in appearance, as if suffering from dropsy. In the long siege that followed, the Romans cut down every tree in the vicinity to make scaling ladders, more battering rams, and other implements of war. Within a matter of months, the whole countryside lay barren. A greater destruction was being wrought inside the city where anyone who looked plump or well-fed was tortured to death. Mothers and fathers grabbed food away from their own children. Thousands searched the streets daily, looking for garbage, and even plucking out grains of wheat from human excrement. In time they started eating their sandals, girdles, the leather from their shields.

There was a widow with a new-born son. Her name was Mary and she came from the village of Bethezub where her father was prominent and wealthy. When the Romans converged upon her village, she gathered together all her belongings and fled into Jerusalem with the babe. A few days later Titus arrived. Along with the rest of the populace, she sought refuge within the old walls of the city but plunderers came to her house every day like ravens. They left nothing. One morning, half-crazed from hunger, her dying infant sucking vainly at her dry breast, she slew him then roasted him over a fire. After devouring half the body, she hid the rest. When the plunderers appeared early the next morning they caught the smell of roasting meat and threatened to kill her if she did not reveal where the food was hidden. She uncovered the remains of her son and they ran from her house panic-stricken.

All this time, the Romans kept pummelling the outer walls with their battering rams. This went on night and day as the harsh sounds of heralds demanded the Jews' surrender. Huge stores of grain were stacked in full view of the Jews to entice them but they refused to give up. Toward the middle of July, on the hottest day of the year, the Romans broke through the north wall and captured the Castle of Antonia which lay only an arm's length from one wall of Solomon's Temple. Titus threatened to destroy the Temple if the Jews did not surrender but they would not be uprooted from their belief that Jehovah would save them.

In the month of August the Romans fought their way inside the Temple, and after a prolonged battle near the entrance to the Holy of Holies, one of the soldiers took a burning brand and threw it into an open window. Wild flames immediately engulfed the sanctuary. Although half the city was now in the hands of Titus, and the once-glorious Temple lay in smouldering ruins, the Jews fought on. Titus could not understand it. He stood on the bridge that spanned the Tyropoean Valley and yelled down to them. 'Oh, miserable creatures, how long can you endure? Your people are dead, your holy house is destroyed, your city is in my hands. Surrender and I will grant you life!'

The Jews did not bother to answer him. Once again the battering rams came crashing against the walls, ladders were tossed up, burning brands flung into the sky. By the thousands, the Romans scaled the walls and started to massacre the Jews. When they grew tired of their own butchery a final order was issued and Jerusalem was leveled to the ground, not one stone left upon the other.

But Origen had never expected to find this . . . a new city . . . a Roman city called *Aelia Capitolina*. Even the ashes of Jerusalem had been plowed under by the Romans. After a brief conversation with a young student, he learned that Hadrian had erected a temple to the Capitoline Jupiter on the exact site of Solomon's sacred edifice. As they walked together through the sparkling city, the student pointed to a theatre, two market places, a

184

temple to Astarte, and many temples to Serapis. "You will observe," said the student, "that there are no Jewish inhabitants in the city. On the penalty of death, they are not allowed to live here."

So completely were all traces of the ancient city destroyed that he had difficulty identifying certain landmarks . . . the Mount of Olives in the east, Mount Scopus in the north, the hill of Golgotha, the pool of Siloam. The young student took leave of him and he continued leisurely through one of the side streets until he caught sight of a young bearded priest. After a few words of greeting, he was directed to a low stucco building further down a vaulted passageway. Its door was half-open. Origen put his head inside and walked in. A small table was leaning against the far wall, several lit tapers stood in the center of the table. A figure in a simple robe of black was kneeling in prayer, his back turned.

Origen said, "Alexandros. . . . "

At first he did not recognize the face, the pointed beard streaked with gray, deep lines formed around the mouth and eyes. "I do not know how to greet you," he smiled, coming closer. "Should I kiss your hand?"

"Origen!"

They fell into each other's arms.

"Why did you not write to me?" cried Alexandros, through tears of joy. "In the name of the Father, I never expected you to come!"

Origen took a chair and sat. The room was drenched with the scent of the burning tapers. "You must be starving," said Alexandros. He hurried into an adjacent room and came back with some bread and cheese, a small amphora of wine. While Origen ate, he beleaguered him with questions about Alexandria, Clement, the college, Rome. Finally he took a chair and sat down beside him. "Origen, why did you come here?"

He told Alexandros about Caracalla, the stone-throwing, the vile names.

Alexandros sighed, "During my stay in Cappadocia, a persecution broke out under Severus and I was thrown into prison."

"How long were you confined?" asked Origen.

"Seven weeks. Soon after I was released, I had a dream . . . a divine intimation."

Origen squirmed in his chair.

" . . . an angel of God advised me to go immediately to Jerusalem. I obeyed. Narcissus was Bishop of Jerusalem at that time and he implored me to become his coadjutor. He was very old and in feeble health. I accepted his offer but when the bishops from the surrounding areas heard about this they objected, claiming that the Church Canons forbade the transference of a bishop from one district to another. They also expressed their disapproval over the presence of two bishops in one city. Thus I had to obtain the sanction of the whole episcopate of Palestine. A synod was convened and in due time I won its approval. Several months after this, Narcissus closed his eyes."

"And now you are the sole bishop of Jerusalem . . . or should I say Aelia Capitolina?"

"Only the Romans use that name. To us, it will always be Jerusalem."

"Do you reside here . . . in this place of worship?"

"No. The brethren have provided me with quarters near the Castle of Antonia. I am anxious for you to see the place. A dear friend has been visiting with me for the past two weeks. His name is Theoctistus. He is Bishop of Caesarea."

"Is the house large enough for the three of us?" asked Origen.

"Of course. It will please you to know that Narcissus left a very large library. It is entirely at your disposal." Alexandros paused a moment. "You did not say how long you plan to remain in Jerusalem."

"It depends on Caracalla."

Alexandros took him by the arm. "We can talk about

186

this later. Come, there are a few places I want to show you before it gets dark."

As they plowed their way through the tight street, Origen spoke at length about Plotinus, about Hippolytus . . . and finally Herais. Alexandros did not remember her until Origen reminded him of Natron.

They moved into a small square, past a plaintive chorus of beggars. Alexandros stopped to bless them and almost immediately hordes of vendors swarmed around them, displaying their wares. Alexandros pulled Origen away and brought him into a cobbled lane so narrow they could touch both walls by spreading out their arms. "We are walking on the Street of David," he said reverently.

Origen teased him. "It is almost as wide as Canopic Way."

With mounting devotion, Alexandros bent down and touch the cobblestones as Origen walked nervously away. Alexandros called him back and they proceeded down the lane.

A fat man of middle age came running toward them, carrying a basket of bread on his shoulders. Alexandros handed him a coin and received two loaves. "For the evening meal," he said to Origen, tucking them under his arm. He led him into an even tighter street that descended by uneven steps into a shadowy lane. Gleaming Nubian faces brushed past them. More beggars appeared, throwing themselves at their feet, crying hoarsely and tugging at their robes.

"It is getting late," said Origen. "Where are your quarters?"

"But Gethsemane is not too far from here."

"Tomorrow perhaps."

Alexandros pointed to a low-slung house of stone that was nestled on a small hill just outside the Gate of Stephen. "That is the home of Mary, mother of Mark. It is one of the few buildings that escaped the wrath of Titus. In its upper chamber Christ ate with His disciples for the

187

last time, and in that same room the apostles gathered together after the Resurrection. The brethren plan to build an oratory there. . . . "

"Alexandros, what do you hope to find here? That house is dead, these cobblestones are dead, Jerusalem is dead!"

Alexandros was not disturbed. "When we remember the dead we resurrect them."

"Please, let us go to your quarters."

"Origen, are you not going to tell me why you did it?"

"Did what?"

" . . . mutilate yourself."

"Alexandros, I buried all this a long time ago."

"When I first heard about it my heart ached."

"What did you hear?"

"That you molested the daughter of an Egyptian Prince. . . . "

"What?"

" . . . and he ordered you to be castrated in public."

"Who told you this?"

"What difference does it make? It was said."

"And you believed it?"

Alexandros did not reply.

Origen let out a sour laugh. "We have said too much to each other. For the last time, let us go to your quarters."

The lamps in the houses were lit and their glow was sending fingers of gold along the street. "It was wrong for me to drag you out here," Alexandros muttered. "I should have realized you were tired from your long journey."

Origen touched him on the hand. Nothing further was said. Within five minutes they stopped before a mud-faced dwelling of two storeys. An old staircase clung to its side. He followed Alexandros up the steps and passed inside as Alexandros held open the door. It was a spacious room. A bald-headed man was sitting at a low table, reading by candleflame. Wooden bowls and cups hung on the near wall; a frayed carpet covered most of the floor. Alexandros spoke to the man and he immediately stood up. Offering his hand, he said to Origen, "At last we meet. I cannot tell you how much I have looked forward to this day. Your name is on everyone's tongue."

Alexandros put the bread on the table and began preparing the evening meal. As they ate, Theoctistus told Origen that he was married and the father of four children. He had a warm disposition and his eyes were perpetually smiling. Immediately after the meal, he went back to his reading.

"What scroll is that?" asked Origen, drawing near.

"That of Matthew."

"May I see it?"

"Of course."

Origen placed the scroll under the candlelight. The parchment was wrinkled and bore the fingermarks of Theoctistus' love. He read a few lines then handed it back to the bishop. Alexandros was still at the table. Origen went to him and said, "Are you angry with me?"

Alexandros shook his head.

"It is not enough for me to know that Christ was born in Bethlehem," said Origen, "that He grew in wisdom and stature at Nazareth, walked these very streets to His death on Golgotha. I am more interested in His words. I remember something Clement once said to us, 'We must be worshippers of hope, not despair . . . life, not death.' "

Alexandros glanced toward Theoctistus. The bishop had fallen asleep and was slouched over the table, his scroll on the floor. Alexandros stooped to pick it up then tapped him on the arm and asked him to retire to his bed. Theoctistus nodded. Alexandros prepared the bed as Origen opened the door and walked outside. From the top of the unsteady staircase he looked out at the darkness which was falling over Jerusalem. For some strange reason, he suddenly felt alone.

In the morning Alexandros said to him, "It is the Lord's Day. I expect you to speak to the brethren after prayers."

"I cannot do it," said Origen.

189

"But everyone will want to hear from you."

"I am sorry."

"You spoke in Rome," interjected Theoctistus.

"Yes, but that was many years ago . . . and I made a complete fool of myself."

Theoctistus adjusted his black headdress. "There is no point in further discussion. You will speak. Come we must be off."

"Are we not going to eat something first?" asked Origen.

Theoctistus was shocked. "It is not proper to eat before prayers."

They came into the street. Toward the east, the sun had just grasped the earth. When they entered the Street of Sorrows Origen was appalled by the squalid dwellings all around him . . . small brown boxes built of mud, dwarfed unshapely palm trees, pigeon houses on the flat roofs, children and donkeys crowded into the tight spaces between the houses, women young in years but old of body pounding maize for bread. . . .

"Jerusalem has suffered much," said Theoctistus. He too had his eyes on the desolate houses, the emaciated bodies.

Alexandros was silent.

The brethren had already gathered inside the dilapidated house of worship. Alexandros greeted each of them before putting on his stole. Tapers were lit and placed on the small table; prayers were sung. At the close of the service Origen faced the gathering and spoke of a chosen son who, after demanding his full inheritance, strayed far from his father's house . . . so infinitely far that his own brother gave up his life in an attempt to find him.

He spoke of the Jew.

Theoctistus stayed three more days in Jerusalem. On the day of his departure Origen and Alexandros accompanied him as far as the ruins of Herod's Place, and remained there until his caravan had disappeared over the Joppa Road. On their return to Alexandros' house, Origen said, "I want you to show me every important site in Palestine."

Alexandros was thrilled. He packed an adequate supply of food into a canvas bag, filled two water-skins, and they set out at dawn of the next day. Later that afternoon they arrived at the remote plot of ground along the banks of the Jordan where Christ was baptized. From there they passed into Jericho. Among the scattered ruins of a destroyed temple Origen detected something glistening, the neck of a bottle. He carefully scooped the dirt and rubble away then pulled it out. "It is an ancient wine jar," he exclaimed.

Alexandros held it up against the light. "There is something inside it," he said. He put his hand into the neck of the jar and withdrew something that was tightly wrapped in oilskin. His eyes shot open when he discovered what was inside. "Origen, it is a manuscript!"

Origen seized it and ran his eyes over the fraying parchment. "It is a Greek translation of the Psalms. What shall we do with it?"

"You found it," said Alexandros. "You must keep it."

Origen tucked it into the sleeve of his robe and followed Alexandros out of the ruins. Soon they came into sight of Bethel. They passed village after village, traversing hills that stretched endlessly into the horizon . . . Shiloh . . . Shechem . . . Jabal.

On the third day they joined a caravan for the long journey into Pella where the Jews had fled after Titus had leveled Jerusalem. The sun was at its highest; Origen was soaked with perspiration. Fleetingly he peered at the sun then teased Alexandros. "I just had a revealing thought. It is conceivable that Christ's work of redemption began on the sun, not here on earth."

Alexandros made no response.

"Since all seven planets revolve around the sun,"

191

Origen went on, "we must place it in the first position. Next to it comes Mercury, then Venus, the moon, the earth, Mars. . . ."

Behind them, Pella was already a speck of white dots poking into the blue sky. They stopped at a small stream and splashed water over their hot faces. "Who knows," Origen persisted, "Christ may be on Mars this very moment?"

"That is preposterous," cried Alexandros. "Hurry, we will never make Scythopolis before nightfall unless we hasten our steps!"

Just before dusk they stopped within a dense wood on the outskirts of Scythopolis. Hundreds of aged sycamores surrounded them. "It was here," said Alexandros, "in this very wood that thirteen thousand Jews were slain by Roman soldiers just before the fall of Jerusalem . . . and it was through this same place that Nebuchadnezzar passed with his hordes of invaders."

"Where shall we sleep tonight?" asked Origen.

"Here, under the trees, and tomorrow we set out for Caesarea."

"Caesarea?"

"We are less than three days away. Theoctistus will be overjoyed to see us."

"But our food is running short."

Alexandros kicked off his sandals. "There are many villages along the way . . . and many springs."

Origen peeled a small strip of bark from one of the trees. "Alexandros, why did you choose to stay celibate?"

"That is a very odd question . . . coming from you!"

"You mean, coming from a eunuch."

Alexandros was hurt. "Origen, I did not mean that at all."

He said, cynically. "You need not apologize. We are both eunuchs . . . I from a razor, you from your fears."

"I do not fear marriage."

"Why have you run away from it?"

192

"I did not run away from it."

"Come now, Alexandros."

"From the day I left Alexandria I have been entrusted with many duties . . . many responsibilities."

"But you have forsaken other things."

Alexandros plunged into silence.

"I have my excuse," said Origen. "What is yours?"

Alexandros put on his sandals and dashed into the heart of the sycamores. When he returned an hour later, his arms were laden with fresh figs. "There is a hidden grove deep inside the wood. It rises before your eyes like a magic island. There are many more figs . . . and dates also!"

"We can gather them tomorrow," said Origen. He put his hand on Alexandros' arm. "I am sorry for what I said. Forgive me. The words must have exploded from my own bitterness."

Alexandros handed him a fig and they laughed. Before falling asleep, they ate all the figs and the rest of the bread in the canvas bag. Several times during the night, Origen was scourged by a looseness in his bowels and he had to make wild dashes into the trees. He felt better by morning. Before leaving, they went first to the grove and gathered a large supply of dates, and much against Origen's desire, more figs. They swung away from Scythopolis and joined a small caravan that had just left the city. Within hours they were walking in the shadows of Mount Gilboa. At its northern slope, near the ruins of Jezreel, they came upon a spring. The frigid water caused their lips to tremble and turn purple. It was here in Jezreel that Saul and Jonathan, along with the flower of their armies, had met death at the hands of the Philistines . . . and when the gray words reached David's ears his lament pierced the veil of heaven, *'Ye mountains of Gilboa, let there be no rain upon you, neither dew, nor field of offering!'*

He could not understand this violent tug toward his childhood.

193

Throughout the next day the caravan made its way across the blistering sands of Samaria. In the afternoon they passed a huge hill that buckled under the weight of a ruined fortress; hewn stones were scattered about like skeletons of prehistoric animals.

At last they arrived on the Plain of Sharon. Breaking away from the caravan, they walked leisurely along the shore of the Great Sea and within an hour Caesarea arose from the scarlet-hued horizon . . . first her low houses of mud came into view then her few flocks of sheep and goats, children at play, old men and women sitting in front of their doors, her dusty streets, her ancient docks.

A melancholic look crept over Alexandros' face. "When last I visited here, I talked with a man who had one hundred and eight years. He remembered Caesarea when she was laid out in splendid streets of granite. Her dwellings were of marble. Her docks were busy day and night. Herod spent twelve years constructing this city, utilizing modern skills and employing his best architects and engineers. Each street led diagonally to the docks. And there, just beyond that small hill, stood a great temple honoring Caesar."

Origen moved his eyes beyond the bleak land, across the sand and wild grass, then back to the desolate city. Everything was decaying . . . the docks, the houses, the animals, the people. "It was in glorious Caesarea that the Apostle Peter baptized the Roman centurian Cornelius, along with his entire household," said Alexandros. "Pontius Pilate kept his headquarters here and rarely went into Jerusalem except for important festivals or to quell a bothersome rebellion."

Despite the barren loneliness of the place, Origen felt a sense of peace as he watched the yellow sand turn purple in the dying sun. A covey of ducks zoomed over their heads, screeching happily, their bellies laden with grapes from a nearby vineyard. He took off his robe and sandals

194

then walked to the water's edge. "I will race you to that sunken pillar," he shouted to Alexandros.

Alexandros disrobed himself and went charging into the sea, kicking up a spray that almost obliterated his slender body. They arched their arms, and at Origen's signal, dove into the water. Origen took the lead but Alexandros kept closely behind, his stroke effortless and smooth, whereas Origen lashed at the sea like an angry Xerxes. With less than a few yards remaining, Alexandros slid past him and was the first to touch the pillar. They swam a while longer before coming out.

Alexandros immediately put on his robe but Origen fell face-down on the hot sand and lay there, chained to a sudden memory. How swiftly life breathes! Only a moment ago he was in Alexandria, lying on a slab of granite that was braced against the Heptastadion, having just discovered the cool waters of Eunostos Harbor. He had never known a more rapturous moment in his life. And then Herais appeared.

"What are you doing there?" exclaimed Alexandros.

He put on his robe and followed Alexandros up a small rise, into a field of golden grass. They were seen by a group of noisy children.

"Bishop Alexandros is here!" one of them shouted.

Alexandros spread out his arms and they came flocking around him, shrieking happily and calling his name while Origen kept on walking. Alexandros joined him in the dust-filled street, his face still beaming from his encounter with the children.

Moments later they were inside Theoctistus' house. The bishop introduced him to his wife Aspasia, a small woman with a kind face who was not given to excessive speech. They had three boys. Thomas, Luke, Peter, and a daughter named Thalia who was sixteen. Unlike her brothers, she had a fair complexion. She helped her mother in the preparation of supper, while the others sat on the faded brown carpet in the front room. Origen noticed Thomas staring at him.

"Why is your hair wet?" the boy asked.

"I bathed in the sea."

"Bishop Alexandros too?"

"Yes."

Thomas stretched forth his hand to touch Alexandros' beard but his father instantly reprimanded him. Everyone laughed, including Alexandros.

*5.*

Three days after their arrival, a ship's master came to the house of Theoctistus, bearing a message for Origen. It was from Demetrius. As soon as Origen broke the seal he felt the coldness of the bishop's hand.

*Alexandria, 21 June, 215*
*Demetrius, the servant of Christ, to Origen.*
*I have been duly informed of your shameless demeanor. The boldness and audacity of preaching before a Christian assembly as a layman, constitutes an offense so grievous it must be immediately condemned. Furthermore, to have committed this unpardonable error while in the presence of two bishops deems it even more flagrant.*
*Under the penalty of eternal damnation, I hereby order you to return in haste to Alexandria and give answer to your conduct.*

He handed the message to Alexandros who read it out

loud for Theoctistus to hear. "Your bishop is totally un-familiar with Apostolic Law," exclaimed Theoctistus. "A layman of your experience and knowledge is often called upon to address an assembly."

Origen walked to the window. "Demetrius has little regard for Apostolic Law."

Alexandros' face turned pale. "This is all my fault. I should not have asked you to speak."

Theoctistus came by the window and touched Origen on the head. "You committed no offense. It is your bishop who is in error. He must not be allowed to flout ecclesiasti-cal laws. I shall write to him and tell him so." He picked up his quill and a sheet of parchment, and went to his table.

Origen raised his voice in protest. "My Lord, I do not want you to get involved in this. It is my problem."

Theoctistus refused to listen. "It is everyone's prob-lem. Demetrius must not be permitted to impose such ignorance upon the Church!"

Origen cast a pleading look toward Alexandros but he made no effort to intercede. Theoctistus carefully com-posed his message, read it over a second time, then handed it to Origen.

*Caesarea, 5 July, 215*

*Theoctistus to Demetrius.*

*I hasten to speak in defense of Origen. Such remarks as yours are entirely without foundation, for wherever men are found with proper qualification to benefit their brethren they are often asked by the bishop of that jurisdiction to address the people. I cite the examples of Euelpis, who while still a layman, was invited for this purpose by Neon at Laranda, and Paulinus by Cilsus at Iconium, also Theodorus by Atticus at Synnada.*

*Therefore Origen must not be judged unwisely or in anger, since it was upon my insistence—and that of Bishop Alexandros—that he address the brethren in Jerusalem.*

*Such conduct is indeed with precedent and is mentioned
repeatedly by the early fathers.*

*Your brother in the Lord,*
*Theoctistus, Bishop of Caesarea*

Alexandros also read the letter then said to Origen,
"What do you plan to do?"

"I shall return to Alexandria as soon as possible."

"Have you forgotten Caracalla?"

"Demetrius would never call me back if the persecutions had not ended."

Alexandros let out a sour laugh. "Do you honestly
think Demetrius is concerned about your safety?"

"I do not know. I desire only one thing, to return to
Alexandria . . . and to my students."

After the evening meal Origen retired to his bed, and
in the morning he bade goodbye to Theoctistus and his
family. Alexandros accompanied him to the docks. While
they waited for the galley to load its cargo, he asked
Alexandros a question that had been on his mind for ten
years, "Why did you leave Alexandria without saying a
word to me?"

Alexandros fixed his eyes on the sea.

"We vowed to go to Athens together," said Origen.

"I knew how you felt about the priesthood . . . how
much you bitterly despised it," replied Alexandros. "I saw
no point in agitating you. And so, I left."

"What makes you say that I despise the priesthood?"

"If you do not despise it," said Alexandros, "why
then have you not accepted it?"

Origen frowned. "Let us not go into that again."

"Your father died for Christ. He did not deny Him!"

Origen started to reply but stopped when he heard a
loud commotion on the dock. Young laborers were busily
lifting heavy sacks and carrying them into the hold of the
galley as wild-shouting merchants flayed them with
curses. Alexandros reached under his robe and pulled out
some coins. Origen refused to take them.

199

"But you must," Alexandros insisted. He put the money in Origen's hand as the master of the ship forbade the merchants from carrying even one more sack into the hold. He asked Origen to climb on board. The anchor was hauled up; the sail lifted. Alexandros ran along the sandy shore, waving his arm, and trying to keep pace with the vessel but he was soon engulfed by yellow sand and sun.

Throughout most of that night Origen remained near the stern of the galley, unable to sleep, his thoughts flitting from Alexandros to Demetrius. He wished now that he had not been so harsh with Alexandros. How foolish to have dissipated what little time they had together in silly argument. What point was served in dredging up the past?

Shortly after the midnight hour he freed his mind and, settling back against one of the sacks, he submitted to the powerful current that was pulling him back to Alexandria.

*6.*

He learned from the master of the vessel, a fierce-looking man with thick black eyebrows and a moustache extending from ear to ear, that Caracalla had been assassinated by a centurian during a military plot and that for a few short weeks the throne of Rome was occupied by Macrinus who had previously filled the office of Praetorian Prefect. The master snorted loudly, "But Macrinus too was slain in an insurrection planned by Julia Maesa, the widow of Severus. She was assisted by the Syrian army. Her grandson, Heliogabalus was immediately elevated to the succession of the Empire. He has an exaggerated devotion to the original gods, and even boasts that he was trained as a high priest of the Sun-god of Emesa."

The galley was passing under the lee of Crete and moving lazily southward. From the moment they left Caesarea the master had displayed an even temper with his crew. He was especially amiable with Origen. He spoke at length about his home in Alexandretta, that he had spent most of his life at sea, had married twice and was childless. He possessed an inquisitive nature and was well-informed on a number of subjects. Heliogabalus irritated him. "He is an idiot. He disgraces the throne with his fanatical beliefs!"

"You too are Syrian," remarked Origen. "Strange that you do not espouse the same doctrines."

The master gripped the rudder so fiercely the veins of his hands threatened to explode. "I am a Christian!"

"What name have you adopted?"

"Ignatius, the blessed one of Antioch who looked fearlessly into the eyes of lions!"

Origen smiled.

"On his first day as Emperor," the master ranted, "Heliogabalus brought out the sacred black stone of Emesa and placed it next to the holy venerations of the Romans, the fire of Vesta and the shields of Mars."

"Why did he do this?" asked Origen.

"To prove that the Sun-god's brilliance could extinguish the deities of Rome."

"Did it work?"

"Of course not."

"You mentioned earlier that Heliogabalus tolerates Christians, and that he even looks upon them with favor."

"Yes, but only because the Christian religion originated in the East. He regards it with special reverence and has even gone so far as to admit Christ into the sacred shrine of his Sun-god." Master Ignatius scratched his stomach and yawned. "But we have talked enough about Heliogabalus. History will take care of him. She never falters."

"And who shall succeed him?" said Origen.

"A better man . . . someone who has been groomed for the purple since childhood, Alexander Severus."

Origen felt a surge of joy when his feet touched the hot granite slabs of the Heptastadion. It was as though he

202

had been away for centuries. Ageless Huldah was standing at her post beneath the Gate of the Moon. She left her basket of flowers when she saw him and came running forward. "It is the season of Sefi," she said, offering him a small bunch of hyacinths. "Somewhere a maiden awaits you. Give her these."

He accepted the flowers but before he could pay her she was gone. He studied the delicate blue petals for a long time then brought them against his cheek. Rhakotis Hill called him. He turned sharply from the Street of the Soma and cut across the Race Course, following the canal that led to the west flank of Rhakotis. He climbed. At the summit, he stopped and shut his eyes. Placing the hyacinths on the throbbing ground, he could hear Herais whisper, 'It will not be this way forever. I will live in a splendid house near Lochias and have four children . . . all boys, handsome and brazen-bodied like you.'

He slowly made his way to Ambrosius' house. Marcella greeted him at the door with a warm embrace. She seemed more radiant than ever, more noble in beauty. "We missed you, Origen. We missed you very much."

"Where is Lord Ambrosius?"

"He was called to the government palace early this morning. I do not expect him until late afternoon."

"How are the children?"

Marcella looked at him with surprise. "They are not children any longer. Anthousa and Anastasia are married."

"Of course. . . . "

"They ask about you always. Their houses are in the Greek Quarter, not too distant from here."

"And Agathi?"

"She is staying with her aunt in Antioch until the end of summer."

Origen started to leave. "Please tell Lord Ambrosius that I am home."

"Shall we expect you for dinner?"

"I cannot say. Demetrius summoned me. . . . "

"Is anything wrong?"

He shook his head.

"Origen, where were you all these months?"

"In Jerusalem. . . Caesarea."

She wanted to hear more but he had already reached the steps.

"I did not tell you about Roxana," she called to him from the door. "She is married and living in Assouan. We plan to visit with her this winter when we call upon Chrysanthus and his wife. Come with us, Origen. It will be a splendid opportunity to see your mother and brothers."

He waved to her from the street then hurried toward the Greek Quarter. Within a short time he was at Demetrius' door. Theophanis answered his knock and let him in. As they passed through the cool hallway, into the room with the foreboding smell of death, Theophanis said. "His Grace is most anxious to see you."

Origen sat on the couch.

"He is very perturbed over your conduct in Jerusalem. . . ."

Demetrius startled them. He came swirling into the room in his brown robes, eyes white with rage. "You had no right to address the assembly," he yelled at Origen. "You are not sanctified!"

"My Lord. . . ."

"Only a duly-ordained priest has this charisma!" Demetrius bellowed. "And I alone have the authority to grant it."

"I was under the impression that it came from God," said Origen.

Demetrius flung both hands into the air. "I will not tolerate your insolence!"

"My Lord, why did you summon me?"

"I want you to resign immediately as Prefect of the college!"

"For what reason?"

"Disobedience."

"Against whom?"

"God!"

Origen reached inside his robe. "I have here a document signed by Theoctistus, Bishop of Caesarea."

"I do not care to see it."

"Then permit me to read it, my Lord."

"I forbid you!"

*"Theoctistus to Demetrius . . . I hasten to reply in defense of Origen. . . ."*

"I command you to stop!"

*"Such remarks as yours are entirely without foundation. . . ."*

With a fierce cry, Demetrius yanked the parchment away from him and tore it to shreds. "Hear me well," he shouted, red-faced. "If you continue along these paths of heresy. . . ."

Origen walked to the door.

" . . . I will drive you out of Alexandria forever!"


It came as no surprise when Heraclas was appointed the new Prefect of the college. He conducted his classes from Demetrius' residence. During the long months that followed, Origen nourished the feeble hope that Demetrius would one day release him from his wrath. On the first day of January, however, Demetrius condemned him, first from the pulpit, then in a long encyclical letter which he dispatched to all the bishops throughout the world.

Ambrosius was his only haven. Origen visited him every day and remained with him until the late hours of night. One evening as they sat beside one of the braziers, Ambrosius said in a gruff voice, "Do you intend to spend the rest of your life cowering under the shadow of Demetrius?"

Origen fastened his gaze on the tiny flames inside the brazier.

"Stand your ground. Fight him!" Ambrosius cried.

"How?"

"Inaugurate your own college. I will help you."

"That is out of the question," said Origen.

Ambrosius was on fire. "Who is Demetrius next to you, a jealous old man who envies the very sound of your name! Unless you put him in his place immediately it will be too late."

"What do you mean?"

"You have permitted him to take the upper hand," Ambrosius exclaimed. "He snaps his fat fingers and you fall obediently to your knees, *'Yes, my Lord. I will do as you command. I am your meek and humble servant!'* "

"I am no one's servant."

Ambrosius smirked. "If he summoned you to his house tomorrow and asked you to journey into a far country would you go?"

"Yes."

"There, you see. . . . "

"But not for Demetrius' sake."

"Whose then?"

Origen hesitated.

"Do not speak to me of your mysterious God!" snarled Ambrosius. "Where was He when Caracalla showed his teeth . . . when your own people stoned you? And now when you need Him most He closes His eyes and allows a resentful old man to grind you into dust. You are a fool!"

Origen again studied the flames in the brazier as Ambrosius got up and paced around the room. Suddenly he let out a loud cry and came running back. "I am the fool, not you! In the name of Serapis, why did I not think of this sooner?"

"What are you trying to say?"

"I have a solution to the whole problem. From this day on, you will start to write, put everything down on parchment. That way you will never be misquoted or attacked by ignorant men!"

206

"I am a teacher, not a writer."

Ambrosius did not pay attention to him. "I will not permit you to dissipate your life trying to prove something to a man who will never acknowledge it. You have mountains of notes. I have seen them with my own eyes . . . commentaries on philosophy, poetry, ethics, logic, the Scriptures. What do you accomplish by bouncing them from one student to another? Put them into books and they will be remembered into eternity."

"But Lord Ambrosius. . . . "

"I want you here at daybreak tomorrow," Ambrosius declared, slapping his hands emphatically against his thighs. He followed Origen across the courtyard and into the dark street. "Daybreak, do you hear? And bring all your notes!"

7.

Marcella escorted him into the large front room early the next morning where a group of men were seated at two long tables. Piled before them were stacks of parchment and rolls of papyrus. Ambrosius stood by the window, arms folded . . . waiting. "What kept you?" he fumed. "You are late!"

Before Origen could open his mouth Ambrosius grabbed him by the arm and brought him between the tables. Pointing to one group, he said, "These seven men are scribes and can take dictation as swiftly as you give it. The seven at this other table are skilled calligraphists. They will make perfect copies of everything the scribes write."

"I do not understand," said Origen.

"You will. Come, it is time to begin."

"But Lord Ambrosius, why are we rushing like this?"

"Gather up your notes and start with this man," shouted Ambrosius. "When he tires, move on to the next."

"I cannot work this way," Origen exclaimed. "I must have time to think . . . assemble my thoughts."

"You have done enough thinking. It is time for work!" He shoved Origen toward the first scribe, a sallow-faced man who kept blinking his eyes and clearing his throat. "Open your notes. Begin!" Ambrosius shouted.

Slowly Origen pulled out his commentaries on the Greek poets. The scribe amazed him. Not only did he keep abreast with each word but he fidgeted impatiently every time Origen paused. One hour fled. Two. Origen did not stop to rest, nor did he lift up his eyes to look at the second scribe, or the third.

By late afternoon he was dictating to the sallow-faced man again. Soon darkness began to enter the room. The servant of Ambrosius lit the wall torches then placed a small lamp in front of each scribe. They worked on. At the midnight hour, when everyone was at the point of collapse, Ambrosius finally called a halt.

They ate.

Ambrosius was so excited he pushed his food aside and started gathering all the sheets of parchment from the scribes' table. "Look what we have accomplished!" he shouted.

Origen was too tired to lift up his eyes.

"There are twenty-two books here!" crowed Ambrosius.

Origen dragged his tired feet toward the table. He sifted through the hundreds of sheets of parchment. It was incredible. A task that would have required him many months to complete, and it had been done in only one day.

Ambrosius was beside himself with joy. "This is but the beginning, little Teacher. The beginning!"

Origen gave him a wan smile. "You are an austere taskmaster."

After the scribes and calligraphers had finished eating, Ambrosius followed them to the front door. "We shall resume tomorrow," he said.

They nodded.

"I have decided to double the wages we agreed upon," Ambrosius added. The fatigue disappeared from the scribes' faces and they bounced out of the house with light feet. Returning to the table, Ambrosius once more appraised the work. Origen could not bear to look at it any longer. "I do not have the strength to walk home, Lord Ambrosius. May I stay the night with you?"

Ambrosius still kept his eyes fixed on the sheets of parchment. "Of course. That way we can begin as soon as the scribes arrive. I do not want you to be late again."

His taskmaster refused to let up during the weeks that followed. Even the nights were not fully granted him for repose, and the space between dawn and the tenth hour which formerly had been spent in study, was now entirely devoted to the scribes. When not dictating, he was kept busy revising and collating manuscripts. Each day led to new labors. Before the end of the year he not only had completed forty-two books of commentary on the Greek poets, but also an extensive analysis of Psalms, Genesis, and Lamentations. In one month alone he produced twenty-six books of exposition on the Gospel according to John. He then embarked on a major work which he fondly called HEXAPLA. It contained six parallel columns . . . the Hebrew text of the Old Testament, the same text translated into Greek, the Septuagint, the translation of Aquila, that of Symmachus, and finally the version of Theodotus. He was greatly aided in the Greek translation by the manuscript he had found inside the wine jar at Jericho.

To the enormous task of the HEXAPLA he also added marginal notes, a large number of which contained allegorical interpretations of Hebrew proper names. He was guided throughout by one precept, *to give each word its deepest meaning*. At times, it seemed he would never finish, for he was constantly undertaking new endeavors, launching out on several dozen scholia that included grammatical notes upon obscure and difficult passages from the Greek plays. He also wrote long discourses on the philosophy of Plato.

Realizing that such a prodigious venture could not be without its faults, he tried to overcome them by giving first the literal meaning, verse by verse, and then moving on to the moral and allegorical interpretations. He was thus able to attain the universal outlook of any given word, and in this way each text became a barrel into which he poured the harvest of his knowledge.

Of all his books, ON FIRST PRINCIPLES remained closest to his heart, for he saw it as the first attempt at a scientific approach to dogma. He wished to prove that each rational soul is a free agent, and that every form of knowledge, whether philosophical or scientific, had to be regarded as hidden treasure which was man's ultimate duty to unearth. It did not matter if this treasure were simple or learned, crude or systematic, because the fruits of wisdom were to be enjoyed by all the universe regardless of talent, wealth, or culture.

Although the demands for such work were excessive, he still found the time to continue the strict vigil over his body, running six miles each day, and eating more sparingly than ever.

# V

Heliogabalus was slain in March of the year 222, and it was his cousin who ascended to the dignity of Caesar. The reign of Alexander Severus was certain to produce a cycle of peace throughout the world. Ambrosius, who rarely dispensed praise toward the purple, never allowed a day to pass without bestowing some manner of eulogy upon the new emperor. Demetrius meanwhile persisted in his vehement denunciation of Origen. Were it not for Ambrosius he would have given in to severe despondency, but his taskmaster kept urging him toward greater goals, relentlessly squeezing every last ounce of energy from his mind and body. To the large number of books already produced, he now added twenty-nine tomes of commentary on Isaiah, twenty-five on Ezekiel, and nine on Joshua. He also completed a long study of ethics, logic, and psychology.

He was interrupted one day in late December by a visit from a pompous government official who delivered a sealed message from the emperor's winter residence at Antioch. It read simply:

> *Julia Mamaea to Origen:*      Antioch, 15 December, 234
>      *It is my fervent wish that you visit me in Antioch. My personal galley has already left for Alexandria with full military complement and will escort you here in safety. Your return voyage will also be assured.*

Ambrosius was overjoyed. He recompensed the scribes and calligraphers then dismissed them until further notice. "You will need clothes," he said to Origen. "Also new sandals . . . but first we must attend to that frightful beard."

"What can she want of me?" asked Origen.

"Who knows?" said Ambrosius. "Do you realize what an opportunity this is? You have a personal invitation from the emperor's mother!"

Origen pondered for a moment. "Lord Ambrosius, please ask the scribes to return."

"Why?"

"Because I have no desire to go to Antioch."

"Have you taken leave of your senses?"

"I am serious."

"In the name of Serapis, a new sky has dawned for you. Think what this will do to Demetrius."

"I am not concerned about Demetrius."

"It is a waste of time arguing with you," said Ambrosius. "You are going to Antioch, even if I have to drag you there myself!" He seized Origen's arm. In the agora he located a barber, negotiated with him, then stood aside while the man cut Origen's hair and trimmed his beard. Ambrosius supervised each stroke as several young boys sat on the cold ground and watched with curious amusement.

From there they walked to the shadows of the Sun

Gate and entered an elegant shop where Origen was fitted to a pair of white Athenian sandals. Several robes were exhibited before Ambrosius made a selection, one of pure white linen that bore an embroidered classical design on the sleeves.

Ambrosius stood back and proudly looked at him. From his shoulders to his toes, Origen was dressed in white. He felt silly, like someone about to be sacrificed.

They returned to Ambrosius' house and after a quiet supper he walked home. He could not sleep. He was so desperate for a place of refuge, he almost felt tempted to escape eastward once again, to lose himself in sand and limitless sky.

Three days later he was summoned to Cape Lochias by the same government official who delivered Julia Mamaea's message. Ambrosius went with him as far as the harbor where two assembled flanks of soldiers were standing rigidly and in full dress on the royal docks near the Temple of Isis.

Slowly Origen walked up the wide plank and stepped into the gilded ship. There was little wind in the harbor and the captain had to call upon the oars, but once they had slipped past Pharos Light a strong breeze embraced them, sending the huge purple sail into the deepest parts of the Great Sea.

Fleets of triremes lowered their colors as the slender galley eased its way into the bustling harbor of Alexandretta. The morning was extremely cold. From one end of the bay to the other, massive mountains flexed their snow-covered shoulders against the shivering sky.

The first official to greet him on the dock was a little Syrian man who identified himself as Petronius, Steward of the Household. Origen felt uncomfortable walking at his side behind two lines of marching soldiers while a crowd of Syrians watched from the square. There were obelisks of many sizes along both sides of the street. Petronius laughingly remarked, "Alexandretta's pillars are more numerous than the desires of mankind."

Origen could not pull his eyes away from the towering mountains. Petronius pointed to the highest peak and said, "On the other side lies Tarsus, the birthplace of the Apostle Paul."

"Have you espoused the new religion?" asked Origen.

"Yes."

"But does this not conflict with your duties at court?"

"The emperor's mother has an open mind," said Petronius. "For this reason did she summon you to Antioch."

"What reason?"

"She wants to find God."

"And she expects me to help her?"

"Of course."

Again he looked toward the mountains. "How far is it to Antioch?"

"Perhaps thirty miles. Do not fret. We will be there before nightfall."

"Across those peaks?"

"We have hill-men and mules at our disposal," said Petronius.

"How about the soldiers? Are they coming also?"

Petronius nodded. "We are glued to their shadows until we reach the safety of the palace. It is Julia Mamaea's strict order."

"This is foolish and unnecessary," exclaimed Origen.

"Look, my friend," retorted Petronius, "life has very little value in these mountains. Bands of thieves and murderers lurk everywhere. But we have no time for conversation. The hill-men and mules are waiting for us."

They moved across the white city, through climbing streets and unfolding hills. The sun was directly above them. When they reached the foothills of Mount Silpius they all had to form a single line. The hill-men led the way

216

on their scrawny ponies while the soldiers held to the rear. Within an hour they were walking on a wide sun-drenched plateau. By this time Alexandretta had disappeared from their view. Thick layers of ice coated their path as soon as they started climbing out of the plateau. The footing became perilous for the animals, and the hill-men had to lead them by hand through deep gorges that glistened with gigantic mirrors of ice. Late in the day, a group of herdsmen appeared before them. Winter was carved in their faces. They begged Petronius for food, and he grudgingly obliged.

Just before dusk they scaled a small mountain village that clung like an eagle's nest to a precipitous cliff. Clay huts hugged terraces that were arranged in symmetrical steps as a protection against the demented winds lashing overhead. It was now unbearably cold. Petronius kept blowing into his hands and stomping his feet. The hill-men wanted to stop and build a fire but he commanded them to continue. They struggled up another incline and at the summit Petronius finally called a halt. Below them lay the Gates of Syria.

Origen went to the very edge of the summit and looked down. Antioch was exactly as he had envisioned her . . . a wide plain spreading itself from the brown shores of a swollen lake, the Amanus River cutting its silvery path westward into Asia Minor under the heedful eye of Mount Casius, clouds of white birds circling over the red tiled roofs, thin spirals of smoke from her many ovens, and everywhere he looked . . . the encroaching mountains. He could not understand why the Romans had at one time expressed a boundless contempt for Antioch. He mentioned this to Petronius. "Nevertheless," remarked the Steward, "our emperors now favor her and regard her as a more suitable capital for the eastern part of the empire than Alexandria. Caesar came here to confirm the city's freedom. At the instance of Octavian, a great temple to Jupiter Capitolinus was erected on Mount Silpius. A forum was also constructed. Tiberius built two long colonnades, Agrippa enlarged the theatre, and Antoninus Pius paved the great east-to-west artery with granite. But it was Hadrian who did most for Antioch, erecting endless rows of colonades, baths, aqueducts and amphitheatres. It is easy to understand why Severus and his mother choose to be here during the winter months. The mountains protect the city from the harsh winds. Her soil is brown and rich, flowers are always in bloom." Petronius stopped for a while, then added, "And of course you know that Antioch was the first to utter the word, 'Christian,' and that the Apostle Peter was her first primate."

Petronius' words flooded Origen's mind as they came into the heart of the city. The soldiers dusted off their uniforms and went directly to a cistern to wash their hands and faces. Petronius and the hill-men fell into a loud argument about wages but in time an agreement was reached. The soldiers were dismissed and Petronius led Origen toward a large iron gate. A command was issued and the door swung open.

"There are baths in the palace," said Petronius. "But we must not tarry. Julia Mamaea will be waiting for you."

"Is Severus here?"

"Yes. He just returned from a great victory in Persia. But I fear that he will not be with us very long. Trouble is brewing in Gaul . . . the Germans are planning an invasion."

Before entering the baths, Origen asked, "What kind of man is Severus?"

Petronius gave him a tired smile. "You will see."

He was escorted into a great hall . . . wall torches burning brightly, servants in rustling robes carrying platters of food and jars of wine, several dozen men and women in noble dress seated around a long wooden table. The emperor in full military dress sat hunched on a simple chair of walnut. He was much younger than Origen had imagined. After Petronius made the introductions, Severus said, "At last you are here. I pray that your journey was not too tiresome."

The emperor introduced him only to the men. "On my right hand sits the jurist Ulpian. I move now to that delicate bird from Nicaea, our illustrious Dio Cassius . . . to Ursulus of the Senate . . . Marcellus, my Chief Marshall . . . Claudian, Governor of Macedonia . . . and our newly-appointed Prefect of Antioch. . . . "

Origen broke in, "Where is your mother, my Lord?" As soon as the words left his mouth a woman at the far end of the table stood up and bowed her head. She was quite tall, gray-haired, and wore a simple robe without adornments. Origen went to her and bowed, "I am honored, my Lady."

She shook her head. "It is you who honor me. I hope I did not take you from your work."

"You did," he said nervously.

"I must explain why I summoned you."

"I already know, my Lady."

She flushed and made no reply. After a while Severus asked everyone to rise. "Friends of Rome and Antioch, I give you Origen of Alexandria."

There was a polite wave of applause and as soon as it subsided, Severus said to him, "I shall now put you to a test. You may sit beside anyone you choose. Who shall it be?"

"If I choose you, my Lord, I might offend your mother."

"Then you must choose her."

"But I would offend you, my Lord. I think that I shall sit with Dio Cassius."

"Why him?"

Julia Mamaea interjected, "Perhaps they have something in common."

"What?" exclaimed Severus.

"History, my son."

When the table was ready Petronius clapped his hands and the servants left the room. Origen took a chair and sat beside Dio Cassius. He was a frail old man with bony cheeks and deep-set eyes. Without looking at Origen, he asked, "I am curious, why did you choose me?"

Origen put a small morsel of bread into his mouth. "I first chose your grandfather."

"Dio Chrysostom? But he has been dead for many years."

"We call upon his orations for study in our rhetoric classes."

Dio Cassius nibbled on a piece of fish. "Did I hear somewhere that you are a friend of Hippolytus?"

"Yes."

"A most remarkable mind, even though a Christian. Tell me, which of my grandfather's works do you like the best?"

"TROICA."

"Strange you should select that. You know, of course, that he was attempting to prove to the inhabitants of Ilium that Homer was a liar, that Troy was never taken."

Origen helped himself to some olives while Dio Cassius toyed with the food in front of him. A chamberlain entered the hall and began pouring wine into everyone's cup. Dio Cassius put his hand over his ear and said, "Lean closer. I want to hear what you know about me."

The wine was red and very sweet. "Your father," said Origen, "was Governor of Dalmatia under Marcus Aurelius. At the age of thirty you became a Senator. After that, you practiced as an advocate at the Roman bar. Pertinax, I think, advanced you to the Praetorship, and for a long while you enjoyed the favor of Septimius Severus. Macrinus then entrusted you with the administration of Pergamum and Smyrna, and when you returned to Rome he raised you to the Consulship. It has been said that you are writing a long history of Rome. . . . "

"It is already completed. Eighty books," said Dio Cassius. "They are divided into decades after the example of Livy. I begin with the landing of Aeneas in Italy and close with the reign of that man who is seated among us tonight, Alexander Severus." He coughed several times then brushed the platter of food away. "It was a tedious endeavor, one that took me many years to finish. I do not think it was worth it."

"Why do you say this?" asked Origen.

"It already had been sharply criticized."

"For what reason?"

"I am told there are too many Latinisms in it."

"So?"

"My critics say this is unforgivable in a Greek text."

Origen took some fish and more wine. "I have one thing to say about your writing. . . . "

"What is it?"

"You reveal an inordinate affection for miracles and prophecies."

Dio Cassius grunted. "That is an odd statement for a Christian to make."

Origen fingered his cup. "I have never been able to understand what that word means."

"Come now. The meaning is quite clear. Christians regard Christ as God!" Without another word, Dio Cassius scraped back his chair and stood up. He went to the emperor, whispered something into his ear, then hobbled out of the hall.

Julia Mamaea was motioning to Origen. As he came and sat beside her a few more guests departed.

"What are your plans for me, my Lady?" he asked.

"I had in mind a series of public lectures," she replied, smiling at a guest who was about to leave.

"Public?"

"If you prefer them to be private. . . . "

"Whatever you wish," said Origen.

She hesitated. "Perhaps we should keep this to ourselves. Would you object if the emperor attended?"

"Of course not. When can we begin?"

"Right away," she said.

"Tonight?"

"Yes."


The household retired early. Although Severus looked drowsy, he did not complain when his mother invited him into an adjacent room. The walls were lined with shelves containing hundreds of scrolls and books. Several busts of Roman statesmen rested placidly on marble bases. Before seating himself, Severus left the room for a moment and returned with a monkey in his arms. "Cicero," he said, peering into the animal's spirited eyes, "we are about to participate in a serious discussion. I want you to pay strict attention."

Julia Mamaea revealed her anger. "It is often said that character is molded in victory. I never realized the meaning of this until a fortnight ago when I looked into your face, Alexander. But there will be more Persians . . . more tests for glory, or defeat."

"The Germans do not frighten me!" shouted Severus.

Origen stepped between them. "My Lord, are there more Syrian Princes in line for the purple?"

"I am the last," answered Severus.

Still agitated, Julia Mamaea walked to a couch and sat down as Severus teased Cicero by keeping a bunch of grapes away from his frantic thrusts. Origen waited until the monkey quieted down. "It is unquestionable that your name will be duly recorded in history, my Lord."

"By whom?"

"Humanity."

Severus laughed nervously.

"From the moment you ascended the throne," Origen

went on, "you prudently surrounded yourself with wise counsellors and advisors."

"This was my mother's arrangement."

"True, but the empire is today a seat of virtue. Morals have been improved, luxury and extravagance put down, taxes lightened, literature and art encouraged, and it is well known that you have preserved an open mind toward religious matters. I heard someone remark that in your private chapel in Rome you keep the busts of Orpheus, Abraham, Apollonius of Tyana, and Jesus Christ."

Severus put down the monkey and slapped its rump to send it scurrying out of the room. "I also tried to erect a temple to the founder of Christianity but the pagan priests prevented me."

Julia Mamaea gave Origen an impatient look. "What are we going to discuss?"

Origen cleared his throat. "Let me begin by saying there are three goals which mankind usually seeks . . . wealth, fame, pleasure. Unfortunately these bring only ephemeral gratification, for when happiness is made to depend upon perishable objects it fails. It is necessary to seek joy elsewhere but before we can achieve this we must purify our sources of knowledge so that we may understand all things without error."

"And how do we accomplish this?" asked Severus.

"If we are foolish enough to believe that we see everything with our eyes alone then we truly see nothing. The same holds true with our other senses."

"I do not follow you." said the emperor.

"It is imperative that we learn to look deeper into things, examine them from all aspects. The face does not reveal what the heart knows. We must accept the fact that even the iota, which is the smallest letter of the Greek alphabet, has its mysteries."

"Are you suggesting that we call upon another sense in this quest for knowledge?" said Julia Mamaea.

"Yes, my Lady."

Her eyes brightened. "What is it? How can we obtain it?"

"We already possess it," said Origen. "It is the sense of awareness. Humanity tends to view the world as an opaque painting on a wall, whereas the true essence of life is *inside* things. Unless we expand the realm of our understanding we cannot venture toward knowledge."

"Does this mean that the eternal truths are buried within our own consciousness?" asked Severus.

"No. The Creator did not furnish us with a glossary of truths. He gave us the incentive to search."

"Then truth does not exist," declared Severus, seating himself on a chair close to the couch.

"Only in the quest, my Lord. When we realize that the mysteries of life are hidden from us, our hearts are then chastised and we learn to pass more humbly through the labyrinths of the universe."

"It is impossible for humility to walk hand-in-hand with science."

"My Lord, who is the wise man, he who claims to know all things or he who admits to nothing?"

"Surely you do not expect us to possess the mind of Socrates?"

"Why not? I would rather be governed by doubt than dogma," said Origen.

"Thus far you have not said one word about Christ," remarked Julia Mamaea.

Origen studied the cold marble floor. "He too passed through the labyrinths . . . but He was guided by a ray of light."

"I do not understand."

"His awareness, my Lady."

Julia Mamaea threw a white woolen shawl over her shoulders. "Perhaps we should return to the subject of truth."

Severus made it obvious that his words were meant for his mother. "Who can bear to know the truth, really know it? I cringe every time I consider the mistakes of the past . . . the cruel words, unjust acts, rude silences. I am even more terrified of the future. . . ."

"Why do you say this, Alexander?"

"Because the world will regard me not as an emperor but as the weak son of a willful woman!"

"That is unkind of you," cried Julia Mamaea, rising to her feet.

The despairing look on Severus' face was slow to leave. His mother walked as far as the door and then came back. Origen felt the tenseness in her body as she sat down once more.

Severus stood up as though addressing his generals before a battle, "Let us speak about God for a moment. I view Him in all things, experience Him in all things. Furthermore I regard myself and every other finite being as a manifestation of the Infinite. This is precisely where Christianity fails. It emphasizes that man should look to a life of future blessedness as a reward for virtue in this life."

"Do you truly believe that God is in all things?" said Origen.

"Yes."

"In nature also?"

"Decidedly. Her order and beauty confirm His own perfect nature."

"Yet this perfection often remains indifferent to human needs."

"What are you trying to say?" asked Severus.

"Certainly nature's breasts cannot feed us all. Even the slightest tremor of her heart causes the earth under our feet to split open. Her tears often drown us; her fickle moods terrify us."

"God alone controls the elements," Severus declared hotly.

"But you just told us that He is *in* the elements. Are you suggesting that He cannot control Himself?"

Severus walked to the door and whistled. The monkey appeared at the threshold. "Tell them, Cicero," he stammered. "Tell them I am an emperor, not a philosopher."

Julia Mamaea's reply shattered the brief silence, "Is it so difficult to be both, Alexander?"

The discussion was resumed the following day. Origen spoke at length about the Creator and His creation. Following his accustomed methods, he passed from the outward to the inward, from the temporal to the eternal. He told Severus that it was just as impossible to think about a king without subjects as it was to consider a God without a creation.

Throughout the long discourse Julia Mamaea remained silent. The friction between her and Severus was still strongly evident but neither of them allowed it to break open.

After the evening meal Severus again devoted himself to his monkey, and when his mother suggested that they continue with the discussions, he declined without offering any reason. Julia Mamaea asked Origen to accompany her into a small room where they talked far into the night about the problem of evil.

He was awakened early the next morning by Petronius. After dressing hurriedly, he followed the Steward of the Household into the great hall and saw Julia Mamaea seated in a chair, her face white and drawn. "I am terribly sorry," she said, "but we must discontinue our talks."

"Is anything wrong, my Lady?"

"The Germans are preparing to invade Gaul. We must depart for Rome right away." She cast him a sad look. "You no sooner arrived and now you have to leave."

"If you have no objection, my Lady, I would like to come with you as far as Alexandretta."

Her eyes flared. "Have you forgotten my promise? My galley awaits you. You shall have an escort to Alexandria."

"But that is not necessary," he said. "I can find some way to get back. The galley and soldiers should remain with you.

She rose to her feet. "No. I will not alter my decision." She looked at him sadly. "I wanted so much to converse with you further. Are you prepared to leave immediately for Alexandretta?"

"Yes."

Platters of food were brought in and placed on the long table. Moments later Severus came stomping into the hall, his heavy sword clanging against his thigh. Origen felt that he had to say something. "Perhaps the situation is not as grave as it appears, my Lord."

Severus strained a smile. "I am sorry about my conduct the other night." He looked out the window toward the snow-capped mountains in the north. Birds were frolicking around the thin cypresses that bordered the stone wall of the palace. "I am afraid this was not a relaxing visit for you," Severus added.

No one had appetite for food.

Severus invited him outside. The morning was mild and free of wind. They sauntered around the courtyard, stopping several times to watch the jubilant birds. Finally Severus said, "What will you do when you return to Alexandria?"

"I have my work," said Origen.

"What kind of work?"

When he told Severus about his writings, the emperor frowned. "Is it worth it, sacrificing your life on books and philosophy?"

Origen did not answer.

"Why do you do it?" Severus grunted.

"I do not know, my Lord."

A cynical laugh escaped from the emperor's mouth. "Perhaps we are all victims of some unseen power which compels us to do these things. Look at me. Do you think I enjoy wearing this detestable uniform everywhere I go?"

He kicked at a stone and sent it toward the cypresses, frightening the birds away.

Origen could not restrain himself.

"What is so amusing?" asked Severus.

"A thought just came to me, my Lord."

"Yes?"

"You may not find it flattering."

"Speak. What is it?"

"There is common talk in Alexandria that you go to sleep each night in full military attire."

Severus tugged free his long sword and slashed through the air. He too burst into laughter. "Do they actually say this about me?"

"Yes."

Again Severus defied the air with his sword. "Tell me, has my mother made arrangements for your payment?"

"Payment?"

"You left your work and traveled this long distance. You should be reimbursed."

"We made no arrangements, my Lord."

"In that case, I shall make payment to you."

Origen objected but Severus raised his hands. "You may have anything you desire."

"My Lord, it is not necessary. . . . "

"Whatever you desire shall be yours," Severus exclaimed.

Origen thought for a moment. "I have a dear friend in Alexandria, Ambrosius by name. He has a sincere admiration for you, my Lord. If you could give me some small token which I might pass along to him. . . . "

Severus unstrapped his sword and handed it to him.

"Not your sword?" cried Origen.

"I insist. Take it to your friend. Perhaps this will dispel all that common talk in Alexandria."

They both fell into laughter.

"Have you ever mounted a horse?" Severus asked.

"Only camels and dromedaries, my Lord."

"There is very little difference. You will ride next to me into Alexandretta."

Petronius had already assembled the soldiers in two long lines that led from the palace, through the gate, and into a wide plain. Mules and horses were brought out. The same hill-men appeared from nowhere and began strapping heavy bags of food, supplies, and furniture to the sides of the mules. The entire household was in the courtyard. Origen was given a horse, a handsome white mare of peaceful disposition, and at last Petronius issued a command. The hill-men led the way, followed by the cavalry, the foot soldiers, and finally the household. At the main gate Severus pulled his black horse to the side and let everyone pass through. Before rejoining the cavalry, he took one last look at the palace.

After an hour Severus pulled up beside Origen and asked, "How do you feel?"

"There is a numbness in my thighs."

"And your rump?"

"That too."

Severus roared.

"My Lord, may I say something?"

"Speak."

"Your belligerence toward your mother disturbs me."

"It disturbs me also," retorted Severus.

"Have you made any real effort to overcome it?"

Severus hunched his shoulders. "Epicurus warns us never to suppress our feelings."

They arrived at Alexandretta just as the sun had reached the middle of the sky. On the docks Petronius once more became embroiled in a heated argument with the hill-men. Severus commanded him to pay whatever they demanded but Petronius still held out until in time an agreement was reached. The servants assisted the dock-

229

workers in loading all the supplies, furniture, clothing and food into the waiting galleys while the soldiers filed into the ships.

The gilded galley awaited him. Before getting in, he bade goodby to Julia Mamaea.

"Your words have given me much comfort," she said.

"Thank you, my Lady."

"I shall especially remember that we must all learn to look deeply into things. All things."

Origen opened his arms and embraced her.

Severus waited until his mother had stepped into one of the galleys and then he too embraced Origen. "You see," he said, his mouth twitching, "what other man is fortunate enough to have his own mother accompany him into battle?"

## 2.

Late one afternoon, in the waning hours of March, his work was halted by the appearance of Ambrosius. His face tugged with emotion. "Word has just arrived from Rome. Severus and his mother were murdered in a field. . . . "

Origen's notes slipped from his hand to the floor.

"Vile Maximinus!" cried Ambrosius. "Barbarous Thracian murderer!" He ran into his sleeping chambers and came back, holding Severus' sword in his hand.

"When did it happen?" asked Origen.

"On the nineteenth day of this month," said Ambrosius, weeping and thrashing the sword at the same time. "Thirteen years of peace have come to an end. Bishop Pontianus has already been transported to the unhealthy Isle of Sardinia, he and his entire body of presbyters. But the persecutions are not confined to Italy. Hundreds have been slain in Cappadocia, in Asia Minor,

Greece and Syria. Alexandria is bound to be next. You must leave right away."

"Nonsense," said Origen.

"Listen to me. Your friendship with Severus and his mother is known to Maximinus. He will seek you out and slay you!"

The thought of another flight was repugnant to him. He did not want to think about it.

"You will be safe in Caesarea," Ambrosius persisted. "I have arranged your passage. A galley shall be leaving at dawn tomorrow."

"What about my work?"

"It can be done in Caesarea."

"But there are no scribes in Caesarea."

"Work on your notes. As soon as the persecution ceases our scribes will be here waiting for you."

He stayed the night with Ambrosius and just before dawn Ambrosius accompanied him to the docks. Origen was still reluctant to leave but Ambrosius shoved him up the plank, past a throng of noisy dock workers, into the ship. It was an unseasonably warm day for March. Behind him, Rhakotis Hill was steaming under a cloud of haze. The sea looked treacherous and gray.

"When you return from Caesarea," shouted Ambrosius from the dock, "I want to see a trunkful of notes!"

Origen lifted his arm in silent farewell.

She was an old galley that shuddered under the heavy pounding of wind and sea. The voyage took eleven full days, almost twice the usual time. Alexandros met him on the docks. Origen was surprised to see him there but Alexandros quickly explained that he had received a message from Ambrosius, fervently requesting him to meet the ship. "But that was days ago," Alexandros added. "What took you so long?"

Origen pointed to the old galley. "The seas were exceedingly rough. At times, I thought the waves would crack her in half."

"This is the fourth morning in a row that I have come to the docks," said Alexandros. "If you had not arrived today I would have feared for your life."

They walked to Theoctistus' house. Alexandros asked him about his meeting with Demetrius and was so deeply upset when Origen told him all the details, he fell into self-reproachment, lamenting and moaning that it was all his fault. Origen clamped his hand over Alexandros' shoulder and said, "I have something wonderful to tell you and Theoctistus. Since last we met I have written hundreds of books." He went on to explain about Ambrosius and the scribes, his commentaries and translations, the HEXAPLA, ON FIRST PRINCIPLES. He grinned when Alexandros gaped at him in disbelief.

After a hasty meal, the three men walked outside. The sun was now dreary-eyed and about to nestle into the hills but the heat of the day still lingered over Caesarea. As they moved along the sandy shore, Theoctistus pointed toward a large stone pillar protruding from the sea. "That is the only remaining evidence of Caesarea's ancient harbor. In many ways, my city once resembled yours. She too had a great seaport; her wide streets led diagonally to the docks; a magnificent temple stood just to the left of the sunken pillar on the very edge of the sea."

Origen tried to envision Caesarea as Theoctistus described her but he could only see tired waves groping toward the graying sand. Everything around them, even the sky, seemed to be touched by death. Theoctistus stopped a moment and asked, "What are you thinking?"

Origen's voice was but a murmur, "How quickly life fades. . . ."

The bishop stroked his beard. "We must be strong and not faint on the road to eternity."

The instant rage in Origen's heart clamored for a bitter

233

retort but he bridled his tongue and followed Theoctistus and Alexandros back to the house. "How long do you plan to stay in Caesarea?" he asked Alexandros.

"Perhaps another day or so. Why?"

"I want to come into Jerusalem with you."

"Good."

There was a long silence.

"Alexandros, do you miss Alexandria?"

"Of course."

"Perhaps when the world is at peace again we can return there together."

There was no response from Alexandros.

The next morning a laborer from the docks came to Theoctistus' house bearing two messages for Origen. One was from Ambrosius:

> *Along with this message, I am dispatching a letter which came to my house from Assouan the day after you departed for Caesarea.*
>
> *I must also mention that Demetrius was here looking for you. He was remorseful and wants you to journey into Greece for the purpose of instructing the Athenians. I lied to him and said that you had left for some unknown destination, and that there was no way of reaching you.*
>
> *Maximinus appears to be slackening his hold on the populace here but it still is not safe for you to return.*
>
> *Please convey my good wishes to your friends and tell them it is my fond hope that we meet someday.*

Origen broke the seal of the second message and immediately recognized Barnabas' hand:

> *Assouan, 4 March, 235*
>
> *Beloved brother, our blessed mother has found eternal sleep. Her end came quickly and without pain. She now reposes on the slope of a green hill that overlooks the Nile. The sun never leaves her face, trees and flowers sing daily over her grave.*

234

*Your name was constantly on her lips, even to the very end.*

*Please know that we are all married, save John, who has entered into the monastic life and lives in the desert with a small group of anchorites. His tent is not too distant and I visit him occasionally, although he makes it quite apparent that he prefers to remain alone. But I am his brother and he must realize that he cannot separate himself from us entirely.*

*We embrace you and think of you always.*

*Barnabas*

After he rolled both messages together, Alexandros asked him. "Is anything wrong?"

"My mother has closed her eyes. . . . "

Alexandros fell silent.

"I am now without father and mother. . . . "

Theoctistus lifted his fingers to bless him. "You still have God."

He felt that he had to escape somewhere, hide himself in the desert and never look upon another human face. Alexandros tried to comfort him but he pushed him aside and hurried out of the house. He ran for one whole hour along the shore, not knowing where he was heading, not caring. Finally he stopped and turned around.

That night at supper he announced that he was leaving for Greece. Theoctistus absently nodded his head but Alexandros expressed sharp disapproval. "You must not do it. Demetrius could be setting a trap for you!"

Theoctistus sat upright now and began stroking his gray beard. "Bishop Alexandros is right. It is not wise to visit a strife-torn country."

Origen refused to listen.

"The Athenians are embroiled in heretical disputes and debates," said Alexandros. "The church of Greece is tottering."

235

"I am not interested in their disputes."

"Then why do you want to go there?"

"To see Clement."

"He may be dead," said Alexandros.

"I must find out for myself."

"But this is foolish. Let me write a letter of inquiry to the bishop of Athens. He will know if Clement is alive."

"He *is* alive. I am sure of it."

"Then why has he not written to you in two years?"

"He may be traveling somewhere . . . "

Theoctistus giggled, "Is it true that Clement fascinated the drawing rooms of Alexandria with his charming wit?"

"Yes," said Origen.

" . . . and that he preached against short skirts which exposed the knee?"

Before Origen could answer, Theoctistus remarked, "Have you ever given serious thought to the priesthood?"

Origen plunged into silence.

"Bishop Theoctistus has asked you a question!" fumed Alexandros.

Origen rose to his feet. "It is late. We are all tired."

"Then you still intend to go into Greece?"

"Yes."

Nothing more was said. His sleep was turbulent that night. Just before dawn his father entered the room, leaned over the bed, and kissed him on the heart. During the morning meal he was so troubled by the dream he told the others about it.

Theoctistus was elated. "God has spoken to you, Origen. You can no longer turn your face away from Him."

"The dream's message is very clear," agreed Alexandros. "Your blessed father will never know peace unless you conform to his wish."

His heart and brain still transfixed on the dream, he followed both of them to the small church that lay adjacent to Theoctistus' house and permitted them to place their

236

hands upon his head. After it was over Alexandros came near him at the holy table and whispered, "How do you feel, Origen?"

He was overflowing with sourness. "My father was martyred decades ago yet I am still trying to please him."

Alexandros was beside himself with joy. "I shall never forget how I felt after Demetrius placed his hands upon my head. I was so happy I could not eat or sleep for weeks. I kept saying to myself, *'I am a priest! I am a priest!'*"

They came outside. Instead of going directly to Theoctistus' house, they wandered across a rock-strewn field that was splashed with bright patches of wild poppies. Further down, several fishermen were mending their nets in front of a house. In the yard, children were playing.

Alexandros was bothered by Origen's long silence. "You have always searched for the truth, and now you have found it," he said. "Rejoice and be happy."

"I feel that I have just taken a withered old lady for a bride." sighed Origen.

They hurried past the docks and came at last to Theoctistus' house. The kitchen was drenched with the scent of food. Aspasia brought out a steaming pot from the oven and placed it on a cloth pad in front of them. Before sitting, Theoctistus chirped, "Come, Father Origen . . . grant us your first blessing!"

*3.*

He awoke the next day with the weight of a hand on his shoulder. It was Alexandros. Through the open window a soft breeze was blowing in from the sea. The song of cicadas filled the air. He went to the water basin and washed his face. He dressed. When they came into the kitchen, he discovered that Alexandros had already filled a goatskin with water. His face was beaming with excitement.

"What is it?" asked Origen. "Why did you awaken me so early?"

"Keep your voice down," Alexandros cautioned. "The others are still asleep."

"Where are we going?"

Alexandros handed him some cheese and several loaves of bread to pack into a large cloth bag. They tiptoed out of the house. Caesarea was buried in darkness but toward their left hand the amber fingers of a new sun were already clutching at the hem of the Great Sea. The olive leaves swayed lazily in a nearby meadow. Birds sang. Within an hour the sea breezes were drowned in a scorching blast of heat. Alexandros stretched forth his long legs to increase his gait, and in another hour they were at Samaria's doorstep. A small spring lay in the shadows of a few palms. They stopped there to eat and rest. Splashes of green pock-marked the place, but beyond that, as far as the eye could reach, there was only pale sand and brown hills. Something pinched at Origen's brain. "Alexandros, why are you doing this? Are you trying to prevent my departure for Greece?"

"Of course not."

"Then tell me, where are we going?"

"To Galilee."

"Galilee?"

"We can reach it in two-days if we do not tarry."

They finished eating then drank from the spring. Alexandros refilled the water-skin. Moving northward, they skirted past Armageddon and came before the rising peak of Gerizim. "Many fascinating tales have been told about that mountain," said Alexandros.

"Are we still in the land of Samaria?"

"Yes," Alexandros paused. "Samaria is the only country in the East where men outnumber women. Just to the west of Mount Gerizim lies Shechem and Jacob's Well. When Golden Alexander conquered Palestine he conferred many privileges upon the Jews but he did not grant these same rights to the peace-loving Samaritans. Instead he commanded that graven images of himself be placed in every town and village of Samaria. Years later he entered the country once again. He looked for his statues then went storming into Shechem and summoned the High Priest. *'Did I not command you to build statues of myself?'* he bellowed. *'But we did, my King,'* responded the High Priest. *'Where are they?'* the conqueror thundered, whereupon the High Priest lifted his voice and shouted *'Alexan-*

239

*der! Alexander!'* Immediately scores of boys, all of approximate age, came running toward them. *'You see, oh great King,'* explained the High Priest, *'we could not give umbrage unto you by erecting statues of dead stone in your honor. Look around. We have made you living statues and have given your divine name to all the male children of Samaria!'"*

Origen laughed, his spirits lightened. As they crossed over the Plain of Esdraelon, Alexandros remarked, "We shall be coming into Cain soon. In another hour we should be inside Nazareth."

They came upon another spring. Several young maidens walked past them with earthen vessels on their heads and shoulders. Innocent eyes. Pure faces. Their winsome smiles brought life and beauty to the bleak land.

They stopped only briefly at the spring. Although Alexandros was impatient to move on, nothing escaped Origen's eyes . . . the fig trees covering the hillsides, almond blossoms spreading their veil over the green valleys, thousands of cypresses stretching their slender arms toward the cloudless sky. Only a short time ago they were in a desert, a place of destitution and death, but now they had arrived into a new land. Alexandros pointed toward a ribbon of white that sparkled in the distance. "There lies Nazareth," he said.

They took lodgings at a small inn, not far from the Virgin's Well, where a humble meal was prepared by the inn-keeper's wife. She also had a warm breakfast ready for them in the morning. Origen left some coins for her and followed Alexandros out of the house. The sky was filled with clouds, the air felt sticky and hot. By midday they had traveled almost ten miles, moving gradually toward the Sea of Galilee. She lay in quiet shadows, her many fishing vessels playing upon her smooth countenance. Occasionally her solitude was disturbed by the flashing and diving of small fish. Along her shores fishermen were busily at work with their nets.

Origen felt an immediate tranquility here. He forgot

about Demetrius, about Maximinus. They walked for some time along the endless shore, past Magdala and Gennesaret, into Capernaum's rich meadows and pasture-lands, its forests of olive trees, fig trees, and vineyards.

They lingered at Galilee for three joyous days.

On the fourth day they returned to Nazareth and stayed the night in the same lodging house where again they were provided with warm food and clean beds. Before setting out the next morning, they spent several hours conversing with the inhabitants of Nazareth. One of the elders brought them into a synagogue, the same place from which Christ was expelled after preaching his first and only sermon to the people of his childhood . . . *'A prophet is without honor in his own country . . .'*

At noon of the following day they were back in Caesarea, exhausted but happy. Too tired to eat, they went straightaway to their beds and, before falling asleep, whispered back and forth to each other, recalling child-hood memories . . . everything they had known and touched together. For the first time in his life Origen felt that he really understood Alexandros.

In the morning Alexandros walked to the docks with him. A twisting ribbon of laborers had already begun to load heavy sacks of wheat into the waiting ship. There was the usual loud bickering between the merchants and the captain.

"Greece expects us both," said Origen.

Alexandros' face tightened. "Keep me in your thoughts, Origen. Everywhere you go . . . everything you see."

The last sack was put into the ship. Origen climbed aboard and went immediately into the hold after waving goodbye to Alexandros. He did not come out until it was dark, until earth and sky were obliterated and he stood alone in the terrifying presence of his own heartbeat.

*4.*

They docked at Piraeus in the first week of May. The earth was bursting with spring. On the busy quay slaves were unloading heavy cargoes while bronze-skinned youths stood beside their small carts, calling to travelers, offering them swift rides into Athens.

Still feeling the effects of the ship's motion, Origen made his way through the wild commotion, crossing the small square. A dirt road brought him past a row of filthy shops and crippled houses, into another square. In its center was a statue of Poseidon, tottering on a cracked base. Across the square rose a temple to Zeus. This too was sadly neglected. On every street corner there were children in rags.

Slicing his way through the agora, he took the north road, moving swiftly and tirelessly until Piraeus sank behind him. A valley of poppies in full bloom met his eyes. Olive leaves shimmered in the distant hills. The Attic sky was cloudless. Hastening his pace, he thought about the ageless dreams that had sprouted from the womb under his feet. It did not seem possible that he was at last in Greece.

He rested a short while beneath a blossoming Judas tree and thought about Alexandros, about Herais, his father, Clement. He could not wait to catch that first glimpse of Athens.

Two hours later he passed through the main gate of the city. Harlots were leaning against the arch, their painted faces following the carts. One of them came forward and threw herself at his feet. She was no more than sixteen. He stepped away from her but like a hare she bolted after him and planted herself directly in his path. Suddenly she drew open her yellow robe and exposed her small breasts. He tried to brush her away, as if with one sweep of his hand he could erase the nightmare of his youth, but she clung to his robe until finally she gave up, her loud curses falling on his back.

He was blinded by the brilliance of the Acropolis, rising above the city like a tower of ivory, awesome and majestic. Losing no time, he mounted the Propylaea steps and placed both hands on a front column of the Parthenon. It pulsated with life. He felt weak with joy and had to sit on a fallen slab of marble. Below him, Athens seethed.

After an hour, he slowly climbed down from the Acropolis and headed for the agora. Buildings and temples of gleaming white marble lined both sides of the street. He was able to identify most of them . . . the theatre of Herod Atticus, the Bouleuterion, Theseum, the stoas of Attalus, Hadrian, Basileius . . . and across the deep bowl of Athens, mighty Lycabettus jutting into the sky.

He strolled across a paved rectangle encircled by lecture halls. Young students in small noisy groups stood in front of each portal, soliciting for their masters. One of them grabbed hold of his arm. He was barefoot and attired in a shattered cloak of burlap. With fiery eyes that defied the authority of the gods, he yelled, "There is no greater teacher in Athens than Cleomenes!"

"What does your master teach?" Origen asked him.

"Life!"

"Does he demand a large fee?"

"The first lecture is without charge."

"In that case. I shall listen to him," said Origen.

The student jubilantly took him through one of the portals and into a large hall where several dozen students were seated around a raised marble platform. Light poured in from three open windows.

"When does the first lecture begin?" asked Origen.

A tall man walked briskly into the hall and stepped onto the marble platform. He too was barefoot. His ruddy face sought refuge behind a bushy black beard. He paused a moment than lifted his hands to silence the applause. "Today we shall speak of pleasure. But not in the spirit of Epicurus. I say that truth is governed only by feeling. When we experience the sweet taste of a grape, our judgment is not misled or refuted. On the other hand, if we attempt to determine the cause of this feeling we fail. And why? Because pleasure, not knowledge, is the only conceivable end of life."

One of the students arose. "Master, I tried to instill these thoughts upon a friend only this morning but he scornfully replied, *'What possible pleasure can you derive from life, traipsing around Athens in those rags, barefoot, destitute?'*"

"How did you answer him?" asked Cleomenes.

"I was unable to find the words, Master."

Cleomenes stretched out his long arms as if to embrace the entire hall. "If we are to become true philosophers we must realize that there is great joy in renunciation. Nature requires every organism to seek its own good. Above all, she calls upon us to select our pleasures, not to abstain from them."

Origen stood up. "Master, what has all this to do with truth?"

Cleomenes squinted at him. "You are new here?"

"I have been in Athens only a few hours," said Origen.

"From where did you come?"

"Caesarea."

"But you speak fluent Greek. Were you born in Caesarea?"

"No, Alexandria."

"What is your name?"

"Master, you did not answer my question. . . . "

"What is your name?" persisted Cleomenes.

"Origen."

A thick silence stuffed the hall.

Cleomenes stepped off the platform and came toward Origen, bowing. "You honor my class, Master Origen. You honor Greece."

He was paralyzed by an awkward embarrassment. The students had stood up in one body but he begged them to be seated. He tried to resist when Cleomenes took hold of his arm and escorted him to the platform. "There is no need for introduction," said Cleomenes, turning to his students. "We all know this man . . . his greatness, strength, and beauty of heart. His many virtues have been attained without hypocricy or pompous prayers . . . and certainly without burdensome dogmas or sacrilegious threats of future punishment. Indeed, they are the products of the subtle force of love."

"Master Cleomenes, you have yet to answer my question."

A wave of laughter erupted from the students. Cleomenes asked for silence. "This is my answer, Master Origen. Socrates identified virtue with knowledge but I say that true virtue is acquired by the denial of scientific study. Man must forget the outside world and concentrate on the inner."

245

"I am still unconvinced," said Origen.

"About what?"

"Moments ago you said that pleasure, not knowledge, is the only conceivable end of life."

"*Inner* pleasure, Master Origen. Wealth, food, and power dethrone the authority of reason. This is why poverty is advantageous. The man of virtue wants nothing from the external world. His real pleasures come from within."

"But even internal pleasures have their opposite in pain," said Origen.

"Yes."

"One is hardly separated from the other . . . truth and error, health and sickness, life and death . . . unless, of course, they exist only in our consciousness. . . . "

"What do you mean?"

"Possibly they are not what they appear to be. What we regard as pleasure might very well be pain. The same could be said about truth and error."

One of the students stood up and addressed himself to Origen. "If pleasures and pains are Platonic illusions what then is real?"

"Perhaps you can tell us," Origen smiled.

The student spun around and faced the class. "This is what I believe . . . first, nothing exists. Second, if there is existence we cannot comprehend it. Third, even if we managed to comprehend it, our language is so limited we could never express it!"

Another student jumped up, looking straight at Origen. "It is said that you are a Gnostic. Is this true?"

Origen's reply was possessed with peace. "Labels terrify me. Indeed I have been accused of many things but this one particularly bothers me. Gnostics are known for their strict adherence to holy rites and sacraments, to baptisms by water and by fire, to sacred formulas, names and symbols . . . to incantations, unctions, rituals. I do not agree with all this. I am not influenced by superstition or fear. If I were to choose between truth and eternal salvation, I would unhesitatingly put my finger on the former."

He stepped down from the platform and walked back to his place. There were more questions from the students, more heated opinions and debates. When the hour drew to an end, he waited for the students to leave and then said to Cleomenes, "Perhaps you can help me find someone. . . ."

"What is his name?"

"Clement."

Cleomenes stroked his beard. "If you wish, I can take you to him."

Origen burst with joy. "Does he live nearby?"

"Yes, not far from the Piraeus Gate."

"Then I must go there right away. Please direct me."

"I shall come with you," said Cleomenes.

"But what about your next class?"

Cleomenes laughed. "Students learn much faster when left alone." He led Origen out of the building and across the rectangle. Near the Stoa of Attalus they crossed a wide street called *Lyceum*. Behind them, beams of light bounced through the golden arms of the Parthenon. Cleomenes stopped to wipe his brow at the Temple of Hephaestus. "We are almost there," he panted. "Another hundred yards and this road becomes two-pronged . . . one leading to Colonus, the other to Eleusis."

They swung to the right following the bank of a trickling stream. Students were reclining on the grass near the water's edge.

"Another fifty yards," sighed Cleomenes. He led the way across a granite bridge, to the other side of the stream. All this time a mysterious weakness was attacking Origen's body. "Did we not just pass over the Eridanus River?"

"Yes," said Cleomenes.

"Then we must be entering the cemetery of Inner Keramicus!"

"Yes. Outer Keramicus is there, just beyond the sacred gate to Eleusis."

"Clement is here . . . in this cemetery?"

"He closed his eyes several years ago," murmured Cleomenes. "His name was so beloved to Athens she entombed him here with her most honored sons."

Origen could not hold back the tears.

"He came almost daily to my school," said Cleomenes. "He often talked about you."

They were imprisoned in a world of gray tombs and enormous crypts guarded by marble lions and finely—sculptured centaurs. Tall steles with winged lions and human faces lifted themselves high above the other tombs. Just then a soft breeze awoke and whistled through a row of cypresses on top of a small hill. The sun began to sink.

His heart pounded when Cleomenes stopped before a marble tomb. Choking with tears, he drew near and read its inscription:

TITUS FLAVIUS CLEMENT
FRIEND OF MARCUS AURELIUS
FRIEND OF GOD

He put his trembling lips to the stone as the earth under his feet began to quake. Cleomenes waited a while then pulled him gently away. At the granite bridge, Cleomenes said, "Dry your tears. Nikolaos must not see you this way."

He looked back toward the tomb and angrily defied a God who could slay a man like Clement, bury him forever . . . stuff his mouth with earth and allow worms and vermin to gnaw away at his flesh and bones. FRIEND OF GOD!

"Nikolaos and Clement were the best of friends," Cleomenes muttered. "His house is not too distant from here. We will come to it as soon as we pass the Stoa of Hadrian and enter into the Street of Athena."

He followed Cleomenes over the bridge. They walked

248

several hundred yards in silence and finally stopped in front of an old stone structure with pitted walls and broken roof tiles. Off to the right, the Acropolis was draped in shadows. Clouds of dust swirled over their heads.

Cleomenes knocked on the door then walked in. An aged man sat on a low wooden bench by a small table that stood under the only window. The room smelled of decaying years.

"I have a wonderful surprise for you, Nikolaos," said Cleomenes, tapping the fragile old man on the shoulder. "One of Clement's friends is here."

Nikolaos struggled to his feet, his bones cracking. "You managed to get here after all?"

"You know who I am?"

"Certainly. Clement was confident that you would come. Yes, to the very end, he was confident." Nikolaos hobbled toward the table and lifted a large package that was wrapped in oilskin and tied with several strands of heavy twine. "Clement left this for you," he said.

When Origen unloosed the twine he recognized the yellowed scrolls of the STROMATEIS. Another manuscript was enclosed, one that he had never seen before: AN EXHORTATION TO THE GREEKS. He unrolled it and began reading.

> 'With you, beloved Athenians, rests the final act . . .
> to choose which is more profitable, judgment or grace. What
> then, is the purpose of this instrument? To reveal wisdom
> to foolish men, to make an end of corruption, to vanquish
> death. . . . '

*5.*

In the weeks that followed, he stayed in Cleomenes' house which was located near the Agora, behind the Tower of Winds. Nikolaos came nightly to visit with them. Most of the time he talked about Clement. Origen was outraged when he learned that Clement had been accused of fleeing from Alexandria during the persecution of Septimius Severus. He tried to convince both Cleomenes and Nikolaos that Clement left under no duress, and certainly not from fear. But they needed no convincing. "People will always find cause to accuse, no matter how virtuous one may be," said Cleomenes. "The Athenians are the worst offenders. Look what they did to Socrates, to Themistocles and Plato, to Pericles, Anaxagoras, Pheidias. The names are legion. They were praised by Athens and destroyed by her. Soon after Pheidias had supervised the construction of the Acropolis, he was prosecuted on false

250

political charges, and before he could disprove them, he died under arrest. The Athenians so harassed Anaxagoras with similar charges that he was compelled to flee the city and seek refuge in Lampsacus where he died in exile. And poor Pericles! After what he did for Athens, she deposed him, prosecuted him on charges of embezzlement, and even made him pay a fine of fifty talents . . . a man of his purity and virtue. This is what Athens has done to her most noble sons throughout the ages. I am afraid she will never change. Never!"

One morning Origen decided to visit Cleomenes' school. He listened with amusement to the youthful boasts of the students, the sharp rebuttals from Cleomenes, and then abruptly the discussion turned to the religion of the Jews. One student, Bassus by name, made the claim that the story of Susanna was not an authentic part of the Book of Daniel and should therefore be considered spurious. By comparing several verses with the rest of the book, he concluded that the writing style in the story of Susanna indicated clearly that it was written originally in Greek, and was not a translation from the Hebrew.

After Bassus sat down, Cleomenes asked Origen to respond. "To examine a language through translation," Origen began, "is like marriage by proxy. . . . "

There was laughter.

"I feel certain that the Greek translators of the text did their utmost to preserve the original Hebrew meaning."

"Then you consider the story of Susanna authentic?" asked Bassus.

"I do."

"In spite of the wide discrepancy in style?"

"Yes."

More words were exchanged between Bassus and another student. At the end of the hour, Origen said to Cleomenes, "You did this purposely. . . . "

Cleomenes eyes were flashing.

" . . . you pulled me out of my grief by discussing the religion of the Jews in a Greek philosophy class."

"So I did," laughed Cleomenes.

Origen looked at him . . . skin and bone in a tattered robe, barefoot, a hovel for a home, subsisting totally on his beliefs.

Cleomenes must have sensed what he was thinking. "Is it not a wondrous feeling to know that we are nothing, have nothing, expect nothing?"

They had not seen Nikolaos for almost a week. One night Cleomenes wrapped some bread and cheese in a cloth, filled an amphora with red wine, and together they went to call on him. His house lay in darkness. Cleomenes found a lamp, lit it, then placed it on a table. Nikolaos was lying on the couch, his face pale.

"Are you ill?" Cleomenes asked.

"I have caught a chill."

"How long have you been this way?"

"A few days."

"You should have sent word to me."

"I did not want to interrupt your classes."

"We brought you a little food and wine."

"That was kind of you but I have no appetite."

"Perhaps you will later on," said Cleomenes. "Do you want me to summon a physician?"

"No."

"But someone has to care for you."

"Father Andreas stops by every evening."

"Who is he?" asked Cleomenes.

"The new presbyter of the assembly in Athens."

"What business does he have with you?"

"We have many discussions."

"About what?" asked Cleomenes.

"Various things. He is an intelligent young man, and very well-versed in the sciences."

252

Origen said, "You must try to eat something, Nikolaos."

"Later perhaps."

Cleomenes poured some wine into a cup for him. "This will encourage your appetite."

There was a knock on the door.

"Is that you, Father Andreas?" called out Nikolaos, propping himself up on the couch. "Come in. Come in. I want you to meet my friends."

The young presbyter looked more like a Roman than a Greek . . . long straight nose, tight pursed mouth, powerful shoulders and legs, proud defiant stance. As soon as the introductions were made, he immediately launched into an attack against the Valentinian heretic Candidus. "This man persistently talks on the nature and destiny of the devil."

Origen remained silent for a long while.

"How do you regard the devil?" asked Father Andreas.

"The devil fell by his own free choice. To say that he is evil by nature is to find fault with the Creator. . . . "

"Therefore?"

"I believe that it is possible for even the devil to be saved."

Father Andreas abruptly moved into another direction. "I have been apprised of your teaching methods in Alexandria and I have this to say to you, faith in God requires no need for study and examination."

"How then do we arrive at a knowledge of God?"

"It is strictly a matter of faith. Either we believe in Him or we do not."

Cleomenes squirmed on the bench. "Surely you are not suggesting that we walk toward Him with blinders over our eyes?"

"This is exactly why the assembly in Athens seethes with strife," cried the presbyter. "The existence of God cannot be proved by syllogism and theory!"

"How do you suggest that it be proved?" asked Cleomenes.

"By faith."

"Which proceeds from what?"

"Faith!" yelled Father Andreas. "Philosophical theories cannot withstand the powerful light of faith. They may hold true for a season but in time they melt away."

Cleomenes laughed. "And what does not melt away, Father Andreas?"

"The words of Christ. They shall remain stamped on the heart of humanity forever."

"But He has been dead only a few hundred years," said Cleomenes. "He has yet to encounter the severe test that Plato passed . . . the test that Socrates and Homer passed."

"And what is that?"

"Time, Father Andreas, that ruthless disciplinarian who knows no beginning, no end."

Again Father Andreas looked toward Origen.

"It may be true," Origen began, "that mankind has been poorly equipped for the pursuit of knowledge but this does not mean that we must give up the quest. If we see some admirable work of art we are at once given to investigate the nature, manner, and purpose of its production. The works of God should stir the same curiosity. Just as the eye seeks light and the body craves food, so too the mind has the natural desire to know the cause of everything it observes. The occupation of our various faculties on lofty inquiries, the very ambition with which we rise above our actual powers, is in itself fruitful and it prepares us for the reception of ideal wisdom at some later stage of existence. Thus we begin with language. We next move into the area of external nature. Sooner or later we must realize that geometry is the sure and immovable foundation of all knowledge. It rises step-by-step into the most sublime mysteries of the universe. The true philosopher must be a student of physics, but only as a preparation,

254

not an end. A much higher goal is reached in moral science. Here we learn to rise above analysis and probing. Real ethics is life, not a theory. Real knowledge lies in action, not in precept. Finally the pursuit of Greek philosophy brings speculation into a vital union with practice. Perhaps this is what Cleomenes meant about the passage of time. But we should go one step further and say that the existence of God can only be proved through the works of human genius . . . through song, poem, painting, sculpture . . . through the tilling of soil, the cultivation of wheat, the building of roads, the construction of temples . . . through procreation and the agony of life. . . ."

"You see God in all these things?" asked Father Andreas.

"Yes. His footsteps cannot be blown away by time, nor can they be obscured by fanatical dogmas and vengeful commandments."

"Then how can we find Him?"

"It is not important that we find Him," said Origen. "It matters only that we seek Him."

"In Greek philosophy and profane works of art?"

"Why not? There is no limit to the places we can search."

Father Andreas looked at Nikolaos. "It is getting late. I have another visit to make. I shall come again tomorrow."

"Please do," said Nikolaos.

The young presbyter addressed Origen. "Perhaps you can attend one of our prayer meetings. Our place of assembly is nearby."

"Perhaps," said Origen.

"The brethren will want to hear from you."

Origen made no reply.

Three days later a deacon from the Christian assembly at Athens brought a sealed message to Cleomenes' house.

*Alexandros to Origen*          *Caesarea, 21 February, 236*
   *Knowing how dearly you love your friend Ambrosius,
I am dispatching this message to you in haste.*
   *Ambrosius arrived in Caesarea only two days after
your ship departed. He was sorely distressed to find you
gone but it grieved him even more when he learned that you
had departed for Greece. With open heart, and upon his
own insistence, he begged Theoctistus and me to place our
hands upon his head and elevate him into the ministry as a
deacon.*
   *On the very next day the terrible hand of Maximinus
struck Caesarea and although Theoctistus and I were somehow spared, Ambrosius was seized because he had insulted
the pagan religion by accepting a Christian office. A young
presbyter named Protoctetus was also taken. Both were cast
into prison and I greatly fear for their lives.*
   *Your friend has sunk into deep despair and now blames
God for his misfortune. I beg you to write to him immediately. Send your message to Theoctistus' house and I
will see that it reaches Ambrosius.*
   *I pray that Maximinus' wrath finds no root in Greece.
My thoughts are forever with you, as are those of Theoctistus and Aspasia.*

In a trembling hand, Origen wrote to Ambrosius and
then asked Cleomenes to find a way of dispatching the
letter to Caesarea. When Cleomenes returned an hour la-
ter, he said, "It is done. The letter will reach your friend
within one week."
   "Did you dispatch it by ship?"
   "No."
   "How then?"
   "By horse and rider, through northern Greece, Asia
Minor, Syria, and Palestine."
   "But I did not want to put you to such an expense,"
said Origen.
   Cleomenes wiped his brow with the back of his hand.
"The man asked nothing from me but a favor."

"A favor?"

"He has a son who wants to enroll in my school. But come, the day is dying. We must eat something before we leave for the assembly."

"What assembly?"

"Have you forgotten? Father Andreas expects you to address the gathering." Cleomenes laughed. "I think that I shall enjoy worshipping with Christians for the first time."

They dined on fish and bread.

It was dark when they left the house. Walking down the Street of Athena, Origen wrestled with his thoughts. "I will meet you at the assembly," he said.

"Where are you going?" asked Cleomenes.

Origen did not answer him.

"But Father Andreas will be disappointed. . . . "

Moving swiftly down the street, he lost himself in the darkness. He could not free his mind from Ambrosius. He started to run . . . down a deserted road, past a row of low-slung houses, across a dew-drenched meadow. One mile. Three more. Several hours later he groped his way up the Propylaea steps of the Acropolis and at the summit, he lifted his heart toward the black night. *'Where has my life gone? Nothing remains of it but bitter frustration and emptiness. I am tired. My once-strong voice is but a whisper. I beg you, take me home to Alexandria. Take me home!'*

He slept inside the Parthenon.

At daybreak, he walked to Inner Keramicus and stood tearfully over Clement's grave but could find nothing to say. He touched the hard stone and heard Clement's thundering voice, *'Indeed, how mighty is philosophy. It makes men out of wild beasts, gives life to the dead, opens the eyes of the blind!'*

"No!" he cried. His embittered voice reverberated through the cypresses, bouncing off every lion and centaur in the gray world of death, and as he fled down the tomb-lined path, past the marble beasts, Clement's words still hounded him, *'No man can walk through life without enduring some manner of pain. Be strong. Be patient. And one day you too will come into the glorious light of peace.'*

In the middle of the next day he walked into Cleomenes' school. The teacher left his platform and came forward to meet him. "Where have you been?" he exclaimed. "I had everyone scouring the city. . . . "

"I came to bid you farewell," said Origen.

"What?"

"I am leaving for Alexandria in a few hours."

"But why?"

"I must go to my friend."

"But he is imprisoned in Caesarea."

"No vessel sails there for at least another fortnight. I cannot wait that long. I went from ship to ship at Piraeus and finally located a galley bound for Alexandria.

"You cannot leave in such haste," said Cleomenes.

"The galley is waiting. I do not want to miss it."

Cleomenes clasped his arm. "I beg you, say a few words to the students before you depart."

"There is no time, Master Cleomenes."

"Please. . . . "

Slowly he turned and faced the students. "I give you the same words that were once given to me by a great teacher." He had to stop and clear the tears from his throat. "Let everything you do be done for virtue, both deeds and words. Learn gladly and teach ungrudgingly. Never hide wisdom from others by reason of a covetous spirit, nor through false modesty stand aloof from instruction. Be first to practice wisdom. Firmly renounce falsehood, guile and insolence. If you look for true knowledge, and ask for it with importunity, you shall receive it."

Cleomenes walked with him as far as the street. Nothing further was said as they clasped hands. Before cutting across the Agora, Origen waved to him, took one last look at the Acropolis, then ran the full distance to Piraeus.

# VI

Hoping to find a galley bound for Caesarea, he went to the docks every day. He hounded captains and merchants. Ships were leaving Alexandria for every harbor in the world but not for Caesarea. "The port is not as busy as it used to be," one of the captains said to him. "Come back next month. I shall be carrying a cargo of mules there. . . . "

"I cannot wait that long."

"Then go by foot," retorted the captain.

He was wretched from frustration and restlessness. There was nothing else to do but send continual messages to Ambrosius, encouraging him to endure his confinement and never to lose hope for freedom.

And then there was Demetrius. Origen tried to see him on several occasions but the bishop refused to grant him an audience. He could feel something lurking behind Demetrius' behavior but he tried not to think about it.

Without the use of the scribes, the quantity of his work suffered greatly but he was determined to throw himself into new projects. In spite of his rigid schedule, he managed to find time late at night to attend to his physical conduct, running through the deserted streets of Alexandria, and along the shore of the Great Sea.

One night he returned to Clement's house after having exhausted himself from a long run around Rhakotis Hill. Theophanis was standing on the front steps. From under his robe, the monk pulled out a scroll and handed it to him.

"What is it, Theophanis. Why are you trembling so?"

"I was told to remain here until you read this document."

"Is it from Demetrius?"

"Yes."

Origen opened the door and walked inside while Theophanis remained close at his heels. Untying the scroll, he placed it under the light of a wall lamp and read:

*Demetrius to Origen:          Alexandria, 6 April, 238*

*It is the decision of two separate Synods convened here in Alexandria under my instruction, in the presence of God and His holy bishops, that you be excommunicated from the Church of Christ, deposed from your fraudulent office as presbyter, and exiled forever from Egypt.*

*Your transgressions are herein cited:*

*1. You have violated the laws of the Church by accepting a foreign ordination into the priesthood.*

*2. Your unholy act of self-mutilation deems you unworthy of such a high office.*

*3. You have continually expounded false doctrines, both in Egypt and abroad, thus bringing dissension and controversy into the Church.*

*Your heterodoxies are herein cited:*

*A. You have persistently tried to reconcile Christianity with profane philosophy and pagan works of art.*

B. *You have espoused the erroneous belief in the final restoration of all souls that includes even Satan, maintaining furthermore that the extension of God's redemption shall reach even those non-existent inhabitants of the planets and constellations.*

C. *You continue to adhere to the hideous dogmas of eternal creation and pre-existence of souls.*

D. *Lastly, you have consistently employed unauthorized methods in giving allegorical and mysterious interpretations to the written word of God.*

*All the bishops of Christendom have been duly informed of the Synod's action, including the Bishop of Rome who was the first to concur.*

*You are hereby cautioned and forewarned that:*

*Any person seen either in your company, or listening to your voice, shall incur a similar penalty. Therefore you are now commanded to leave Egypt and never to return.*

*May God have mercy on your fallen soul.*

*Demetrius, Bishop of Alexandria,*
*By authority of the Holy Synods*
*Convened at Alexandria.*

Shocked and confused, he placed the scroll on the table beneath the lamp as Theophanis slowly edged his way toward the door.

"Wait," said Origen. "I am coming with you."

The monk's eyes widened with horror. "No. The bishop never wants to see you again!"

"But I must answer to these charges," said Origen. "He has no right to do this."

Theophanis had already flung open the door and was lost in the night. Again Origen picked up the scroll and read it. Suddenly a bitter laugh escaped from his mouth. *He was no longer a priest!* With an abundant surge of spirit, he brought the scroll close to the lamp and watched the flames devour it. Quickly he started gathering all his notes

261

and what few belongings he possessed into a cloth bag. He lingered for a long time under the fig tree in the courtyard where Herais had whispered, 'It is a beautiful day. . . . ' Remembering Clement's manuscripts in his bed chamber, he went after them, picked up the cloth bag, and came out into the street.

At the Heptastadion his body started to tremble. It was here that he had first kissed Herais but now, as he stood on this sterile rock and looked across the harbor, the piercing eye of Pharos mocked him. Further down the Heptastadion, he stopped before a ship that was moored to the dock. Men were moving in and out, stuffing her bowels with heavy sacks. He asked one of the laborers where they were bound.

"Caesarea," came the husky reply.

Amidst the loud bedlam, he climbed on board and spoke to the captain. The captain gruffly nodded his head and Origen put the cloth bag behind a wall of sacks. He kept Clement's manuscripts under his robe until the ship began to move.

Within the hour Alexandria was gray against the sky. Rhakotis Hill had disappeared behind the two huge obelisks that were still barely visible near the Caesareum. Pharos Light alone remained clear and whole, stretching its long fingers toward him, calling out his name. But soon it too was swallowed by the malignant darkness.

He fell into a disturbed sleep. He saw himself standing before a fearsome abyss, heard violent echoes . . . and then his father was revealed, austere and unforgiving. He wanted to cry out to him, but his voice was lost in the hollow echoes that resounded in his ears, *'Father, you must believe me . . . I am not a heretic . . . I am not a heretic!'*

262

## 2.

He learned from Theoctistus that Ambrosius was still imprisoned. The dungeon was located only a few miles from Caesarea, on the road to Armageddon. Origen wanted to go there immediately but Theoctistus warned that it would not be safe even though Maximinus was no longer Emperor of Rome. "Gordian ascended to the throne when Maximinus and his son were murdered in their tents near Aquileia," Theoctistus declared.

The old bishop described Gordian as a man of great learning and accomplishments, the grandson of Marcus Aurelius. Although he had yet to show any animosity toward Christians, it was still conceivable that his feelings could change. But until then, Theoctistus felt that Origen should not be seen on the streets during the daylight hours, especially where crowds congregated.

Origen reproached himself daily, knowing that Ambrosius was but a short distance away. He tried to lose himself in work but the writing was slow and tedious. He kept at it however and in time produced additional commentaries on the Greek poets. He labored continually on certain books of the Old Testament. In the Book of Numbers, he compared the struggles of the Israelites with the conflicts of the present world. In Joshua, he drew many parallels that gave allegorical meaning to Israel's capitulation and defeat. His target throughout was the man of false virtue, the Christian unduly proud of his faith, the Jew who gave liberal offerings to the Temple but nothing to suffering humanity, the pagan who looked down upon slaves.

It seemed strange to him, writing in Theoctistus' house. The old bishop and his wife resided there alone now. All their children were married and living elsewhere in Caesarea. Occasionally they would come and visit, bringing their own children.

Theoctistus and Aspasia were constantly at his side. At night, they all sat in the front room discussing many subjects. One evening Theoctistus returned from his daily walk to the agora and announced that Gordian had decided to look upon all Christians with favor. Origen was jubilant. "This means that Ambrosius could be released soon!"

Theoctistus agreed. "I shall write immediately to Bishop Alexandros and ask him to come here. He will know what to do."

Origen ate with appetite that night. After the meal he was overcome by a peaceful fatigue and went quickly to his bed. For the first time in months, he fell into a sound sleep.

Alexandros arrived by camel six days later. He looked thinner than ever, his beard now entirely gray. Aspasia hastened to prepare him a meal but he announced it was imperative that he get to the prison before nightfall.

264

"I am coming with you," said Origen.

Alexandros forbade him. "It is best that you remain here."

"But the persecutions have ceased. I have been walking freely in the streets for several days."

"I insist that you stay here until I return."

"Will Ambrosius be with you?"

"I pray."

Origen nodded. He walked with Alexandros as far as the camel while Theoctistus remained by the door, blessing both Alexandros and the beast until they were lost in the darkening horizon.

Aspasia put a platter of food before him but he was to restless to eat. He paced back and forth from the front room to the door while the night swallowed Caesarea.

The hours passed.

Aspasia again implored him to eat but he shook his head. Theoctistus yawned. After extracting Origen's promise that he awaken them as soon as Alexandros returned, the old bishop and his wife retired to their beds. Origen walked outside. Sky and earth were one. Toward the west he could hear the soft lapping of the sea. A dog howled. He started to run, across a sandy field and into a narrow street. Heading northward, he stumbled past Caesarea's ancient theatre and then stopped. Distant voices ruffled the night. They grew louder, more distinct. There was the sound of rushing feet, a loud cry, "Is that you, little Teacher?"

His heart tore itself asunder.

The following morning Alexandros and Theoctistus led Caesarea's assembly in prayers of thanksgiving. Alexandros asked Origen to assist them from the beautiful table but Origen tautly reminded him that he was no longer a priest. Alexandros did not pursue the matter.

After the prayers, all the brethren gathered around a table in Theoctistus' yard and partook of bread and olives.

265

Testimonies were given. When the young presbyter Proctetus gave accounts of the suffering they had endured, it brought tears to the eyes of the brethren. Throughout the meal Ambrosius spoke hardly a word. After the brethren had departed, Alexandros took Ambrosius by the arm and all three walked along the sea. Ambrosius kicked at the sand and turned upon Origen. "I warned you about Demetrius but you refused to listen!"

Origen picked up a stone and hurled it into the water.

"He has humiliated you before the world!" Ambrosius shouted.

Origen picked up another stone. "Demetrius no longer worries me. I am still free to teach anywhere in Palestine, also in Asia Minor, Arabia and Greece."

"What about your writing?"

"While you were confined in prison I managed to complete many books. And in a few days, I shall engage myself in a debate against Celsus."

"Who is he?"

Alexandros loudly retorted, "That same Epicurean whose fanatical reverence for the past inflicted the cruelest attack upon Christendom!"

Ambrosius fumed. "From where does this Celsus come?"

Origen laughed. "He closed his eyes more than eighty years ago."

"Then how can you debate him?"

"He will be represented by the Roman philosopher Fabian."

"In the name of Serapis, what good can come from all this if Celsus is dead?"

Again Alexandros interjected. "His rude accusations must be disproved. The early apologists were unable to do so . . . Justin, Aristides, Ignatius."

"Why?"

"Because they did not deign step down from their theological positions."

266

Ambrosius glared at Origen. "If these great men failed, how can you succeed?"

"I intend to meet Celsus on his own ground, philosophy."

Ambrosius ignited. "You are a fool. Open your eyes. You have been branded a heretic . . . scourged, mocked, exiled from your beloved city . . . and now you seek to defend a church that has done these cruel things to you!"

"Must you blame the church?" said Alexandros.

"Brother Bishop, Demetrius *is* the church! I ask you in all sincerity, what can Origen gain from these foolish debates . . . forgiveness, propitiation for the sins he has never committed?"

Alexandros tightened his lips. "Dear Ambrosius, we must learn to pity our enemies and not hate them, pray for them and not curse them."

"Stop preaching to me! I am sick and tired of empty promises and false hopes. When are you both going to learn that all your efforts are in vain . . . all your questions, your schools, your philosophical arguments?"

Alexandros looked toward the sea. "I never expected to hear you talk like this, Deacon Ambrosius."

"Do not ever call me that again!" Ambrosius yelled, his gaunt face trembling.

"But you *are* a deacon. My own hands lofted you into that exalted position."

Ambrosius scowled. "I have only one position, Brother Bishop, to return home . . . to my wife and family. As soon as my feet touch Alexandria, I will fall on my knees and thank Serapis."

"You must not say these things!" exclaimed Alexandros.

"And why not? I have put your God to the test. Do you expect me to trust in Him? How can I? He abandoned me when I needed him most. Stop deluding yourself. Your God will never survive in this world. If the Romans do not slay Him, evil Christians like Demetrius shall. Do you know how an ignorant man like this became a bishop? Do you? When his predecessor Julius lay on his death bed an angel of the Lord came to him and told him his successor would be that man who first brought him a bunch of grapes. Demetrius heard about the dream and so, this peasant . . . this ill-bred boor who could neither read nor write, rushed to bring his bunch of grapes to Julius, and straightaway was proclaimed Bishop of the Great See of Alexandria!"

"You are God's deacon," Alexandros reminded him. "We are all His servants into eternity, and should not lose heart when men persecute us or say vile things against us or even kill us. Nothing can separate us from His love."

Ambrosius walked away from him.

Later that night, before retiring to their beds, Ambrosius put his hand on Origen's shoulder and said, "Am I still your taskmaster, little Teacher?"

A tear burned its way out of Origen's eye.

"I still think it is absurd . . . fighting this dead man."

"What are your plans, Lord Ambrosius?"

"I must return immediately to Alexandria."

"You will miss the debates."

Ambrosius stirred. "If you are wise, you will come with me."

"Have you forgotten?" said Origen sourly. "I can never go back to Alexandria."

"Then get all your notes together."

"For what reason?"

"We will resume our work as soon as I return."

"You plan to come back here . . . to Caesarea?"

"Of course. With Marcella and the scribes!"

3.

It was his good fortune that Theoctistus had a copy of
Celsus' TRUE WORD, and although he was familiar with
the book, he gave it more diligent study. Celsus had always been convinced that every phenomenon in the material world was the direct result of natural causes. Epicurus
had taught him that alleged miracles wrought either by
God, demon or magic, were false manifestations of ignorant and superstitious minds. In this spirit Celsus wrote the
TRUE WORD. Because his arguments were powerful, his
style ironic and captivating, it was very clear to Origen
why the book had met with such great success.

Deeply immersed in Celsus' book, he fell violently ill
one morning from an attack of dysentery. The very next
day both Theoctistus and Aspasia were ravaged by the
same disease. Somehow Alexandros managed to escape.
He ministered to all their needs, cooking and washing

their bed clothes, reading to them each night under candleflame.

On the day of Fabian's arrival from Rome, Origen's condition had not improved and Alexandros represented him at the official greetings on the dock. When he returned home, he announced that masses of people had already poured into Caesarea from all the surrounding towns, and although the debates were not scheduled to begin until the next morning, many spectators had made their way into the ancient amphitheatre and were prepared to sleep there through the night.

Origen asked him about Fabian.

"He is a large man, robust of body," said Alexandros. "He dismissed my salutation with a haughty toss of his head and went directly to the high government officials who were waiting on a large platform." Alexandros broke into a laugh. "several times I saw him pull out a small mirror and he meticulously combed his hair."

"It should be an easy matter for me to defeat an adversary whose prime concern is the mirror," said Origen.

Alexandros became serious. "Origen, I do not think that you should leave your bed tomorrow."

"Nonsense," said Origen. "It is too late to postpone the debates. I must go."

His condition was much worse the next morning. Although he managed to dress and eat a dry piece of bread with a cup of herb tea, he felt so weak that Alexandros became alarmed and insisted he return to bed. "Look at yourself . . . you will never be able to stand before thousands of people under a burning sun!"

Origen shook his head. "If the debates are postponed, Fabian will claim the victory."

"They need not be postponed."

"What do you mean?"

"I can take your place," said Alexandros.

"That is impossible. You have no time to read Celsus' book. Fabian will cut you to shreds."

"I have already read that despicable book. I know every word. As for Fabian, he does not frighten me. God will shield me from his blasphemous tongue."

Origen stumbled toward the door.

"Where are you going?" shouted Alexandros.

"I am coming with you. I may be too ill to debate Fabian but nothing can keep me away from that amphitheatre."

"Very well," Alexandros sighed. "But you must promise that you will sit in the shade . . . and if you become ill. . . . "

Origen had already stepped outside.

The streets were packed with people. Children and dogs followed the long lines across the agora and up a winding hill to the amphitheatre which was now filled to capacity. Those who could not get inside had climbed a high hill overlooking the front of the amphitheatre, while others perched themselves on trees and great boulders.

Before stepping into the center of the amphitheatre, Alexandros arranged for Origen to seat himself in a shaded place along the first row. Origen's legs felt numb, his stomach churned. The spinning noise of the huge crowd abated when Alexandros and Fabian drew lots for the first speaking position. Fabian won. Coming forward, he raised his hands for silence and began. His voice was powerful, his stature arrogant and defiant. He was exactly as Alexandros had described him.

"People of Caesarea, sons and daughters of the Hebrew prophets, what madness possessed you to leave the Law of your fathers and accept a fool who called himself *Messiah*? Can you conceive that we who were also looking for a Messiah should not have recognized him? His own followers were not convinced, otherwise they would not have betrayed and deserted him. If he could not persuade those who daily saw and spoke with him, shall he convince you now that he is gone? *'He suffered,'* you say, *'in order to de-*

271

*stroy the power of evil.'* But have there been no other sufferers? Was he the only one? *'He worked miracles,'* you say. *'He healed the lame and the blind, he brought life to the dead.'* But is it not written in your own books that miracles can be wrought by others? You say, *'he prophesied that he would himself rise from the dead.'* And yet the same is said of many others. Zamolxis told the Scythians he had come back from the dead. So Pythagoras told the Italians. Rhampsinus claimed he played dice with Ceres in Hell, and even showed a golden handkerchief which Ceres had given him. Orpheus, Protesilaus, Heracles, Theseus . . . all are said to have died and risen again. But did anyone really rise? Or shall we say that all these stories are fables and only yours is true? Who saw your *Messiah* after he arose? An hysterical woman who had the reputation of a harlot, and some of his own companions who dreamt of him and were deluded by their enthusiasm? All the world was witness to his death yet only a few friends witnessed his resurrection.

"Let us examine the person and character of your *Messiah*. He was born in a small Jewish village. His mother was a poor woman who earned her bread by spinning. Her husband Joseph divorced her for adultery with a soldier named Panthera but he agreed not to abandon her. Thus the child was carried into Egypt where he mastered the healing arts. Soon he returned to Palestine and began claiming he was God. The story of his divine parentage was taken from the myth of Danae. Who was it that saw the dove descending upon him in the Jordan? Who heard the voice declaring him the Son of God? He was asked in your own Temple to give a sign of his divinity but he had none to give. *'He cured diseases,'* you say. *'He restored dead bodies to life, fed multitudes with a few loaves.'* But are these not the common tricks of Egyptian wizards performed every day in your market places for a few obols? They too drive out devils, heal sicknesses, call up the souls of the dead, provide suppers, cover tables with platters, and make things seem what they are not. We do not call them Sons of God. They are rogues and vagabonds!

" *'Come to me,'* says your *Messiah, 'ye who are fools or children, ye who are miserable.'* The thief, the burglar, the poisoner, the robbers of temples and tombs . . . these are his proselytes. Does he look upon the just man who has held steady from the cradle in the ways of virtue? Why must sinners have preference with him? Is it not a known truth that persons with a proclivity to evil have so formed their habits they are notoriously past cure, and neither punishment nor tenderness can save them? *'God must come down to earth to judge mankind,'* you say. But why would God do this? He already knows all things. The everlasting order of His universe does not need to be judged or set right. He is all-perfect and all-blessed. If He leaves his present state to come down as a man among men He must pass from blessedness to unblessedness, from perfection to imperfection, from good to evil. However we know that no such change is possible, for change is the condition of mortality. God cannot change and still remain Himself. He cannot seem to change while He remains unchanged, for then He is a deceiver.

"You are all like so many ants creeping out of a hill, or frogs sitting around a pond, or a congregation of worms on a dung-heap that claim to have had the secrets of God revealed only to themselves. *'Only for us,'* you say, *'did God leave the circuit of the sky. He considers only our interests and forgets all other created things. To us alone He sends messenger after messenger, for we are his children and are made in His likeness. And when some of us have sinned, He either comes or sends His Son to burn the offenders and give the rest of us frogs eternal life!' ''*

Fabian was interrupted by a loud burst of laughter from the crowd. He waited until it died down:

"People of Judah, who are you that you should claim such high privileges? History knows you as a colony of Egyptian slaves who revolted and then settled in a corner of Palestine. In your own account of yourselves, you assert that God made man with His own hands and breathed life into him. He then put him to sleep, took out one of his ribs and made a woman out of it. Having thus created them, He gave certain orders which a serpent tempted them to disobey. And then there was a deluge, and a marvellous ark in which all manner of living things were assembled, with a dove and a raven to act as messengers. The history of your patriarchs follows . . . children singularly born, brothers quarreling, mothers plotting, a story of Lot and his daughters which is far worse than the banquet of Thyestes, one of the lads goes to Egypt where he interprets a dream and becomes ruler of the country.

"Like Euripides, you too exclaim, *'The day and night are ministers of man!'* But why more of man than of ants to whom night brings sleep; and day, food? Are we lords of the animals because we capture and devour them? Do they not equally chase and devour us? Will a higher place be claimed for man simply because he lives in cities and rules himself by laws? So do ants and bees. They too have their rulers, their wars, their victories, their captured enemies. They too have their cities, their division of labor, laws of punishment, cemeteries for their dead. No, people of Judah, the universe was no more made for man than for the lion, the eagle, or the dolphin. One created being is not better than another, for all are but parts of a great and perfect whole whose constant care lies in the hands of the Creator. He does not forget it, or turn from it when it has become corrupt. He is never angry with it, never threatens to destroy it.

"If you are tenacious of your traditions you are not to be blamed. But if you pretend to the possession of special secrets of knowledge and refuse as unclean a communion with the rest of mankind, you must be taught that your own dogmas are not unique. *'We worship the God of heaven,'* you say. But the Persians also sacrifice on the hilltops to Dis by whom they mean the circle of the sky. It matters little whether we name this being Dis or Most High or Zeus or Adonai or Sabaoth or Ammon. As for your customs, know that the Egyptians and Colchi were circumcized before you. The Egyptians furthermore do not eat swine's flesh nor the flesh of many animals. The Pythagoreans touch no meat at all.

"You claim that God, through Moses, promised you prosperity and earthly dominion. He bade you to destroy your enemies, sparing neither old nor young. He even threatened you with destruction if you did not obey Him. Yet your false *Messiah* condemned riches, condemned earthly domination, counseled you to care no more for food or raiment than the ravens or the lilies of the field, invited you to turn the other cheek if you were smitten on one. Either Moses was wrong, or your false *Messiah!*

"You dream of another world, as in some Elysian field where all riddles will be solved and all evil put away. You say, *'Unless God can be seen in the form of a man how are we to know Him?'* But these are the words of flesh, not of reasonable men. Then only can you see God when you close the eyes of the body and open the eyes of the mind, and if you seek a further guide upon the road, avoid those quacks and conjurers who promise to show you ghosts. Put away your vain illusions, your magic formulas, your lion and your Amphibius, your God-ass and celestial door-keepers in whose names you allow yourselves to be persecuted and impaled. Did not Plato say that the Architect and Father of the universe is not easily found?

"If you cannot comprehend these truths, I bid you to remain silent. Cover your ignorance. Call not those blind whose eyes are truly open, nor those lame who run. If you must have a new doctrine, at least adopt an illustrious name that is better suited to the dignity of a divine nature than that of your impudent *Messiah*. If Heracles and Aesculapius do not please you, there is Orpheus. He too died of violence. There is also Anaxarchus who was beaten to death and mocked. *'Pound on,'* he yelled to his tormentors. *'You can pound the sheath of Anaxarchus but himself you cannot pound!'*

"Your ancient heroes are more presentable than the one you have chosen. *'We are God's special people,'* you say. And yet you have not a yard of ground to call your own. You are persecuted and are only safe when you keep concealed. If you are found, you are executed. Why? Because you stubbornly shun the demands of earthly life. We do not ask you to abandon your belief in God but you must also obey the princes and rulers of this world. A monarch is enthroned upon earth to whom God has committed the sceptre. If you refuse to acknowledge him, refuse to serve under him in the state or in the army, he has no other choice but to punish you because if all were to act as you do, he would be left alone and the empire would be overrun by barbarians.

"Your notion that all the world can be brought to one mind in religion is the wildest of dreams. It cannot be. The very thought reveals your ignorance.

Your chief duty on earth is to defend your sovereign, in the field and in the council chamber. . . . "
At last Fabian stopped.

The wind that had been swirling over Caesarea for three days now reached the intensity of a storm, bending trees and flinging clouds of dust over the city. The crowd in the amphitheatre started to scatter. Origen made his way to Alexandros while Fabian tried to comb his hair. Alexandros yelled into Fabian's ear, "Perhaps you should continue tomorrow."

Fabian's words penetrated the fury of the storm, "The position of Celsus has been presented."

"You have finished?"

"I have."

"Then I can begin my argument tomorrow."

"Do as you wish," Fabian snorted. He had now abandoned all concern over his hair. Tossing his head back wildly, he charged into the howling wind and disappeared in a gust of sand, his robe trailing behind him.

Origen was seized by a severe cramp in his stomach and slumped to his knees. Alexandros cried, "You are pale and trembling. This was insane. I never should have permitted you to come here!"

He helped Origen to his feet and together they leaned into the wind, groping their way along the west wall of the amphitheatre. By this time the audience had dispersed, only a few stragglers remaining.

In the street, they were thrown back by the howling wind and it took them almost an hour to cover the three hundred yards to Theoctistus' house.

## 4.

He felt much better the next morning. The storm had subsided, the sun was shining. With tottering steps, he walked to the amphitheatre and sat in the same place. Alexandros was very nervous. During the morning meal, he had said to Origen, "If Christianity truly proceeds from God why should it fear one man? What harm can Celsus do? Perhaps these debates serve no purpose. Did not Gamaliel stand up before the Council in Jerusalem when Peter and the other apostles were about to be executed, and did he not say, *Ye men of Israel, refrain. Let them alone, for if their teaching be of men it will come to nought. But if it be of God, ye cannot overthrow it, lest ye fight against God!'* "

"If such be the case," said Origen, "there is no point in going to the amphitheatre. Let God take care of Celsus."

"This is not a joke," said Alexandros. "Celsus rendered a mortal blow to Christianity. He must be condemned in public!"

278

"And will you do it through philosophy or Holy Writ?"

"God will enlighten me," said Alexandros.

The amphitheatre was again filled to capacity. Alexandros greeted Fabian but the Roman turned aside and took his place on the marble bench, fixing his eyes upon the crowd. After a long silence, Alexandros began,

"I trust what little I have to say does not provoke another storm. . . . "

There was raucous laughter.

"I need not remind you that the words you heard yesterday were not those of my esteemed opponent but were first uttered eighty years ago by a philosopher named Celsus who had little regard for the spiritual life. The evidence of truth concerning any religion is not the testimony of one or more persons who saw or thought they saw some indication of a supernatural presence. The real evidence is the power with which a religion can cope with moral disease, lift it out of grossness and self-indulgence, into higher and more virtuous spheres. Christianity has effected this in a manner that no creed or system of philosophy can ever accomplish.

"Christ dawned as a sun upon the world if we are to judge Him by moral and not physical law. We err when we seek to examine His physical body because it is the inner man who is made in the image of God, not the man of flesh. The highest speculations of the Greeks are mere theories. They still continue to nourish ancient beliefs, still persist in sacrificing a cock to Aesculapius. Their beautiful syllogisms may transform a few students into philosophers but the crude words of Scripture have transformed multitudes, making the coward a hero, and the wicked good.

"I rise up to defend the character of Moses. I say his writings are inspired, his record true. My opponent has made false accusations against the people of Judah. Unlike the Romans and Greeks, they have never found delight in games, nor the theatre, nor horse races. Their women have never sold their beauty. From their earliest years they were taught the blessing of spiritual realities; they have always believed in the immortality of the soul. They are indeed wiser than those philosophers who, after their most learned utterances, continually fall back upon the worship of idols and demons. The people of Judah have forever looked to one God, and in this sense alone are chosen.

"My friends, a new life has come into the world. It grows like a grain of mustard-seed, and the earth is green under its shadow. It is said that the overthrow of a government is swift and sudden but the regeneration of character is slow and painful. There is not one school of philosophy, one pagan festival, one ritual, one mystery that can alleviate the miseries of mankind. It is true that nature is inexorable. She never pardons. She punishes mistakes as harshly as she punishes crime. But the strong and successful are not always good, the weak are not always wicked. The genius of Christ has forbidden the strong from seizing the helpless and making them slaves. It has brought mercy into the world, and has blessed mankind with love and forgiveness. Eventually we must all understand that evil is death, that to forsake it is the resurrection of life. . . . "

Fabian launched a sharp rebuttal. "The Scriptures are echoes of Greek tradition. The idea of Satan originated in Pherecydes, the story of Babel is a plagiarism from Aloidae, the Christian concept of heaven adulterates Plato's world of ideas. . . . "

Alexandros made his rebuttal brief and when he finished, he turned to Fabian and offered his hand but the Roman spun away and marched out of the amphitheatre.

Within a few days Origen recovered from his illness but both Theoctistus and Aspasia were still not strong enough to care for their own needs. Alexandros meanwhile kept to himself, avoiding all attempts that Origen made toward conversation. Now that he had most of his strength back, Origen resumed the vigil over his physical attitude and began running a few miles along the shore each day.

One evening, after Theoctistus and Aspasia had fallen asleep, Alexandros broke his long silence. "Origen, I cannot hide something that has been burning my heart since the debates."

"What is it, Alexandros?"

"I have this terrible dread that Fabian defeated me."

"Nonsense. You gave a powerful argument against Celsus," said Origen walking toward the window. The sky was cloudless. A soft breeze brushed against his face.

"I am leaving for Jerusalem tomorrow morning," said Alexandros.

"What is your hurry?"

"I have been here too long. I must return to my people."

"Alexandros, stay a while."

"Why?"

"So that we can talk. . . . "

"What good is talk?" said Alexandros sourly. "I should be in Jerusalem, and you should be in Alexandria with your students and your work. It makes me ill when I see you concealed in this remote place, your talents buried under the ominous shadow of Demetrius. You must put an end to it."

"To what?" asked Origen.

"Hiding in this old house, conversing with two old people, writing a few lines each day, running along the shore like a young athlete. What are you trying to prove?"

Origen did not answer.

"Origen. . . . "

"Yes?"

"Will you promise to do something for me?"

"If I can."

"I want you to defeat Celsus."

"But the debates have ended. Fabian has returned to Rome."

"I am not asking you to debate anyone."

"What then?"

"You must write a book against Celsus."

"Ambrosius has already asked me."

"Are you going to do it?"

"Yes."

Alexandros came to the window. "I thought that God would surely enlighten me in those debates . . . that He would fill my tongue with the appropriate words so that Celsus would be crushed once and for all. But I was wrong. I should have met Celsus on his own ground, as you had intended to do. This is why I want you to write that book. You will not fail me, Origen? You promise?"

"Yes."

They retired to their beds in silence. At daybreak, Alexandros departed for Jerusalem, and for one whole week Origen was mired in gloom. On the first day of August Ambrosius returned to Caesarea looking haggard and forlorn. "Little teacher," he murmured, "Marcella is dead. . . ."

"What?"

"She died while I was imprisoned . . . I never knew until I returned to Alexandria."

Origen was at a loss for words.

Choking with tears, Ambrosius suddenly asked, "Have you started that book yet?"

Origen shook his head. "I could not begin without you."

"In the name of Serapis, must we wait another eighty years before Celsus is put in his place? How did the debates go?"

Origen told him about the dysentery, about Alexandros and Fabian. He did not have time to finish. Ambrosius rubbed his hands gleefully and shouted, "I am glad you were sick."

"Why do you say that?"

"Because you would have made a fool of yourself. You are not a debater. You are a philosopher and a writer!"

As they passed the Agora, Origen asked, "Is Demetrius still alive?"

"He lives and reigns," ranted Ambrosius. "But he is a very old man. Once he is gone, you shall be free to return to Alexandria."

"That depends upon who will succeed him.

They stopped in front of Theoctistus' house. "When do we start on Celsus?" said Ambrosius. A spark had ignited in his tear-stained eyes.

"Whenever you say," replied Origen.

"Tomorrow at daybreak!"

They started up the front steps.

"Lord Ambrosius, the Celsus book must be the best of all. . . . "

"It shall be."

Half-way up the steps, Ambrosius again rubbed his hands. "Let me go first. I want to surprise them." He tried to take the steps two at a time but stumbled and almost fell. He did not look like the Ambrosius Origen had always known. The uncertain gait, the stooped shoulders, gray hair and trembling hands belonged to someone who had grown old overnight.

*5.*

Origen felt that he was sinking in a whirlpool that year. New problems unfolded, new dilemmas and impasses, and throughout these long ordeals Ambrosius tried to keep his spirits high. "Our luck will change, little Teacher. I tell you, this is a good year, the thousandth anniversary of Rome's birth!"

"It certainly has launched itself in a very auspicious way," said Origen sharply. "One Emperor already murdered by a band of mutinous officers, another slain in battle . . . and the vilest of all, sitting on the throne this very moment. . . ."

"It is much too early to judge Decius," said Ambrosius. "Besides, nothing you say can discourage me. I am convinced this will be a very good year for us. Look what we have accomplished already. You have established your own college here in Caesarea and in a very short time it has rivalled that of Alexandria, drawing students from every corner of the world. Yes, Demetrius has attempted in many devious ways to close it down, exerting his influence with those encyclicals to the bishops of Palestine and Syria, and even with those false accusations about your disobedience, immoral acts and heresy. . . . "

Although Origen still nourished a deep resentment and anger against Demetrius, he reacted with a firmer dedication to his work. Fortunately, Ambrosius was able to procure the assistance of three scribes, one having an extensive knowledge of Hebrew and Greek. His name was Jacov, a fragile hunch-back in his early forties. With his help, he completed a new series of commentaries, homilies and scholia. But it was his book, AGAINST CELSUS, into which he poured most of his energy . . . and when he faltered, Ambrosius was constantly at his side, nudging him forward, page after page.

He was flattered on the last day of classes when a student named Gregorius delivered a panegyric praising him and his methods. Later, Ambrosius walked with him to Theoctistus' house. In the middle of the street, Ambrosius abruptly stopped. "Little Teacher, I know how much you reproach yourself for not having a wife and children. . . . "

Origen tried to cut him off but Ambrosius held firm. "You must never feel this way. You do have a wife, *the Greek language*. She has borne you many offspring . . . tall, short, slender, fat, scholarly, wise . . . more than two thousand. I counted them myself. They fill one entire wall of the Mother Library in Alexandria!"

They reached Theoctistus' house.

"This does not mean that you should sit on your hands," Ambrosius declared. "Your wife is a fertile woman. She does not stop at a few thousand."

"But how fertile does she think I am?" retorted Origen.

Ambrosius slapped him on the shoulder. "You are a bull, little Teacher . . . a powerful and irresistible bull. This is why she married you!"

6.

Somehow he felt no deliverance when word of Demetrius' death reached Caesarea. It was as though a large
part of his own life had died. As everyone expected, Heraclas succeeded to the bishopric and quickly made it known
that he intended to continue Demetrius' battle against
him. Origen tried not to think about this. He remained
steadfast at his work and kept a relentless watch over his
body, running many miles each morning and eating only
one light meal each day.

One morning he returned to Theoctistus' house and
found a message on the small writing table. Theoctistus
said that it had been delivered by a dock worker. Origen
did not recognize the handwriting.

*'I was present in Athens during your discussion with*
*Bassus in which you claimed the authority of that part of*
*the Book of Daniel containing the story of Susanna. I re-*

*mained silent at the time but now feel obliged to urge with vivacity my strong objection.*

*In my mind, the story of Susanna is wanting in gravity and contains many internal improbabilities. The prophetic inspiration which you wrongly ascribe to Daniel differs considerably from that of the authentic book. Therefore it is my strong conviction that the writing style alone clearly indicates the book was written originally in Greek, and could never have been a translation from the Hebrew.*

*I pray that you take my words in the spirit of truth.*
*Julius Africanus*

Ambrosius took the letter from his hand and read it. "Who is this Julius Africanus?" he asked.

"I never heard of him," snapped Origen.

"He is from Nicopolis," responded Theoctistus, after he too read the letter. "He has a reputation as a chronologist and is known to have written several tomes beginning with the Mosaic account of creation and concluding with the reign of Macrinus. Some regard him as a genius with details. In one separate volume he listed all the winners of the Olympic games from the time of their inception. But you must not let Africanus upset you. His eye is too close to everything and therefore blurred with distortion."

That night Origen wrote a reply to Julius Africanus, refuting each objection and citing long passages from the original Hebrew text that contained a play on words which indeed the translators tried to preserve. He fixed his signature to it, sealed it with wax, then ran to the docks and made arrangements to have it delivered at once to Nicopolis. Aspasia and Theoctistus were still sleeping when he returned but Ambrosius was waiting for him in the kitchen. "Where did you go?" he asked.

Origen kicked the door closed. "I have just made an utter fool of myself."

"What do you mean?"

"I wrote to Julius Africanus."

"So?"

"All the way back from the docks I kept thinking about his objections. He spoke the truth. Every point he made was valid."

"You can always write him another letter."

Origen paced around the small room. "I cannot understand myself. After all these years, I still hate to be corrected."

On the very next day Alexandros came to Caesarea for a visit. He looked very tired. From the sleeve of his robe, he drew forth a letter and gave it to Origen. "It was passed on to me from a merchant in Alexandria," he explained.

Origen went outside and read the letter under the sun. It was from a former student who was now the Bishop of Bostra, Beryllus of the black face. Under the threat of excommunication, he wanted Origen to journey into Arabia and defend him before a Synod that was prepared to examine his theological views.

At supper Theoctistus repeatedly warned him not to go. "It is too long a journey."

Ambrosius agreed. "I urge you not to leave Caesarea at this time. You were right, Decius is a savage . . . and he knows how friendly you were with Severus and his mother."

"But Beryllus was one of my students. He needs me and I must go to him."

Ambrosius lost his composure. "You are willing to jeopardize your health, your new college, your work . . . for this black man in Arabia?"

"Yes."

Early the next morning he assigned himself to a small caravan that was bound for Pella. The journey was even longer than he had anticipated, requiring four full days. At first he did not recognize Beryllus. He had put on much flesh. During the evening meal Beryllus reminisced about their days together in Alexandria. He had a remarkable memory, recalling events that Origen had long forgotten. Although it pleased him to see Beryllus' face beaming with excitement, he finally had to interrupt him. "Beryllus, what are we to say to the Synod?"

"The truth," said Beryllus.

"And what is the truth?"

"I agree that Christ was the Son of God. I do not deny His incarnation."

"What do you deny?"

"His human nature."

They walked outside together. The first stars had already appeared. A soft breeze was blowing across the western sky. After a long silence, Beryllus said, "It is impossible for me to believe that Christ had two natures."

"Why?"

"Because God is a spirit. He could never become a person in Jesus Christ."

"You want to strip all humanity from Christ?"

"Yes."

"Cast away His entire human nature?"

"Yes."

"His suffering and death?"

"Yes."

"But what does this leave?"

"Exactly what He had from the beginning . . . his divine nature."

"Perhaps you should defend yourself before the Synod."

"Is this how you feel about it?" asked Beryllus. "Would you have me confess that I am wrong?"

"It is not a question of right or wrong. My position differs greatly from yours."

"What is your position?"

"If Christ has no humanity, He holds no interest for me. I am drawn more to His human nature than to His divine."

"How can you say this?"

"Because I cannot imitate a God. No one can. But I will follow a virtuous man to the ends of the earth."

Later, as he lay under the covers of his bed, listening to the sounds of the desert, great waves of confusion and doubt crashed against his brain. Who was he to expound on Christ? How could a heretic save a man from excommunication?

He did not fall asleep until an infinite voice at last comforted him: *'If a man have a hundred sheep and one be gone astray, doth he not leave the ninety-and-nine and go into the mountains to seek that which has gone astray?'*

There was no need to go before the Synod. The next morning Beryllus dispatched a letter to the bishops, reversing his position. On the day of Origen's departure from Bostra, an attack of dysentery rendered him so sick and weak he was compelled to remain with Beryllus five more days. At Pella the dysentery flared up again and for three days he sustained himself only on water and a few herbs.

When he came into sight of Caesarea, he had to be assisted all the way to Theoctistus' house. His body was burning, his feet and hands trembled.

"In the name of the Father," he heard Alexandros cry out. "Origen, you are ill!"

He slumped on the rug.

Alexandros held him in his arms until his eyes slowly focused upon the table, the chairs . . . upon Theoctistus and Aspasia standing near the hearth.

"Where . . . where is Ambrosius?" he stammered.

Alexandros pointed toward the bed chamber. "There, lying down."

"But it is midday. Wake him up."

Alexandros' words quivered. "He is not well."

Clouds of nausea gushed over his head.

"The physician was here this morning," Alexandros murmured. "He said it is only a matter of time."

Origen dragged himself across the room. Ambrosius' face was the color of wax. His mouth hung open, grotesquely twisted to the side.

"Let us pray for his soul's repose," said Alexandros, standing before the bed. Theoctistus and Aspasia joined him.

Origen stumbled away from them, from the sterile incantations and hollow petitions . . . to a place where he heard his own heart cry out, *You must not take him away!*

After a while the others walked outside and he returned to Ambrosius, measuring each breath that leaked from the drooping mouth. He placed his hand on the gray forehead and just then the lips started to move. He slid to his knees and whispered, "Lord Ambrosius, what are you trying to say?"

The words slipped from the sagging lips, faint and harsh, "Little Teacher. . . . "

At that moment the breathing stopped. The eyes sprung wide open. Ambrosius had come face-to-face with Charon.

A few hours later, Alexandros and Theoctistus chanted prayers in the small oratory next to Theoctistus' house, and at sundown Origen called upon all his stamina and accompanied his taskmaster to a place under a solitary olive tree on a peaceful hillside. It was in full view of the sea.

7.

The frightful arm of Decius now extended into Caesarea. Theoctistus begged Origen and Alexandros to flee and seek refuge in the coastal city of Tyre, sixty miles to the north. They agreed but insisted that Theoctistus and Aspasia should come with them. "No, my children," said Theoctistus, blessing them. "We shall stay here in our home, and die here if we must."

They traveled by ship to Tyre. It was a short voyage. The instant they stepped off the dock they were seized by Roman soldiers and bound in heavy chains. That same afternoon they were thrown into the depths of a filthy dungeon.

Alexandros bore his suffering nobly. Every day Origen tried to buoy up their spirits by reciting long passages from the Greek poets, and when his memory failed him, he fabricated lines of his own. Alexandros did not discern the difference.

Despite the meagre rations, Origen kept rigidly to his schedule, rising early each morning while the guards slept, dragging his chained feet from one wall of the dungeon to the other. He lost all awareness of time.

One day they learned from a new arrival of prisoners that Theoctistus was martyred in Caesarea, dragged along the streets by two ferocious horses until his heart expired. Origen took cold that night and could not eat the one piece of stale bread that was thrown at him. Alexandros tried to minister unto him but he too fell ill the next morning. Origen managed to drag him away and carefully place him against the wall. He took off his own robe and threw it over Alexandros. Sitting at his side, he tried not to think about the dry vomit that clung to Alexandros' beard, the acrid smell of excrement that festered the dungeon.

"Origen!"

"What is it?" he asked.

"I must return to Alexandria. Please take me there!"

Origen held him tightly in his arms. "Yes, Alexandros. We shall go there together."

Alexandros' eyes were crazed with fear. "We must go now!"

There was a painful silence.

"Origen. . . . "

"Yes."

"Can you see it?"

"What, Alexandros?"

"Pharos Light . . . there . . . towering over the Great Sea. Let go of me. I must climb it. Let go!"

In the morning, a guard dragged his rigid body away. From that moment on, Origen held no desire for life. He openly defied the guards by chanting David's psalms in their presence. They whipped him with heavy straps, fastened an iron collar around his neck, distended his feet on a cruel instrument that left him almost crippled.

He withdrew into his childhood and imagined himself walking down Canopic Way toward his martyrdom as thousands cheered. But his own exalted joy was heard only by the guards who came again and tortured him with deadlier violence. Remembering Plotinus, he tried to convince himself that suffering had its virtue . . . that it obliterated the face of time until aeons fell away like dead leaves from a tree.

The death of Decius redeemed him from his wretchedness. He was taken by cart to the house of Photius, a presbyter in Tyre who also had been confined in the same dungeon. The wife of Photius nursed his wounds and fed him, and soon he was able to walk as far as the agora with the help of a cane. Within one month, he was hobbling along the shore, one hundred yards each day.

A message was delivered to him one morning. It was from Dionysius, a former student who had just succeeded Heraclas to the bishopric of Alexandria. He took the letter with him and slowly began a painful trot along the sea. He went no more than thirty yards when he felt a powerful stab in his chest. Dropping to his knees, he waited for the pain to subside.

Two young boys were playing near the water's edge. One of them recognized him and came racing forward. "Master Origen, is someone chasing you?"

"No." The word slipped from his throat in harsh denial.

"But we saw you running along the shore. . . . "

In time the boy moved away, leaving him with the acrid specter of himself . . . running . . . all his life running . . . running from Alexandria . . . from his father's ominous presence . . . from dreams and illusions . . . from the unhealing wound in his groin . . . from Herais. . . .

The burden in his chest was unbearable. He scooped up a little water from the sea and tossed it over his face. He tried to get on his feet but could not do it. Dionysius' letter was crumpled in his hand. With great effort he brought it close to his eyes.

*Dionysius to Origen*　　　　　　*Alexandria, 28 July, 254*
　　*Beloved Master, it is my sincere wish that you return to Alexandria where your name is once again spoken with respect and admiration. . . .*

A flood of gall poured into his heart. He tore the message to shreds and dropped the pieces into the sea. Again he tried to get up but failed.

He put his thoughts on Tyre.

She was not unlike Alexandria. She too was built on an island and had a long causeway connecting to the mainland. Behind him, huge billows of purple smoke poured out of her dye factories. Whole decades passed before his memory like streaks of light flashing across the universe. He beheld Alexandria, vibrant with the colors of Sefi. He walked down the full length of Canopic Way, stopping before the Soma of Golden Alexander, now the Museum, the Mother Library, the Caesarium, the two obelisks near Antirrhodos, the guilt-laden Temple of Serapis stained with his father's blood.

His mother's hands reached out for him, her eyes overflowing with forgiveness. He called out to his brothers and then ran toward the Great Sea and Pharos Light. He climbed the massive boulders of the Heptastadion and there, amidst a galaxy of Grecian suns, Herais' smile sparkled before him. As their hands met, their hearts, restless oceans swelled under his feet. . . .

He closed his eyes.

# EPILOGUE

As late as the middle ages, Origen's grave in Tyre was an imposing monument for visitors. His name still lingers over the ruins of that ancient city, and today, natives of Lebanon point out the place where he lies buried.

The controversies that hounded Origen throughout his lifetime grew more intense after his death. The cruelest attack was launched by Bishop Epiphanius in the fourth century. There were many others, their cause greatly strengthened when Jerome, influenced by the surging tide, turned against his once-honored teacher.

The disputes erupted into open battle in the sixth century, and blood was shed over the gentle Origen's name. Under the jurisdiction of Emperor Justinian, Origen was anathematized by the Fifth Ecumenical Council at Constantinople in 553. Soon thereafter, all of his writings were systematically sought out and destroyed.

The loss was immeasurable.

Fortunately, some Latin translations survived—those of Hilary, Jerome, and a few others. The greatest number comes from Rufinus of Aquileia who has been unjustly maligned by scholars for his hyperbole and overabundant zeal. Historians now praise Rufinus. Indeed, his diligence and dedication saved from final ruin the precious name of a great man.

# A Small Bibliography

*The Ante-Nicene Library*, Vols. X, XXIII.
G.W. Butterworth, *Origen on First Principles*.
Dio Chrysostom, (Loeb Classical Library).
Jean Daniélou, *Origène*.
Clement of Alexandria, *Stromateis, The Exhortation to the Greeks*.
Eusebius, *Ecclesiastical History*.
E.M. Forster, *Alexandria: A History and a Guide*.
Edward Gibbon, *History of Christianity*.
Charles Kingsley, *Alexandria and Her Schools*.
S. McKenna, *Plotinus: The Enneads*.
John Patrick, *The Apology of Origen*.
Philo, (Loeb Classical Library).
James Pritchard, *Egyptian Mythology*.
M. Rostovtzeff, *Caravan Cities of Egypt and Palestine*.
H. White, *The Monasteries of Natron*.

And the few extant writings of Origen:

*Against Celsus.*
*Hexapla.*
*On First Principles.*
*The Epistle to Julius Africanus.*
*Exhortation to Martyrdom.*
*The Commentaries.*
*On Prayer.*

ITALY

ROME

Naples
BRUNDISIUM

MACEDONIA

EPIRUS

ATHENS

CORINTH
ACHAIA

SICILY

SYRACUSE

MEDITERRANEAN
(THE GREAT SEA)

N

W — E

S

| 0 | 100 | 200 | 300 | MILES |

| 0 | 100 | 200 | 300 | 400 | 500 | KM |

- - - - - ORIGEN'S TRAVELS
............. LIMITS OF ROMAN EMPIRE

THE WORLD OF